Watch for More Novels

by Jonna Ellis Holston

from Indigo Sea Press

indigoseapress.com

Toggle

By

Jonna Ellis Holston

Perseverance Books
Published by Indigo Sea Press, LLC.
Winston-Salem

Perseverance Books
Indigo Sea Press, LLC
302 Ricks Drive, Winston-Salem, NC 27103

Copyright 2016 by Jonna Ellis Holston

First Perseverance Books edition published April, 2016

Perseverance Books, logo, and all production design are trademarks of Indigo Sea Press, used under license.

For information regarding bulk purchases of this book, digital purchase and special discounts, please contact the publisher at indigoseapress@gmail.com

Cover design by Pan Morelli

Manufactured in the United States of America
ISBN 978-1-630663-22-3

For all the women who dare.

—Jonna Ellis Holston

*"We have to continually be jumping off cliffs
and developing our wings on the way down."*

Kurt Vonnegut

1.
Early Fall 2012, Headed East

Chica had been cooped up in the Camry for the past four hours.
I fastened her leash and *Little Dog* pulled me as if getting to some
unusual odor left on a boundary of old tired grass was the most
important part of this entire trip. I had to stop for a minute. Damn,
this stupid hip stiffens up when I drive too long. I gave each glute a
good stretch and breathed in the scent of old salty marshes and
asphalt. It was a large lot for a tiny station on this peculiar
man-made island, a beach-free key in a sea-breached lea of uncut
country collards. It was an oddly pretty place, gold under the blue of
the sky.

The delivery van pulled in close to the entry. A beautiful
brown-skinned man stepped out and began to unload cases of novelty
treats, cream cycles, Nutty Buddys, and those yummy chocolate
covereds. Chica, always investigating, led me closer to the truck,
sniffing and flashing her sweet brown eyes, fully expecting to be
rewarded with dairy. He bent down to pet her then returned to his work
lifting and stacking. Thin and muscular, with a high and well-formed
ass, I watched this specimen as his biceps flexed, then his triceps, bis
and tris, back and forth. Good God, I was glad for the breeze.

My thoughts were an easy read. "Young man," Annie said as
she walked from the store and grabbed my arm, "you have no idea
what kind of danger you are in." She led me toward the car and
called back over her shoulder. "This woman *really* likes ice cream."

"Didn't he have beautiful arms, such pretty mocha-caramel?" I
tried to turn for one last look.

1

"Damn, Sophie. For chrissake, what were you planning to do, tie him up and have your way with his fudgicles? Put your tongue back into your mouth and get in the car."

I sighed. Only a few short years ago, I'd have happily hung flashing neon "no trespassing" sign around my neck; now I'm panting like a dog-bitch at a gas station lusting after strange men.

"Okay, Sophie, the truth — how long has it really been since you've been made love to?" My right hand must have twitched, some kind of tell. "I mean by a man," she added.

"Okay. Okay. It's been probably-definitely been, well, I don't really know how long it's been, since maybe 1996 or '97."

"That's long."

"Annnnnnie…" I started the car and headed east.

"I don't want to hear it. You need to have sex, Sweetie. If *any*one I know needs to get laid, it's you. You're doing that thing with your nails again, please stop. You realize that it atrophies without use, don't you?"

"What atrophies?"

"Your vagina."

"Vaginas don't atrophy. Vaginas atrophy? Are you kidding me? Vaginas atrophy?"

"You studied anatomy? You gotta use it or guess what?"

"I suppose I learned that vaginas atrophy but I must have filed it away with the stack of information I thought I would never need to remember."

"What are you waiting for? You have had ample opportunities, I know you have."

"I'm practicing self-love at the moment. I think it might work out. The sex is pretty good, and I never have to worry if I'm being faithful."

"Quit joking."

"I wish it was funny. Who would have thought that a time would come when getting laid would be a problem? When we were young we had so many guys to choose from, you never expect that will ever end. Then one day you're old and randy and your right hand becomes preferable to most of the men you meet."

"There is nothing wrong with masturbating but you'd have much more fun sharing it with someone," she said. "So have you gotten smaller, narrower inside?"

2

"Yes, my vagina is smaller because I *don't* have someone to share it with. So what am I going to have to do, get a bag of carrots and start with the smallest one and move up?"

"Well, a bag of carrots would work or you could be like a normal woman and use a device. I'd be happy to take you shopping for a dildo because I know you don't have one."

"How do you know that?"

"Well, do you?"

"Do I own a dildo? You are asking me if *I* own a dildo." I didn't own a dildo.

"Sophie, watch the road, please!" She reached up to the dash and sighed deeply.

If a person's appearance portrayed an accurate description of their true self Annie would be a retired history teacher who had never missed a Sunday of church in her life. She is darling, polite and a loyal friend. But Annie engages in some kind of kinky sex lifestyle. Bren and I were nebulously aware of her tastes and I (I can only speak for myself) was a little jealous. Not so envious about the sex (which was probably great and I *should* have been jealous of it) but of her courage and her choice to be who she is regardless of the judgement or opinions of others. I tried to imagine what that kind of freedom would feel like after so many years of... pretending.

She had had a long-time man-friend, Mounty, this much we knew, but there was more. Bren and I had imagined the specifics of her sex life and I said that I would try to get Annie to disclose some of the particulars of this, ah, ménage de trois? quatre? cinq? Truth is- we didn't know what the fuck Annie was into.

"What was so wrong with those guys you dated last winter? Weren't you attracted to any of them? Will was okay, wasn't he?"

"Ya, he was okay, but it's so easy to become entangled, start nesting, you know? I didn't want to become entangled with someone I already suspected was a liar."

"You don't *have* to get entangled."

"I don't choose to get entangled. It just happens to turn out that way."

"How would you know? You haven't made love with anyone in actual modern history. It's not like you intend to have anybody's children so there is no need to nest. Can I make that clearer?" She sucked on her e-cig. "Just do it."

"Easy, right?"

"If you only knew how easy it is to get laid. Put an ad on Craig's List that says that you have a narrow vagina and guess how many men would answer it. You'd have men competing for you, young guys, gorgeous guys, if you *only knew*."

"Oh, God, I couldn't do that."

"Why not?"

"Because there are nuts out there and diseases."

"I could set you up with someone safe. Hell, I was talking with a guy last week who was complaining that all the women he's been with have pussies that you could drive a tank through. He hardly knows if he's even inside them."

"What?" I spit. "How do you even know people who say things like that in public? And how derogatory toward women is that?"

"That's just judgment."

"Well, isn't it derogatory?"

"Believe it or not, Sophie, there are places where people can be open and honest about who they are and can speak their truth without having to worry about excessive social correctness."

"Where, like orgies and sex clubs?"

"Why does it matter if you aren't interested?"

"I can't do that stuff. I'm not even sure if I can handle the missionary position without shitting the bed."

"What about somebody else? Has there been anyone else that you liked enough to be with?"

"I was attracted to a married guy in Wally World and that cute young guy at Stella's party — also married. A good-looking man with mega abs in a cut-off shirt was examining celery at Whole Foods the other day and nearly made my knees buckle. Do you want me to go on? Oh, and Chuck. Let's not forget Chuck."

"We need to get even with Chuck. What he did was terrible. Think of a really evil practical joke." My active mind was already scanning the realm of possibilities. "I still can't believe he did that."

"He did it," I said as we whizzed the high bridge over the Intracoastal. I watched a lone sailboat going out to sea.

"Sophie, the road! Watch the road. I should never let you drive."

"Sorry."

"Honey, you keep finding faults with every man you meet. Just find a guy, do it and get it over with. So you fell off the horse with your marriage. Get back on the flipping horse and ride."

"It's not that easy."

"It's easier than you are making it. You're practically inventing reasons not to get laid."

"There has to be some element of trust, don't you think? I just can't find some random guy and have meaningless sex with him."

"All sex is meaningful; you just don't have to get involved with the guy."

"That's easier to say than to do, I think, even harder to believe. Besides, I can't be like Letta, she's hideous."

"Letta has lived here all her life. She knows everyone in town and everyone in town knows she's easy. A guy strikes out with the babe at the bar, he's still horny, but Letta is willing and available. Of course she gets laid a lot. She's still youngish and kind of cute."

"And desperate, how old do you think she is?"

"Mid-fifties, maybe, the boob job didn't hurt her chances."

"Her boobs are fake?"

"Haven't you ever hugged her? They should be redone."

"I never hugged Letta."

"Mmmm, I don't suppose you have."

"I don't know, Annie. Maybe I'm not supposed to have anyone right now." I bit my lip.

"You'll find somebody but you have to be open to it for it to happen. All I see you doing is closing off possibilities." She paused thoughtfully and sighed. "Sophie, can I ask you a personal question?"

"Can I ask *you* a personal question?"

"This is very personal and yes, I'm asking permission."

I swallowed and took an audible breath. "Okay, go ahead."

"Are you sure you are over Jim? Could you still be in love with him?"

"Jim? Jim Chase? Jim Chase, my ex? I'm not in love with Jim, how could you think that?

2.
Let's Back Up Eight Years

Jim and I had twelve wonderful years together... unfortunately; we were married for twenty-six.

We grew apart... he cheated... yadda-yadda.

Fourteen years of a cheating husband can kill you, no joke, because witnessing a slow-death marriage is brutal on a soul, like inexorably slow slices, infecting and re-infecting, perpetual wound debridement. A hacked amputation would have been kinder. Already in an emotionally weakened state, I became a vulnerable hotbed for illness and I got sick, unable-to-diagnose sick, maybe I'd never-work-again-kind-a sick, maybe even an all-in-my-head-kind –of sick. That's when he set serious pursuit in motion. My husband expected much more from life than a bedridden wife. He wanted financial security and a fully functional, contributing partner. Surrounded by choices of fine Southern women, he started his quest for the upgrade.

I'd stood on that marriage like it was rock solid footing. Corroded by bimbos and time, it washed out as easily as cold wet clay and I slid downwards onto a man-hating trail of shadowy bogs full of quicksand and boundless patches of poison ivy. I had little personal savings, lived in a poorly-maintained home with two children, mounting debt and bad plumbing. By the time the divorce papers were delivered, it was almost a relief because ... after that ride I hated Jim and wanted him buried.

Misty helped me through the gamut of feelings one experiences. She told me she read somewhere that "getting divorced is like waking up every morning as a captive in the hold of a pirate ship. You're completely off-balance, usually nauseous and any minute you expect another flogging."

He was gone, ran off with Edith, Edith, with legs up to there and a Doctorate's salary. Now I faced fear, the unknown. I had to be independent, prioritize and learn to conserve. I quit most of my

6

medications, discontinued the children's' extras like Karate and dance. Junk food completely disappeared from my home. Cable TV had to go, so I didn't see very much of my kids for the remainder of their high school years, but the bulk of my work with them had been completed and I knew that any real influence I had in teenage-land was purely imaginary.

So I ate healthier food. I got more exercise and I began to get better. And I cannot emphasize the importance of eliminating stress because when that irritating factor named Jim left the building I began to feel sane again. Hell, once that shithead was gone, even the plumbing got better.

I had even designed a product which I intended to market to other man-haters. It was a small doll made of really squishy plastic. It had a small but powerful magnet in one hand and metal pieces in his head, his heart and in his groin. You could stretch his hand out and release it to predict if he was thinking from his head, his heart or his penis. It came with a set of magnetic letters so you could assign an appropriate initial for an adjective to describe him, post it on his tee shirt and change it as needed to accommodate a new description of the type of asshole the real man in your life was at any given moment. He was called the Adj Man, and voodoo pins were suggested in the derogatory, albeit very funny, packaging.

I had envisioned women all over the country squeezing them, wringing their necks, throwing them against the wall and violently stomping on their little six-inch bodies. Voodoo was just an option.

It was a twisted idea.

I was twisted.

My friends saw me through. They helped me reach for humor as we cut through the red tape and bullshit that was my divorce. My adopted sisters were from elsewhere, big cities mostly. Like me they came to this small town, their circumstances varied. They were smart, had experience, wisdom, education; all of them had been through divorce. When I was too sick and drugged to read his divorce agreement, they combed through the pages, shared their expertise. It was they who found the hidden legal bear traps.

My chief expert in divorce advice was my friend, Bellamy Hays. This woman saved me from financial hell and she propped up my spirit with tales of her own divorces. Those crazy stories often seemed to be the only hold I could grasp. Her father and first two husbands were attorneys; she had been through it all and again so she was familiar with divorce law (and a plethora of lawyer jokes).

Bellamy is intolerably beautiful, a leggy San Diego blond who never cooked a day in her life until she moved to this town. We originally buddied up to travel for food. In those days we had to drive to either Greensboro or Winston-Salem for simple fare like bean sprouts and avocados or to find a leg of lamb and real imported feta cheese for holiday dinners. I taught her what I knew from growing up in a Greek kitchen and she customized it, California-downsized it and increased the nutritional value of the revered Mediterranean diet by making the salad with spinach instead of iceberg and lightly steaming the vegetables instead of simmering them down into moosh, like I do.

Food, restaurants in this and the surrounding towns have improved a lot in recent years. There are plenty of good Mexican restaurants and that means good margaritas. The margarita is not my usual drink of choice but Sunday nights are much more festive when my friends and I enjoy one with fajita and chips. Chicks with a couple of margaritas, a better life boat can't be found anywhere, nor is one needed more desperately than here in Kernersville.

Misty Lewis was the first real friend I made here after Jim's job took me away from all that I knew as sane and normal. We were neighbors. Both of our husbands had been relocated to Kernersville by the same company. We hoped they'd be friends but putting them in the near vicinity of each other resulted in a head-to-head bullfight oozing with testosterone and usually ending with both of them brandishing food utensils, gardening tools, car accessories or other representations of suburban manhood.

Misty is naturally gentle and trusting. Her husband Jet was meaner and more devious than Jim's worst day on steroids (no, he really was on steroids). Jet hid all his money, wouldn't pay alimony and she lost her home. But in spite of everything Jet did to Misty, she was able to find forgiveness. She's a much more tolerant human than I am.

8

I struggle with forgiveness. Well, maybe struggle is not the right word here. To be truthful, I like to keep my grudges. My people can store up enough vengeance for another three-part series by Mario Puzo. Curses, the evil eye, this is part of my heritage. I have always tried to suppress that part of myself. I still have the violent thoughts (sure, how can you help that?) but I believed in the words, "as you give, so shall you receive", so if I ever acted on those tendencies I used the *practical joke* approach. I could get the last word in and have a good laugh about it. I could even be sneaky enough so that no one would know that it was me. This way I could be a better person, a better parent and role model for my children. And if there *is* a judgement day (or reincarnation) and I have much to atone for, all I have to receive is a few good jokes played on me and it's all a bunch of laughs, right?

Misty had part-time office hours as psychotherapist, but I think that talking me off the famed ledge of lunacy was full-time for her. She suggested that I do what she did, make "forgive and release" my mantra. That, she claimed, is the way she forgave Jet. She repeated that until a mantra refinement was in order, and she then tailored subsequent affirmations that evolved in order to suit her needs. She says that thoughts are choices we make, part of our free will. If her mind wonders to something unpleasant from the past she catches herself and brings her mind back to something happy and lives in the present. She continues to strive towards complete forgiveness so having a mantra to fall back on helps her.

Sometimes I flirt with forgiveness but I'm still angry. I play the bad memory tape then hit rewind and play it again. And so far I'm sticking with my basic story, that men are sacks of shit, boiling sacks of smelly, faithless sloth shit.

3.
Fast Forward to More Recent Times

But there comes a time after divorce where you start noticing how handsome a sack of sloth shit can look in his jeans and polo shirt with the tight sleeves against biceps. Maybe it's unbuttoned, and his chest hairs are all out and exposed. You don't want to notice, but there it is.

Now there are obstacles. I'm fifty pounds overweight and this is a huge impediment to a healthy self-image. Having had the words "man-hater" practically engraved into my breastbone, there is an expected amount of teasing that I will receive from my friends. Am I willing to rise above it all because I have remembered that once upon a time I liked men and enjoyed their company?

Never is such a long time; to a woman my age, it *seems* so very much longer. You know how guys say that women get better-looking at closing time? I'm beginning to think about sex more as I get older. I have major amorous feelings and it's nearly last call at the bar. It feels like my chance for love, for one last great passionate love is quickly growing nigh.

The randy sixties, all the misery of menopause is gone and I'm hornier than a spring-loaded rabbit. I don't remember this stage being addressed in the adult female developmental textbook that I was required to read for psychology class.

So if your desire to experience passion is greater than your dislike of the object that makes you cognizant of said passion, it is time to reconsider firmly-held opinions.

"You may want to soften your stance from never to maybe. You might consider dating when it feels more safe and comfortable," Misty told me one Sunday night.

"If a man ever did to me what Jim did to you, I'd force him into my upright freezer and lock him in."

"That's pretty severe."

"Your man fucked every skank in town. And you *knew* he was screwing around. I'd have hit him over the head with a frozen thigh bone left over from the previous tenant."

That's my cool friend Bren. Titanic in both drama and style, this retired New York cop raised three children on guts and salary. She's trustworthy and she asks the questions I never seem to think of asking. What I love the most about her is that she doesn't believe in being overly good. So if you are up for raising hell, you call Bren.

Bellamy was on her way in the door. "Hey, girls, sorry I'm late. I had to go to three stores to find tomatoes that smell like tomatoes," she gave kisses all around. "So have we found Sophie a date yet?"

"She ain't ready to start dating and anyway, where? Where you gonna find a man in Kernersville?" Bren asked.

"Lack of evidence does not prove evidence of lack. I think that's a science law, Sophie. Isn't that a science law?" Bellamy asked.

"How do you know that? It's called Ferme's experiment."

"There are thousands of men in this area, and you have not met every one of them, Bren. You haven't even seen most of them." Bell turned to me. "So how about it, Sophie, do you think there's a man for you in this big wild universe?"

I know a fair bit about the universe because I grew up watching Carl Sagan on TV. Carl Fucking Sagan. I was riveted by Carl Sagan, amazed how his head with all those brains and teeth and eyebrows could balance on that thin turtle neck in a sweater, ever defying the laws of gravity. I was, however, listening so I can tell you that there are billions and billions of stars in this galaxy, and they have found hundreds of billions of other galaxies beyond the Milky Way. The universe is huge; it's beyond huge.

Right now I live in Kernersville and star power is in short supply. It's small, *small.* It's sort of like living in a town in a book — Hobbiton of The Shire works well. Certain things are very important here, like pumpkins and fireworks, gardens full of vegetables and beer.

People from Kernersville are not particularly adventurous. They might travel as far away as Bree but rarely will they trek as far as Rivendell. The women I hang out with have already been through the toxic airs of Mordor and we are not planning a return trip.

I complained that there is a shortage of nice available men here. This is probably true throughout the country and there are many, many, older single women who need partners to love them.

I've become aware that the bell curve of probable outcomes for a single woman of my age group is not very encouraging. The bulk of the statistical data under the bell curve suggests that we will most likely face a decline in health and mobility, a shrinking of opportunities and social connections as we grow older. We are expected to face pain, illness and loneliness as we age. I hope to be the outlier, one of the few who land at the slightly open edge of the curve. I want to exit the world of probability and enter a realm of possibility. I want to believe that anything is possible, even at my age.

Annie said, "If finding a man is important to you, you have to get creative. Our generation is 50,000 fellas short from the war in Viet Nam. That amount is not even comparable to the World Wars, of course, and I have no idea how many are still hospitalized from their injuries or chemical agents or how many are homeless."

"She is probably as much to blame for the scarcity as the Viet Nam war," I said, tipping my thumb at Bellamy.

"That's a valid point," said Bren, "yet Bellamy assures me that there is someone out there who is the perfect man for you, Sophie."

I think Bellamy believes in a world full of magic where some heavenly force (like baby cupid angels?) is united in constant attempt to bring souls looking for their mates together, after all, she is from California.

"That's right. We're putting it out to the Universe for you," she said. I imagine she waved her invisible sparkly wand skyward.

Billions and billions.

Bellamy believes in love. Misty believes in and has found both love and a monogamous relationship. Bren is willing to encourage me to take care of business, at least. And Annie has a movie all her own.

So I, Sophie Pappas Chase at age, I-don't-even-wanna-tell-ya, am going to choose to have faith, maybe even go out on a limb. I have decided I'm probably-definitely going to date at some time in the near future… maybe.

I have good reason to be indecisive. It would be the first time I have dated since the seventies when I met and married Jim. For me to even contemplate entering the dating scene is a giant leap. I found the dating scene intimidating and confusing when I was young, when my body was firm and my face without wrinkles, when my hair was soft and thick and my feet weren't so big and bunioned, and varicose veins? Don't even let me get started on those.

And what if I did find a great guy in Kernersville? A possible outcome of one of those dates could be having sex with the guy. I pondered that possibility and nearly wet myself. "How would I ever *dare* to take my clothes off in front of a man?"

"Hang on," Bren's hand rose in a placating gesture. "It's just a date. Taking off clothing is optional."

"That's right," Annie added. "A woman has to be careful now. Every man you date has had several, maybe lots of partners and the baggage to match. You have to be careful and discerning. "

"Haven't all the nuts been culled out by now?"

"Don't you be too sure about that," Bren jumped in. "There are plenty of nuts out there… and predators."

"You'll know when you have found the right man when you feel comfortable enough to *want* to take your clothes off," Annie said. She munched a tortilla chip.

"I had a ten-pound, twelve-ounce baby later in life and I never lost the baby weight." I pictured my big dimpled butt and the apron of fat hanging from my lower abdomen. It was ugly. "I'll never feel that comfortable with a man again!"

"You will when you're ready, Sophie, and it will happen. You still look good," Misty encouraged.

"I look better in clothes." My nose wrinkled up in a half smile. I knew that I needed to join a gym but I was too fat to have the nerve to walk into a gym. I began to reconsider.

Doubts have a way of creeping into existing doubts. It's probably the Law of Attraction to blame. Misty has been explaining that to me.

But I was absolutely committed to making several positive changes in my life. I had already cleaned up my diet, began walking my dog more often because that needed to be done, and I had to start *somewhere*. After I lost some weight and got some more of my confidence back, maybe I would get serious about dating.

Bren downloaded some old music for me, a playlist of music that you cannot resist dancing to, the kind of music that made you remember how it felt to be young. That's the kind of music, old time rock and roll and Motown. Motown, when Marvin loved Tammy and everyone loved Smokey. Diana was Supreme. Gladys had Pips and the Temptations were — tempting?

Bren told me this really embarrassing story from when she lived in the city. She'd put on some extra weight so in the evening, after the children were in bed she played Motown tunes and dance to them like nobody was watching. Bren is a busty and booty-ful woman of color, so keep that image in mind. Years later, when the two firemen who lived in the apartment across the street were moving out, they took that opportunity to ring her doorbell and personally thank her for the years of entertainment that she had given them from the not-so-private view into her front room window.

I remembered to close the blinds but I danced, I danced and it was fun, joyful.

Quarter inch by quarter inch, the lost relic of waist-line made a comeback. Guys began to look again and young man actually flirted! Now I gotta say that I was surprised at that, how many young men paid attention to me... and that crazy little thing called lust tickled away at my imagination. Like the guy at Stella's party, he was young and cute and he had everything exactly where it should be on a man (except my hands). Positioned in Stella's bay window he resembled the cover of a romance novel, and he looked at me the way guys used to look at me.

I joined the gym the next day.

I remember loving sex, I wanted to love it again. What happened to me?

Misty said that it was the anger I felt for Jim. She said that anger, fear and hate are similar emotions that manifest differently and that when you are feeling those emotions love cannot or will not exist.

Annie didn't agree. "Anger is passion, and many a heated argument has ended up in the bedroom. Passion is hot stuff. It can warm your bed, for sure, but it could also incinerate the whole room!"

"I got the anger part down pretty well, Annie. It's the passion part that I lost."

"Then get it back cuz it feels good." Annie widened her eyes.

14

"Can we have more details?"

"Quit it, Bren."

"Well, I'm just saying that we are your friends, and you can tell us. You trust us, don't you?"

"It's got nothing to do with trust. Are you asking me to kiss and tell?"

"Well, ya, I am. Does that offend your sense of decency? You want to know, don't you?" She'd turned toward me and I bobbed my head enthusiastically.

"Leave her alone," Bellamy interrupted. "We are not talking about Annie's private life."

Misty brought us back on point. "Love and passion, sure we all want it, but in the right proportion. Can you imagine feeling love when you are being chased by a drunk with fists like anvils?" That's what her life with Jet was like. "After I tried to understand Jet's behavior, after I began imagining … well I am never going to know what it was like to grow up in an alcoholic, abusive home like Jet did. I try not to think about what he endured."

I suppose I could start understanding why Jim cheated. I'm not excusing his behavior but *understanding* it. He had the chance to be the "it" guy in town, and he went all Tiger Woods. He was still handsome, had a great smile and a good sense of humor. Almost as soon as we came to this town, the women were all over him. Most men, if given the choice between a fat sick wife and unlimited number of willing young females would choose the latter.

I know that I am better off without him, hadn't loved him for years so could I really blame him? "So, what if the roles were reversed? What if we were in some parallel universe where men got fat bellies, saggy breasts and bottoms and then they became totally undesirable? Then, say we moved to a place where sexy, young gorgeous men were all over me. And if Jim got really, really sick, would I have slept around and left him?"

Emphatically, no. I stated silently. *Maybe.* I almost wavered.

So now I work on forgiveness like I work out my body. Neither happens overnight. It's a continued process interspersed with bouts of failure. I find anger issues resurfacing about as often as I get an urge for a donut. I try to resist both. Sometimes I fail but so what? It gets easier; at least Misty assures me that it does.

4.
Close to Last Christmas

With work and diligence I managed to lose forty pounds and I had a much lighter heart. I don't know which the heavier burden was. The forty pounds was like carrying a preschooler everywhere. The heavy heart was like carrying a disease. It was a holiday gift from me to me.

El Mejor is a restaurant but we call it "the bar" because it's become the local watering hole for this town. Amid the faux frescos of Mexican women chopping cilantro and pressing tortillas hung colorful lights and festive signs wishing "Felice Navidad". An extra margarita diet cheat was in order for me and the girls took advantage of my alco-cheer.

"An online dating service sounds fun, like shopping for men catalog style," Bellamy supersized. "It's the best way to maximize the amount of guy choices you have available at any given time."

"I tried that and it lasted just a week. The guys on the site fell into two categories: the 'I like to hunt and fish type' and the 'I love long walks on the beach and sunsets with a glass of wine and reading Jane Austen books, type'. Guess which guy is telling the truth. There were so many 'long walks on the beach' guys that I think there must be a book out that tells men how to attract stupid women on stupid dating sites," Bren scoffed.

"Or they really like walking on the beach. Most people do, you know," Misty said. "I think dance groups or dance lessons might be the way to go for you, Sophie."

"Ya, you like to dance," said Annie. "Why don't you try contra dancing or swing?"

"Maybe you could go with me, Bren, and shake the boo thang." We all snickered about the firemen story and knuckled each other.

"How about joining a book group?" Annie asked.

"Nope, they're full of woman trying to get away from their husbands." Bellamy survived four divorces and her last husband's death. "I used to join book clubs when I was with Phil because he liked to watch those fishing shows." She sipped her drink.

"Hardware stores," said Stella. She made her occasional cameo appearance. "They're full of men. Letta met one just last week at Lowe's. She was acting all stupid-like and she had enough nerve to ask a man to explain the mechanics of a male/female connection."

I gasped. "I bet that sparked his wiring!"

Loretta "Letta" Steele. Letta has a little bitty baby voice. I find grown women who talk baby talk in public extremely irritating. I believe that if one feels an overwhelming urge to coo infant speak, then they should do it in the privacy of their own home. But the guys seem to love her.

"I might someday learn to say something that suggestive to a guy, but I'd never pretend to be that stupid." I had trouble keeping the disdain from my voice but my friends knew what had passed between Letta and me.

"Sports bars?" someone suggested.

"That's only legitimate if you enjoy sports. I really don't," Annie answered.

I used to love the Red Sox and the Bruins, but even when the Hurricanes won the Stanley Cup, I was as lackluster as the average North Carolinian. "Maybe I could do that. I like the fights. Maybe I could go someplace to watch boxing matches."

"I'm telling you, computer dating is your best chance and you're keeping current," Bellamy reiterated.

"Church is the best place to meet decent men, everyone knows that," Stella offered.

"No way," Both of Bren's hands went up this time. "Church is for worship, for feeding the soul and nourishing the spirit. It is *not* a meat market." This is when my gut began to talk back.

So what if everywhere in the world is as sacred as a church… everywhere? And here I sit contemplating the idea of entering a new old man meat market. Just how willing am I to pretend to be who I'm not in order to find a mate? It feels like I have been who I *am not* for most of my life. I want to be myself, be loved for myself.

Wait, did I just say "old man meat market"? Eeeuw.

"Just do what you love to do. What makes your heart sing? Pursue your own interests and expand your horizons. Have you ever thought about taking a class? Is there any volunteer work that you have been intending to find the time for? You love animals; they are a great ice breaker. Find more local events, get out more and then ask your friends if they know anyone to introduce you to."

"You know any men you can introduce me to?"

"Nope, not a one," was the blanket answer.

"Sophie, you must have had lots of dating experience before Jim." Annie sucked on her e-cig.

"Well, dating was easier when we were young. If you met a cute guy you slept with him and if you liked him, you asked him what his name was. Boston in the sixties and early seventies, stuff was happening." I nodded and drifted to old memories.

"Well, you have to be choosy now," Bren reminded, but I saw her hide a smile. "You've seen what some women will to do for a man these days. Choosy is a good thing."

"Well, if you mean Letta, I'm leaving." We regarded Stella with our heads tilted; our eyelids raised and lips pursed shut. "Okay, maybe she doesn't always do the right thing but at least she's honest about it. How many times has she admitted that if she's not here on Sunday nights, she's off chasing a man?"

Silence.

"Okay, so she is usually out chasing men; but we have known each other our whole lives, and she is a good Christian woman who sits next to me in church every single Sunday."

I tried to not roll my eyes. It would take a lot more than sitting in church to make Letta into a good person. I decided to change the subject. "Stella, you have been married the longest. Can I ask you a question?"

"Sure."

"Is Wes good to you? I mean, does he help you around the house or do you have to pour his whiskey while you're soaking his shorts?"

"Wesley doesn't drink whiskey. I don't expect him to do any of the inside work, but he does fix things and he cuts the grass most of the time. He is a complete gem and I wouldn't trade him for anything in the world."

"Oh, you cater to him. I've seen." Bren wasn't buying it. "It's just like most of you Southern women do."

"If you are going to bash the South, you can go back to where you came from," she managed to say that sweetly.

"It's not just here. It's like that over most of the country, most of the world really," Annie commented.

"Stella, I'm not bashing the South. I like it here but I think it was different up North. Most husbands of our age lived with woman's lib. They helped with the kids, the housework and cooking, at least a little. Misty, did Jet change his habits when you moved here?"

"Jet used to do more, and he was less abusive when we lived in Vermont. It wasn't as acceptable as it is here. What about in Michigan, Annie? Did you have to do all the housework?"

"I'll admit that I did way more than Vern, but he would help sometimes. I sure did all the cooking. He helped me wash the dishes if he were feeling amorous."

"Doing dishes was foreplay for Vern? That's a new one on me." Bren mimed enough to get us giggling.

"Not foreplay, really; he'd get flirty and bump into me. Sometimes he'd put on a little music, then we'd dance together and one thing would lead to another. I got all three kids from washing dishes with Vernon! What about in California, Bell?"

"My husbands knew I was no cook. If they wanted to eat they either cooked it themselves or they took me to a decent restaurant. As for housework, we had housekeepers. And I'd have left at any sign of abuse. You know that."

"What did you do with your time? I don't imagine you stayed home much," Bren asked.

"I went to the beach. I went to yoga. I had lunch with my friends, ordered take out. You know?"

"No, I cannot even relate."

"Well, I had no kids but I did things, had hobbies. I thought that was a normal life. It's what I knew." She had our attention. "Well, if I had to pretend that I cook biscuits and fry chicken to get a fella, I'd be dead in the water."

"I don't think you have to worry about cooking biscuits, Bell."

Kernersville is a great place to grow a family, but I had a hard time adjusting to living in the South; I didn't understand the South. It's different, in a collard green, black-eyed pea kind of way.

Moving here *did* piss off my mother. Our move to North Carolina may have been the beginning of her decline.

Expensive health care and the subsequent nursing home were sure to consume every bit of the considerable wealth she had amassed in her lifetime. I remember how Jim watched her assets dwindle. It ate at his grasping little heart. Once he actually asked me if I thought she would rather live with us.

"With us? Would *you* rather she lived with us? Would you really want her cursing and spitting the evil eye at these good people?" I asked him. "Besides, she'd annoy you enough and you'd probably want to kill her."

"Ya, I'd want to kill her but think of all that money."

Mom liked Jim. He was handsome, and that was pretty much all it took. Jim hated her. She was domineering, demanding and would brood if she didn't get her way. She was "too much," he would say. Too much like him, I think.

5.
Sunday Evening before Christmas

"Miss Sally's party was great, wasn't it? I don't know how she does it at her age. How old you think she is?"

"And she knows all the best bluegrass pickers in the area," I said.

"I never thought I liked bluegrass," Bren said, "but in the middle of all those musicians it feels like it goes right to the heart. That music has honesty."

"Honesty." I considered the comment for a moment.

"I don't know how else to describe it, like the blues has honesty."

"I've never thought about it like that but it fits," I agreed.

"It looked like more than music was moving you last night. Who was that young guy you were flirting with?" Bren asked.

"*He* was flirting with me. I met him once at Stella's and he's married. Anyway, I wouldn't want some guy that young."

"Why ever not?" Little Annie asked. "Who would it hurt?"

"His wife," Bren said as she filled another tortilla.

"I don't know. The guy was as dumb as pellets. What would we talk about?"

"I could think of something dirty to say to him," Misty smiled.

"Ya, I could whisper naughty thoughts," Annie giggled.

"It just wouldn't feel right. What do you think, Bell?"

"If you hit it off with a younger man then I say, go for it."

"Have you considered writing a list of the qualities you want in a guy?" practical Annie asked.

I could see that this might have some merit although it also might be limiting. "I personally would not feel comfortable dating someone excessively handsome. When I met Jim, I thought he was the handsomest man I had ever seen and he turned out to be a shit."

"So you don't want handsome or young? What's wrong with you?" Bren challenged.

"Nothing wrong with handsome," Bell agreed.

"So what do you want?" Annie asked.

"I don't really know what I want. Let's start with someone I'm attracted to. I dunno. Let's ask Misty. Misty, tell me what it is that I'm supposed to want with love and a partner, maybe sort of spiritual with great tantric sex maybe, and everything and everything else."

"Quit making fun of me."

"Well, you gotta admit that most of this woo-woo psycho-spiritual weirdness is..."

"Most?"

"Some."

"Like what?"

"Well, there was that crazy pelican lady that you took me to see." I rolled my eyes at the others.

"Oh, she was completely harmless and sort of sweet."

"She wore barrettes that bobbed around her hair with sparkly angels and she bragged about them! She could hear trees talk and...woodland creatures... gnomes or something. And what about that alien implant guy?" I turned and glanced at the others. "You don't want to know."

"I don't want to know." Bren surveyed the ceiling.

"I also took you to the past-life-regression hypnotist and that medium who you loved."

"That's true," I said to the others, then turned back to Misty. "So how do I get what I want when I only know that what I want is something good?"

"I'm beginning to believe that the answer to all questions, Sophie, is self-love, self-love and acceptance. I'm thinking that we all get what we are. If we are secure and fulfilled, then that's what we get."

"Which is just a tiny bit different than feeling rejected and filled with self-loathing; I'm glad you pointed that out."

"You are making fun of me again, and I still love you," she tittered.

"Misty, I was faithful to Jim. I didn't get what I was then. I got a cheater."

"Are you suggesting that you were not just a little deceitful with Jim?"

"In what way?"

"You could have honestly confronted him when you first had

suspicions. Instead, what did you do? You snuck around and followed him with a camera. You told me you used to check all his phone messages when he was in the shower."

"That's deceitful," Bren agreed.

"So you are saying that it was my fault he cheated?"

"It's not your fault he cheated but you have to accept a degree of culpability if you weren't honest with him. You pretty much allowed him to cheat. I'm just saying that it could have gone another way. It's possible he would have stopped if you had fought for him."

Annie interrupted when I started to protest. "That's all ancient history. Let's get back to finding you a man right now."

"I can tell you this, finding a guy is simply a numbers game," Bellamy stated.

"Unfortunately the odds are not in our favor," Bren said, lips pursed.

"So how do we increase our odds?"

"You give them what they want."

"Which is?"

"Men are basically simple creatures. They want arm candy," Bellamy said.

"They want a woman that makes them feel manly."

"Or to be spanked!" Annie bated.

"Or they want their mothers," Bell again, "or toys."

"They want blonds with big tits," said Bren.

"I think we need to spin that differently," Misty stated. "Men are seeking the same things we are: shared warmth, understanding, comfort, loyalty, trust, companionship and to feel loved."

"By a blond with big tits!"

"Oh, Bren." Misty's hands hide her face.

"Well, men are visual creatures."

"So I will ask again, what do you want in a fella, Sophie?"

"Annie, I don't know, I would like a man who is nurturing rather than selfish," I said.

"And lots of guys are nurturing. Do you expect a guy to be nurturing?"

"I don't think I have ever had any man who was nurturing. I seemed to do all the nurturing in my relationships and then I'd feel used. It would be nice to have someone who would rub my back and pour the coffee for me. That would be a change."

"Well, if you are going to find that nurturing man, you first have to have a first date." Annie stated the obvious.

"I love first dates. They are so full of promise," Bellamy sighed. "I've met drop-dead gorgeous men that I felt no attraction to and homely men who have amazing sex appeal. My advice is to be open, be honest and just be you, the open honest you, that is."

"Well that's the point, isn't it? Being our honest and true self is not always easy," Misty said. "Really, Sophie, the best dating advice I can give you is to learn to love yourself first. If we can love ourselves — all the so-called ugly stuff — maybe we become more lovable *because* of our imperfection. Would you want a guy who was perfect?"

"Like that would happen," I replied.

"I wouldn't. He'd drive me nuts," said Bren. "But you've got to remember what Elvis said, "Don't be cruel" and in front of you may sit "a heart that's true". If he says something really stupid, cut him a little slack. You have said something really stupid before; you know you have!"

"She's right," Annie added. "People are nervous on first dates. Live with it. So you've had time to think about it, what are you hoping for in a guy?"

"I want a guy with a sense of humor. I'd want him to be bright and generally optimistic. An interest in the arts, movies and music is a plus; and I hope he would enjoy cooking with me. I have an adventurous spirit and get enthused easily. It would be great if he were up for new adventures also. The last thing I need is a man with a closed mind and a narrow comfort zone."

"So you *have* been giving this a considerable amount of thought and yet, I noticed, that you did not add *trustworthy* to that list," Bren caught.

"Or sane," Misty added.

"Oh crap, I didn't, did I? And trustworthy and sane, of course."

We explored it from another angle. What is unacceptable behavior? We called it the *deal breaker*. For me unacceptable behavior is unkindness. Is he rude to the waiting staff? How does he treat animals? Is he intolerant, homophobic or show sexist tendencies? I'd rather be with a kind heart. If I found a guy with a really kind heart, I would be willing to overlook an awful lot. I can see a movie and laugh with the girls. I would really like a man to do what Jim never did, and that was to listen to me and honor my feelings."

"Okay, listen," Bellamy said. "There's a New Year's Eve singles party at the Roof Top Club, so why don't we all go to the Roof Top and Sophie can meet some men and actually flirt with them."

"I'm not sure I remember how to."

"Just watch me. Smile a lot. Flirting is just gazing into a man's eyes when you talk to him and giving him an occasional compliment."

"Holy crap."

6.
Christmas Bell

"Auntie Bell's here, Auntie Bell!" She ran up and hugged Bellamy around the hip. Bellamy lowered to one knee and kissed the girl.

"Merry Christmas, Shayna. Did Santa bring you everything you wanted?"

"Uh-huh, I got a doll house and seven dolls. Seven, can you believe it? And four of them are Barbies."

"Of course I believe it. You are a very good girl, practically an angel. What a pretty dress. Is it new?"

She spun holding onto the golden cap sleeves then fell into Bellamy's arms. Bell caressed a chubby brown cheek that had some sticky stuff on it. Shayna was her favorite. "And I got an Easy-Bake oven too. Jessie got a punching bag. He better not be punching me. Granny says he won't if he knows what's good for him."

"Bellamy!" Bren came out of the kitchen, wiping her hands on a towel. She hugged Bell. "Merry Christmas."

"You too, Bren. Where is Charles? I need him to help bring in my gift for the children."

"It better not be something big. You spoil them enough."

"Oh, like you don't."

"Charles, come here now and help Miss Bell. "

"Sure, Merry Christmas, Miss Bell." Charles was the oldest of Bren's grandchildren — seventeen and tall, athletic, handsome; and he'd inherited Bren's wide bright smile.

"Merry Christmas, Charles," she hugged him and they walked out the door. "Have you been checking out colleges, Honey?" She asked as they walked out to Bellamy's Lexus.

"Yes, Miss Bell, I'm hoping to go to Appalachian State."

"For football?"

"Oh, ya, but I'm gonna major in political science."

"I didn't know you were interested in politics. Grab that box and I'll carry the wine."

"Oh, the kids are going to love this."

"I hope so. But you're too old for gingerbread so here's something special for you." She handed him a gift card for the mall.

"Thank you, Miss Bell; you know what I want."

"Yes, you want to choose your own gift! You're welcome, Darling, it's my pleasure. Political science, really?"

"Yes, Miss Bell, and maybe law school after."

"I'm so proud of you." She hugged him affectionately then Charles picked up the box and carried it up the front steps to the house."

"Oh gosh, look what Auntie Bell brought." The children screamed with excitement. "Did you make that?" Bren asked her.

"Oh hell, no," she said quietly. "I could never make one of these."

Charles placed the box on the counter. The children gathered wide-eyed to watch Bellamy take the candy-covered gingerbread house from the carton and place it on the kitchen table.

"That's beautiful, Bell."

"And I brought huge chocolate chip cookies too." Five designer cookies wrapped in cellophane with big red bows were distributed amongst the children.

"They're pizza size!" Shayna exclaimed, and all the children screamed and jumped around crazily. "Can we eat them, Granny, can we eat them now?"

"Not until after dinner, you can't. You know that," Bren told them. "Just what they need, more sugar treats," she rolled her eyes.

"But you have to share with Charles, because he didn't get one," Bell insisted.

"Charles didn't get one because he's been bad," Shayna tattled.

"That's not possible, I'm sure," she said withholding her amusement.

"Oh Lord, you don't know the half of it. Uncle Lenny will tell you. Listen, could you keep the little ones busy while I get dinner on the table?" Bren's daughters, Larissa and Audrey set the oversized dining room table wishing their brother, Charles Senior, could be there too. "Kids, take care of Auntie Bell. We can't have her sitting alone, can we? Like that would ever happen in this house."

The younger children surrounded Bellamy, patting her face and stroking her soft blond hair. Bell delighted in the tussle and she hugged each of them in turn. She settled the baby in her arm and little Abel on her lap. Alicia and Shayna teetered on the arms of the chair, and Jessie sat quietly to the side.

"When I was a little girl, I lived in a place where it never snowed."

"Then how did Santa get his sleigh to your house?"

"Santa is magical. He doesn't need snow and ice because the reindeer can fly, can't they?" They nodded. "But we used to hang so many lights outside just to make sure he couldn't miss our house." She nibbled Abel's cheek.

"Did you have a tree?" Alicia asked.

"We had a tree that changed colors."

"What kind of tree changes colors?" Jesse eyeballed.

"It was made of aluminum. Do you know what that is?"

"Like aluminum foil?" Alicia asked.

"Yes, Darling, you are so smart, shiny and silver just like aluminum foil."

"How did it change colors?"

"It had a big round light and a color wheel that turned around on top so it would be green, then turn to pink and then blue."

"Sounds pretty."

"Not as pretty as your real tree and yours smells so nice."

"Then why didn't you have a real tree?"

"Because where I lived there weren't many pine trees, I lived in California. Have you ever heard of California?"

"Oh yes." Alicia nodded knowingly. "That's where all the movie stars come from. Were you a movie star, Miss Bell?"

"No, Darling, I wasn't a movie star. Why would you think that?"

"You are as pretty as a movie star."

"Thank you, Alicia. What a sweet thing to say." She kissed her and then tickled Abel's belly, making him squeal with delight.

Uncle Lenny was a thin, elderly and man. He made his way slowly, bent-backed, and seated himself at the head of the table where he watched his family gather. He nodded affectionately as the children were seated, bibs were tied and napkins placed on their laps. Finally when all were seated and the platters of food were passed and the plates were piled high, Larissa said the blessing. The family tucked in, and conversation flowed as only happens in a large close family. He nodded with approval and pride.

"Mom, this is delicious," Audrey complimented and many nodded in agreement.

"Your daddy and momma would be so proud of you if they were here today."

"Thank you, Uncle Len."

"Nobody can cook like you do, Granny. Did you see the pies she made for desert?" Charles asked.

"Save room. I have apple, sweet potato and pecan."

"Only three, Mom? That's not nearly enough."

"Don't worry, Audrey. There's ice cream and cake and five giant cookies. And there is a whole gingerbread house if you're still hungry after that. Do you want a roll, Bellamy?"

"No thanks. Charles, are you still working at Harris Teeter?" Everyone froze, forks hovered in midair.

"Oh no, here it comes again," said Audrey and she pursed her lips.

"It's not my fault." Charles tried to hide his smile. "Besides, nothing happened. I don't understand what Uncle Lenny is... "

"You're right; you don't understand, boy," Len frowned. "Do you even understand how hard it was for the black man here in the South?"

"You're from Harlem, Uncle Len. How would you know how hard it was here?"

"I'll swat you, boy. I'll swat you good. Fifty, sixty years ago men were lynched for less than that."

"What's lynched?" little Alicia asked.

"Nothing you need to know about. Eat," Bren said firmly, directing a finger at her plate.

"That was sooo long ago! And I'd like to see you try and swat me, Uncle Len."

"Charles," Audrey admonished, "you do not speak to Uncle Len that way." Everyone but Lenny seemed to be muffling their amusement.

"Sorry, Aunt Audrey. Sorry, Uncle Len."

"Alright, who is going to tell me what this young man did?" Bellamy asked.

"Oh don't tell Miss Bell. Pleeease don't tell her," Charles begged.

"Uncle Len went to Harris Teeter and saw all these middle-aged women flirting with Charles at the register," Audrey shared, pressing her lips tight to prevent a smile.

"I watched it happen over and over again, old white woman batting their eyelashes and him all smiling back at them with that big white grill of his. And to top it off, his little blond cheerleader girlfriend was waiting patiently till his shift ended," Len complained. He was now hiding a smile. "I'll swat you, boy, just on general principal. Nobody should have it as good as you, Charles, nobody."

"You just wait until Jessie's my age. The girls are already waiting in line for him!" Charles said. Jessie peeked up and smiled shyly.

It had been a long and tiring day. Bellamy sagged into the sofa. She held up the dark red sweater Bren gave her. She always thought she looked slutty in red but she might wear it.

She set it aside and opened the bag of gifts that the children had made for her, took each one out and arranged them on the coffee table before her: a plastic beaded bracelet, a cardboard star, a picture of a tree torn from a coloring book sparkled with glitter. Little Abel's was a wad of scotch tape and red tissue paper that was barely recognizable. She stared into her half-decorated tree, gulped from a glass of vodka then placed in on the table next to the gifts. Bellamy Hays held pillow tightly against her chest, fell into the soft plush of her sofa and achingly, brutally she wept.

7.
The Roof Top Club

We met at Bellamy's house. Bren, in basic black, helped Misty with an earring which had caught on the edge of her silver cocktail dress. Annie's small frame wore a deep red, lacey short thing. I reconsidered my blue skirt and white top. Okay, it wasn't a plain white top, but compared to Annie, Bren and Misty, I looked like a girl from Catholic school.

Crap.

Bellamy descended the staircase in a gorgeous purple dress, short in the front and multi-leveled in the back. She was a vision of lavender sparkles.

"Purple haze . . . ," Bren sang out. "Great dress! Now tell us how we can fix Sophie's attempt to repel men with her wardrobe choice."

Bell studied my outfit. "The skirt is a little long, but I have a top that might work with it. Come upstairs. We have time."

Bren and Annie were passing the time with a deck of bird spirit cards they found on Bell's coffee table. They were laughing as they matched people they knew to the birds in the deck.

"You're always drawn to those," Misty said. "Every time we're here you pick up those bird cards."

"That's because they are so freaking funny," Bren replied.

"Animal magic is as old as time," Misty said.

"And pagan."

"It's more about having an encounter with an animal and what that means for you. You would not be laughing at animal totems in front of Native Peoples, would you?"

"I agree with Misty," Bellamy said from the stairs. "You are part Native American, Annie; I'm surprised that you are poking fun at this. And Bren, there is just no hope for you."

"Sophie, that top is great on you. I think you might attract some of this here *cock* magic." Bren pointed at the spirit card.

31

"Let's go, Bren, we're taking my car." Bell tried to ignore her. "Cock magic? Really, Bren."

Bell's dark blue sparkly thing was cut a little too low, and maybe it was more than a bit tight on me, but there was cleavage and the guys looked at me, asked me to dance. Bren was certainly at no loss for company. Men flanked her. She smiled coquettishly and flirted. I don't know how she pulls it off at her age, but men, I've come to find out, are usually at Bren's mercy. She's more than a flirt; she's a complete tease.

The DJ played great dance tunes. The food was delicious: salmon or roast beef. I'd had a few glasses of wine, but since I danced so much, I felt a little indulgence was allowed. A tower of cookies, cream puffs and chocolate-covered strawberries were calling out to me but I was saved by Bell.

"What do you think of that guy in the tux?" I asked Bellamy.

"What guy with the tux? There are about twenty of them," Bren commented on her way to the restroom.

"That tallish one on the right."

"Oh, he looks smart," Misty said. "A lot of tuxedos here tonight, nice to see."

"It's some of that *penguin* magic going on."

"That was cheesy," I said.

"And predictable," Bellamy followed. Bren had been drinking dangerous martinis. Bell reminded her that she'd be paying for them in the morning.

The tallish one on the right came over and asked Bellamy to dance. She was graceful in spike heels, and more than a few fellows were checking her out. I wore sensible dance shoes with two-inch heels, kind of frumpy; they were *dance* shoes.

So I flirted a little, sort of remembered what it felt like to enjoy—anticipate—the next dance, the next face, the next body.

I met a man named Albert who seemed quite charming. I accepted his invitation to go watch his chess game at a coffee shop on Wednesday afternoon.

And I met Kenny. Kenny made my heart pound. I was trying not to smile too widely as midnight approached. We lingered at the end of the bar when the band announced that it was five minutes to midnight. "You know what that means?" he asked.

"It means that, in five minutes I get to kiss you?" I was flirting; it was that easy!

"Should we begin now?" His jacket had been shed, and his tie loosened. He placed my hand on his damp chest and we began to sway gently to the music. He smelled like sandalwood and heaven, and I could feel his heart beating with his hand over mine. "This minute will never happen again. Let's make it last," he said, and we did just that. I could feel his breath tickling in my hair. His lips brushed my forehead, then again. I think I might have moaned as his mouth found my temple, and I felt the warmth of his body against mine. His lips edged closer to my ear and, oh God, he felt fantastic.

The crowd began to count down, and we entered each other's breath space deliberately, sensuously... we melted into our first kiss, a kiss marking the passing of the old into the New Year. I smiled in expectancy of what was yet to come: 2012, a new year, a new me.

The chess game on Wednesday was boring. Albert seemed overly grateful that I held his captured pieces, but it was a first date so I cut him some slack. We sat for a coffee afterward, and he asked lots of questions, what I did, where I lived, and how many square feet in my home. I told him a little about myself, that I was a bead artist.

"I build structures using tiny beads, some under a millimeter. I combine ancient indigenous techniques with new precision-cut beads. It's done under high magnification and is very labor-intensive."

"So you make what with these beads, jewelry?"

"Some is, well, most is jewelry."

He seemed interested and asked if he could see my work. We made plans to meet Saturday afternoon for bagels. It didn't feel exactly comfortable; but it was only a first date.

On Friday, Kenny met me at a darling little Indian place loaded with ambiance. It was not too crowded that evening so we were able to sit for hours drinking decafs and talking. He told me several times how comfortable he felt with me. I felt nervous, like I should run out and wash my car or get a manicure. He had been impeccably dressed at the Roof Top and he was impeccably dressed now. I wondered if he were always perfectly pressed and perfectly matched. He obviously spent a lot of his money on clothing. I mentally assessed my wardrobe and realized that if I tried to dress this well on every date with Kenny I would run out of outfits by Thursday.

I agreed to go to hear a jazz band with him on Sunday while mentally fretting about apparel, wondering if my black slacks were clean.

We walked into an obsidian night with thousands of tiny cut stars. He protected me from icy winds and wrapped his fine jacket around me. I slipped my arms into the soft silk around his back absorbing his warmth with my body. His lips lingered on my upper cheek where the bone curves in towards the ear then kissed and kissed, over again, in just that... one... lovely spot. All my nervousness melted away.

"You have such beautiful hair," he whispered and slipped his hand behind my ear separating the locks with his long probing fingers until his palm cradled the back of my skull. He held my hair firmly with his fist as his mouth traced my cheek then those gorgeous full lips found mine.

Whoa, baby.

The good people of Kernersville have finally come to realize that bagels do not come from the freezer section of Food Lion. I had been travelling to Greensboro, where there is a much better selection of bagel places. Bagels with cream cheese and lox were among the foods I missed the most when we moved to Kernersville. I kept asking where I could get them and got replies like, "Anyone who likes bagels ain't never had a good biscuit." This is sort of like saying that anyone who likes Monopoly has never played a good game of Scrabble.

It was just after two when I met Albert. I showed him a few of my beaded pieces. He studied them, complemented me and said that they should be in a gallery. It was nice to hear the praise.

He claimed that he was from Arizona, but nothing about him seemed Southwestern. I listened skeptically as he spoke of the years he had spent on the west coast of Mexico.

"They would love your beadwork in Mexico."

"Really? In Mexico?"

"Mexicans are famous for beading. They would love your work."

"Mexico is a rather impoverished country, and I'm pretty sure that they have their own style of beading which they are fairly proud of."

"There is great wealth in Mexico when you get into the large cities. Mexico is so romantic. We should go."

"So what are you doing here in Greensboro?"

"An old manse, I'm refurbishing an old historic mansion."

He was hinting that he was wealthy. I had my doubts. I figured that if Albert truly had wealth and the means to travel, he'd be doing this with a much younger and prettier woman.

We talked through most of the afternoon about art, and again, he asked me many questions. How long had I been beading? What got me started? Did I have a studio? Then Albert reached into his case and handed me his resume.

"Your resume? Gee, and most guys just bring you flowers.

"I want you to know who I am. You're an artist, and I want you to see my credentials. My mother was a famous oil painter and I managed her gallery for many years. I know art and I can show you how to get well-known in the art world, how to get your work in the better galleries." The resume was peppered with misspelled words and bad punctuation.

Then he went for the close. He asked me to come back to his place for dinner and suggested that I spend the night with him. The manse, he told me, was just about a half-hour east and we could pick up some barbeque on the way.

"I can't spend the night with you. You hardly know me. I could be a hatchet murderer."

"Come back with me and I will get to know you," he smiled.

"And I have a dog that I have to walk and feed."

"A dog can go without food for one night. It won't hurt it at all. You'll love Mexico," he said, again, "and I can't wait until you see the manse."

"I'm going home to feed my dog. Good night, Albert. By the way, have you ever been to Mexico?"

"Yes, of course, it's on my resume."

"You know you misspelled Mazatlán?"

35

Smooth jazz played and the saxophone was powerful. I purposely appeared a little disheveled for this date to gauge Kenny's reaction. If he noticed he never let on. I felt more relaxed about my appearance and about my messy car. Kenny was long-limbed and solidly built. I admired beautiful thick eyelashes over his soft brown eyes. And that mouth, those lush lips framed his warm white smile. I imagined what he'd look like naked.

That night, I met the girls at El Mejor and gave a full report.

"Sophie has had four dates this week *and* she's won a free trip to Mexico!"

"That is nothing to joke about, Bellamy. She could have been abducted and sold into white slavery."

"Oh, Bren, that's just the cop in you. Women our age don't get kidnapped."

"Oh, really? You think woman our age don't get taken for their life's savings? What if this Albert had taken her to Mexico and forced her to empty her bank account? Then she'd disappear and no one would ever know what happened to her."

"I wouldn't have gone to a foreign country with a perfect stranger. Do you think I'm that stupid? Ya, his stories didn't seem plausible. I got a weird vibe."

"You better listen to that vibe. Promise me you will be careful. There are a lot of lonely women and more than enough men to prey on that loneliness. You have been out of Boston for too long, and you better get your *streetwise* back."

"I listened; I had a little *street* on." I felt silly saying this but I managed an acceptable hand gesture. "And may I point out that I'm not in some border town tied to a chair, half-starved, smelling tacos. Give me a little credit."

"So what about this man, Kenny?" Misty asked. "Are you going to see him again?"

"I don't know. He didn't ask for a third date. Maybe he did notice the funky clothes."

"E-mail him. Tell him how much you enjoyed the music. You have to let him know that you like him. We all need a little encouragement. It's not all up to the guys like we were taught by our mothers."

"Bellamy's right," Misty added, "it's okay to show your

interest, but that will be the third date."

"Ya, the third date."

"It will be the third date," she repeated.

"What does that mean?" I studied their faces.

"You know, sex gets initiated," Annie told me in an exaggerated whisper.

"I'm not having sex with him just because it's the third date. That's insane."

"It's not insane. It's a rule," said Bren.

"It's not a rule. I don't have to go to bed with him because it's the third date."

"Of course you don't *have to,* but expect him to make the move."

I thought about that a while and e-mailed Kenny that evening.

Our schedules didn't match, and then he got the flu so it was a while before we met again. Eventually we arranged a brunch. I'd been tempted to go shopping for a new outfit but I resisted the urge. He either liked me for myself or he didn't. I was determined to be myself.

It was a Sunday afternoon when we met at Sweet Potatoes on Trade, in the center of the arts district of Winston-Salem. I liked his choice of restaurants. It had banging sweet potato fries and a great omelet, but I can't say my knees were continuing to buckle.

He complained about work, began to tell me about age discrimination in the office, how he had been passed over for a promotion by a younger woman and how white men had so little chance any more (waah, waah, poor baby).

The conversation segued to his men's group (I didn't even know they had men's groups) where he learned about something called 'the death of a thousand cuts'. I didn't like the sound of that so I asked him not to tell me about it, especially while I was eating.

"No, it's really nothing violent. It's figurative."

"Fine, but this better not be violent. I do not like to hear violent and disturbing stuff, okay?"

"Okay," he spoke rapidly, "there really is an Asian torture that is called death of a thousand cuts and they do eventually die from it but… "

"You tricked me! I didn't want to hear this. I told you I didn't want to hear this and you tricked me."

"Yes, but the violent part is over. It's a metaphor for life, how it cuts you down over time, bit by bit."

"That is just as disturbing, and I specifically asked you not to tell me that."

Maybe I was overreacting but I don't want to hear or see violent stuff unless it's highly fanaticized, like the orcs in *Lord of the Rings* or wizard dueling in the Harry Potter movies. I never had cable TV reconnected because I don't like to hear all those crazy, over-ly-sensationalized news items that I accidently stumbled upon while surfing the channels. It's the real stuff that gives me the creeps. When I hear about violence, unpleasant stories or even something exceedingly boring, I go to the mental Bahamas. I visualize soft breezes and palm trees waving. I bask in the sunshine and imagine the gentle cadence of the waves rolling in and out.

He apologized. I thought I made my point, but our third date had not taken a romantic path.

The following week we made an evening date and I expected that this would be the night when we would first make love, the first time since my marriage. I was excited at the prospect, nervous still, but ready. We went to an alternative theatre and saw a Japanese art film called *Rashomon*. I thought the photography was brilliant, but it was violent, murder and rape… and it was peppered with uniquely disturbing sexist scenes that are characteristic of old Japanese films. Honestly, I spent half the picture in Barbados.

"Have you seen this movie before?" I asked as we exited the theatre.

"Yes, it's a classic."

"You don't find this movie violent, disturbing and sexist?"

"Oh, come on, Sophie. They didn't even show the gory parts." He clearly wasn't listening.

Deal breaker.

"Are you telling me that you gave up perfectly good sex with a handsome man because you didn't like the movie he took you to?" Bren asked.

"I did, didn't I? Oh what is wrong with me?"

"Call him back."

"No, it wasn't meant to be, I mean, I don't care if he watches violent films. I care that he took me to one after I made my feelings about it clear. I didn't want to see that any more than I wanted to hear about the death of a thousand cuts or him whining about how unfair the workplace is for white men."

"I've heard about the death of a thousand cuts," Bellamy said. "They cut you in the most sensitive places and…"

"I'm in Aruba; I don't want to hear this."

"Then go to the Aruba in the ladies room so Bellamy can finish telling me."

Misty followed me. "I agree with you. If it doesn't make me smarter, happier, slimmer, richer, better in some way, I don't want to hear it either."

Carlos delivered drinks as we rejoined the gals. Bren had the extra-large margarita. "I think I'll have one of those also, when you have a chance, please," I said.

Misty wasn't drinking because she had given it up for Lent. Bren and I were planning to get stinking drunk for the full forty days of Lent. We were trying to convince Annie to join us since we already had a built-in designated driver in Misty. But Bellamy, who was usually up for any kind of party, seemed uninspired.

"You gals have fun. I gotta go," she said and she left that quickly.

"What's wrong with her? Is she feeling okay?"

"February," Bren said plainly.

"Crap, it's February. I forgot, February."

"Oh ya, February… again… this is getting old." Bren swallowed. Bell's favorite husband died in February. Every year at this time she gets tearful and overly sentimental.

"Misty, can't you set her up with some mourning therapy or something?"

"I have offered, and I could help her but I can't make her come. I think this is more of a guilt issue with Bell."

"Why would she feel guilty about Eddie's death? She cared for him in every way possible, stayed with him to the very end," Annie asked.

"Bellamy is extremely beautiful, and being that pretty is not as easy to live with as one might think."

"I'm beautiful and I love it," Bren stated.

"Yes, you are beautiful; your beauty shows in your personality, your confidence and your inner light. But Bellamy is *ridiculously* beautiful, Grace Kelly beautiful, Marilyn beautiful. Most women who are that gorgeous have some guilt attached to it. They often sabotage themselves in some way so it's very common for gorgeous women to become alcoholics, drug addicts, have multiple marriages."

"And multiple orgasms."

"Bren, I'm serious. They can even become suicidal."

"Like Marilyn."

"Yes, like Marilyn."

"Why? Why would they do that?" Annie asked.

"It's complicated and everyone is different; but it is common with beautiful women."

"Well, she is gorgeous," Annie said. "She's just going to have to endure all the attention that comes with it."

"And all the orgasms."

"My mother was Ava Gardner, drop-dead gorgeous. She could flash a flirty smile and the world opened before her."

"And you have often told me how mean and unhappy she was, haven't you?"

"Oh, she was mean alright and cold. I don't think she had one maternal gene in her whole body. Kathryn and I were just props that Mother could dress up, show off and then store us safely in our rooms. Fortunately, my room had a window that I could sneak out of," I chortled. "Fortunately, any hidden, less than perfect DNA in the family gene pool fell to me."

Mother called me her ugly duckling, and I suppose I learned to find humor in that early on. It was the only way to deal with the lunacy of Pappas family life. I think maybe my older brother Nick was the only child Mother really cared about. My sister Kath is also gorgeous and she has been in and out of the shrink's office her whole life.

"Hey, there is Stella! Hey, Stella, come on over here. I haven't seen you in an age. Where's Letta?" Bren was always happy for added company.

"Letta is out having dinner with that guy she met at Lowe's Home Improvement. They have been hot and heavy ever since."

"Gee, that's great, gives me hope every time one of us finds love." She turned to me and mouthed the word "slut".

"What's his name? Do we know him?" Misty asked.

"Al Predo."

"Al Fredo? Sounds saucy," I slurred. There was way too much tequila in me. "Hope she orders linguini."

"Not Al Fredo, Predo, Al Predo, like pray he has doe."

"Good, the wives of Kernersville won't have to trail their husbands like they usually do."

"That's not very nice, Sophie." Stella wagged her finger like a nice little church lady. I didn't care.

"With an Italian name like that, he's not a local boy," Bren asked.

"He's from Philadelphia or Jersey or some one of them Yankee places."

"That's what I need: an Italian man, a nice, dark, handsome, passionate Italian man who talks with his hands and yells, 'Ay, you-comin'-out or what?' I want a man who cooks red gravy and meatballs."

"That's just what he sounds like. That's so funny," Stella giggled.

"A man who cusses, 'Aye, Fuck-face, you gonna eat?', hmmmm. That's like a warm fuzzy to a Boston girl, very North End."

"Well, how about that old Italian guy that lives in your neighborhood, what's his name, Joey, the one who has all the dogs?" Misty reminded me.

"You mean that fat old guy with the eyebrows? He's even got a hairy back."

"They all got hairy backs now. Hair growing where it wasn't and none left where it used to be. I got an early day tomorrow." Stella gathered her belongings. "How long has it been since you had a boyfriend, anyway, Sophie?"

"Sex is so last century." I had to be pretty tipsy to admit that, especially because there was a chance that it might get back to Letta. Stella nodded her good nights and left the bar.

"Letta's getting laid, and I'm not." I wanted another drink, but it was the last thing I needed.

41

"Annie and Misty are getting laid, and you are not," Bren stated.

"Well, how long has it been since you had a date, Bren?"

"I don't need to date because I have Leroy."

"Who is Leroy? How come I don't know about Leroy? Misty, do you know about Leroy?"

"Shush, keep it down. You don't know about Leroy because Leroy is a secret. He comes over when I call him. We have sex and he goes home."

"He's a friend with benefits?" Misty asked. "Bren, can you do that, keep your emotions out of a sexual relationship, separate the two?"

"Oh, that wasn't the hard part. The hard part was yelling the name Leroy in a fit of passion. Oh, Leroy, Leroy, Leroy." We snickered. "So I'm having sex regularly and you are not."

"I am not," I admitted and I have not for an embarrassingly long time.

"Well, that old guy Joey must be looking pretty good to you by now. He's got nice big arms, and I bet he's got some meatballs."

8.
When I Met Letta

Stella has lived here all her life. In some ways I envy that because there is no question that she belongs where she is. I usually feel displaced, geographically challenged.

She and I met at our daughters' school and I liked her right away. She is a kind and intelligent woman, very gracious, the quintessential Southern woman, if you will. Knowing that I was new to the area, she invited me to her home for coffee and pie after we picked the kids up from school. I was eager to make friends in Kernersville so I accepted right away. Our girls played nicely together and our sons were close in age so we arranged some quiet time with good conversation in her den. We talked about the children mostly and she asked if I had been to Korner's Folly.

"It's a very interesting historic home," she told me. "It's three stories high, but there are about seven different levels. They call it the strangest home in America."

"Oh, that must be that unusual building on Main Street."

"I'd love to show it to you, and you may as well get to know other historical sites in the area. Have you been to Old Salem yet?"

"Stella, I haven't been anywhere yet."

"Oh, you have to visit Old Salem. It's the first Moravian settlement in North Carolina."

"What's a Moravian?"

"Oh, you don't know who the Moravians are? They came from Bavaria, I think, maybe Czechoslovakia. They settled here and were very talented craftsmen. People came from all over to trade with them, and the village thrived. It's a fascinating place. They built the first woman's college in this whole country. Washington slept there, at the tavern, not at the women's college."

"I'd love to see it." I was excited to have made my first friend in my new town, and I looked forward to getting to know her better. "Say, why don't you and Wes and the kids have dinner with us this Saturday?" I asked.

"That would be nice; we could see if our husbands like each other. It's always good when that happens."

And so I made plans for my first dinner party. It had been Mother's opinion that I would always be an outsider in North Carolina, but I was more than happy to prove her wrong.

I shopped half the day and cooked the other half, resulting in a lovely wine-baked chicken with green beans and artichoke hearts, freshly-baked spanakopita and a home-made apple pie for dessert. I thought that even the most finicky eater would have something on the table that they would like, and hopefully they would be willing to try something new.

I expected them at seven, and the phone rang close to that time. "Hi, Sophie, Wesley has a problem at work and he was called in just now so he can't make it for dinner."

"I'm so sorry. You and the children can come, can't you?"

"Oh yes, but my friend Loretta's here. She just broke up with her boyfriend, and she's feeling sort of blue. Would you mind if I brought her along?"

"Bring her, absolutely; we're happy to have her." And I was. I was excited to meet one of Stella's friends.

They were a little late, but the dinner wasn't ruined. Jim and I met them at the door. Loretta Steele had beautiful clear blue eyes and a sweet smile. I welcomed her warmly but when she turned towards Jim I watched her pupils dilate and glint. Her bottom lip dropped considerably. She caught herself gaping and changed her expression to an admiring, upward beam. She didn't seem like she was nursing a broken heart to me. By the time we were seated at the dining room table, she had unbuttoned her blouse and there was a considerable amount of cleavage exposed above a tiny pink camisole. Jim was admiring the view. Actually he couldn't keep his eyes off the view.

"Yuck, what's that?" Wes Jr. asked, pointing at the artichoke hearts.

"Try it. If you don't like it, you don't have to eat it."

"If it's on his plate, he has to eat it," Stella warned. I cut a tiny piece for him to try before I served and he liked the flavor which was sweetened by wine and richened with butter. His younger sister, Emma Jane, was willing to follow his lead.

Martha and Johnny convinced them to try the pita without mentioning that the green stuff was spinach. Johnny expressed his enthusiasm, "I'd rather have pita than chocolate cake, any day."

"Would you like a piece, Loretta?" I asked her.

"Everyone calls me Letta," she said then peeked up at Jim. "Really? It's better than cake?" The end of her question was ear-piercingly high. She took a cautious bite and wrinkled her nose.

That annoying voice was almost reason enough for me to know that she and I would never be friends. I couldn't imagine wanting to meet her for coffee or a drink if my sense of hearing would be thusly assaulted. An instinct suddenly crawled up my back and there it was the vibe, suspicion that his tiny woman could be an incredibly large threat. Something about her put me on high alert (besides the fact that she was flirting with my husband with her boobs practically hanging out at my dining room table).

Women had flirted with Jim in front of me before, I was used to it. Even Mother acted like she was thirty years younger when she was near him. But this woman felt like a wild animal that could spring on me at any moment, or maybe I was the animal waiting to leap.

I sat back and observed this strange being. Outwardly she was adorable, but her smile was unsettling with small uneven teeth that looked as if they could gnaw through metal. Her eyes fascinated me. They were certainly among the prettiest that I remembered seeing; also the most expressive and she eyed my husband with more hunger than she showed for dinner.

"So what church do you go to?" That was usually the first question a Southern person asked when they met me. So far, only Stella had not.

"We haven't found a church yet," Jim answered. That was so out of character for Jim. He was brought up in a rigidly religious setting. His father regularly beat him with the Good Book for faltering on scripture which he was made to recite daily. He feared that father until his death; he then swore that he would never set foot in a church again. Jim hated church.

"We don't go to church," I admitted, hoping that it would not be an impediment to Stella's friendship.

"You mean you haven't found one yet?" Stella asked.

"No, I mean we don't attend church."

Letta understood my answer, and she viewed me like I was a primitive life form in need of stalwart modification. I watched her eyes transform. The blue remained vivid but the irises rearranged like patterns on a quilt immediately recut, or the focus of a camera lens turned slightly to the left and quickly refocused on a completely different view. Maybe they sharpened or blunted, but I saw ice-cold scorn in them, hatred and judgment directed at me.

"You ain't takin' these young'uns of yours to church?" Letta shrilled. Stella's children inspected mine for defects.

"You got to go to church, Darlin', got to have a church family. That's how it's done here," Stella said, "and, besides, that's the only way you're gonna get to heaven." She seemed to have genuine concern for my soul and those of my family. "You do believe in Jesus, don't ya? Why don't I pick y'all up this Sunday and bring you to our church as my guest?"

I gently explained that I promised my grandmother that I would never leave the Greek Church. This was a convenient story, you know, like a lie. I had practiced and repeated my church-lie to Southerners almost daily and it sent Letta into fundamentalist fury.

"Your *grandmother* ain't going to help you get into heaven."

I narrowed my eyes. "Are you suggesting that my grandmother isn't in heaven?" I thought to argue, but I controlled the urge. I wanted Stella's kids to like my kids and wanted Stella to like me, but I was never going to be like them and everyone at the table was aware of it.

"Every single word in the Bible is the absolute truth from the very first word to the very last and you got to read it every single day." Her finger might have dented the table and her voice was glacial-ly high. Thin blond hair hovered with static electricity. She looked like a screw-eyed lunatic and sounded like a cartoon alien. "Don't you even care about your own kids' salvation?" she appealed to Jim.

"Now, Sophie, It wouldn't hurt to visit church," Jim said smiling at Letta. She was already sizing me up, gauging just how tightly my claws were imbedded into my husband.

"Y'all need to be born again or you ain't got a prayer," she told me.

"Well, we don't have that tradition in the Greek church. Once seems to work well enough." I thought of my devout and saintly grandmother.

"What Bible do you read?"

"The Greek one," I lied.

"My family's been reading King James since the time of Christ."

"How smart of you." God she was stupid.

After dessert the children went outside to play. Stella wanted to sit out on the deck to watch them catch fireflies and maybe to rethink our acquaintance. I wanted to sit out with her and repair any damage the church issue caused but I didn't want to leave Letta alone with my husband.

Jim had never given me the slightest suspicion that he would cheat. He was always home in the evenings, never travelled without the family, but my antennae were up and I didn't trust this high-frequency bitch one iota. I walked out to the deck with Stella and set down drinks. I then invented a reason to go back inside in order to eavesdrop. I peered around a corner and heard Letta ask Jim if he liked her new jeans. She turned to show him the back. "Can you tell that I am not wearing any underwear?"

Holy shit!

Back outside, I asked Stella, "Does she act like that around your Wesley?"

"Ya, but she don't mean anything by it. That's just her way."

"Well, I think she means it with Jim."

"She's just naturally flirty."

"She just asked my husband to check out her butt. What part of that did I misunderstand?"

"Oh, maybe I better take her home."

Stella yelled to the kids that it was time to leave. They'd collected their belongings with a fuss while I found a jar for Wes and Emma's bugs. Jim walked them out to the car. Stella buckled the kids into their car seats as he opened the passenger door for Letta. I was suddenly glued beside him.

"It's a real shame that you ain't born again," she said with her frosty voice and eyes that didn't match her words. She gave me a full top to bottom checkout and I saw in her face that she thought I'd be easy competition. Then she smiled as if nothing would make her

47

happier than to think of me burning in hell for all of eternity.

I said nothing to Jim, but I watched. Sunday morning he invented a reason to go in to work. After he left, I took the kids to my neighbor Alice's home then I drove to and patiently waited outside of Stella's church. As they exited I watched my husband succumb to the flattering attentions of a large-breasted blond who gazed at his handsome face with rapt devotion.

"Bet you remember your scripture now," I said aloud.

I bought the smallest camera I could find.

The crispy brown leaves on the Old Salem common crunched underfoot as we walked towards the Tavern. We ate traditional Moravian chicken pot pie as Stella explained Kernersville to me. People were pretty much alike when she was young. Every family was eating the same kind of food, they shopped at the same few stores, had the same belief system and values. They were a homogenized society. Catholics were exotic and maybe a little scary. She met her first Jewish person only recently. There was a certain safety in knowing everyone in town they all acted alike, no surprises.

Then came the invasion of the outsiders. People from all over live here now. I'm what they call a "halfback", definitely Yankees but we moved here from Florida. Up North, too cold and Florida was too hot. Both had high crime rates so we halfbacks moved to North Carolina in droves. Sometimes we were graciously received and sometimes treated like shit. There are many people here who have been taught since birth to fear outsiders and to hate Yankees in particular. Some of them, especially those like Letta, are just a few borderline clicks away from a psychotic incident due to the rapidly-forced assimilation. Their entire belief system, their very way of life has been assaulted with discernible thought, historic fact and scientific findings.

I'm from Boston. I love Boston, the Back Bay in particular. Prudential Center to the Charles River and Mass. Ave. to the Public Garden is the stretch of land that is dearest to my heart. Would I move back if I could? Maybe, probably not; but it's still home.

I miss Florida. I liked living so close to the beach and having lots to do. It was hot but breezy and a warm rain punctuated the afternoons. I'd have stayed but the drugs and gang-related crime activity convinced me that it wasn't the place I wanted to raise my kids. Up North and in Florida most everyone I knew was Catholic or Jewish, Italian or Greek. We are diverse and fiery people. We laugh loudly, cry hard, yell and cuss. Southerners, I find, often don't like me much unless I keep the communication filter turned on way up high and the voice soft and sweet or, in short, act like I'm someone else. I acted like someone else for years for the sake of my kids, for the acceptance of my family and to be allowed to teach scientific method at the kids' elementary and middle schools.

9.
Send for Candy

Through Facebook I had reconnected with an old friend from high school and I invited her to visit. Her divorce had become finalized just before Christmas and I thought she might appreciate a change of scene. Februarys are pretty mild in Kernersville. The crocuses are already popping up, the jonquils on their way. Because she'd retired from the airlines she was able to cut a buddy pass. She was here by the end of the week.

We talked about old times, who married whom, who cheated on whom and with whom, who died and how. But mostly we talked about Woodstock. Candy Annella and I went to Woodstock together a million years ago and she's the only one that I can share that memory with.

Anyone who tells you that Woodstock was the best time they ever had was probably not there. Everyone that hillside was covered in a mixture of upstate New York mud and cow shit. Hell, we were thankful when it rained, we could collect clean water to drink and wash off some of the dirt. No food, no shelter, it was a disaster but with all those great bands it was a cool disaster. We survived it by people pooling their resources, sharing marijuana laced brownies and LSD cider... sustenance.

Freaks were very practical, all their clothes were wet and muddy so they took them off and walked around naked. It seemed perfectly natural at the time. Candy and I kept ours on and nobody cared either way, except maybe the guys we came with. They disappeared almost immediately, went off to find the cooler girls, the ones with no clothing on.

Candy and I downloaded some old rock songs and acted like hippies, giving each other the peace sign, dancing freestyle like we did in the sixties. Now we're in our sixties, and I'm still wondering how that happened.

I introduced her to the gals on Sunday night at El Mejor. Stella had a family thing but Annie, Misty and Candy seemed to like each other immediately. Misty loves most everyone, and Annie is so adorable, everyone likes her.

"Oh, here come the B's. They're driving into the lot now." Bren parked and they got out of Big Red, Bren's humongous SUV. She wore a mocha fudge jacket and slacks with beige gloves. Bellamy's outfit was all cream: cream skirt with a thick Irish cable knit sweater-jacket with a dark brown belt. They reminded me of the yin and the yang. I considered my old jeans and comfy sweater and assured myself that I was more appropriately dressed than they.

"Hey, sorry we're late," said Bren. "Are you Candy? I'm happy to know you. This is Bellamy Hays and I'm Bren Sykes. How was the trip?"

"Oh, it was okay. It's a trip to see Sophie and I couldn't pass that up."

"I've known Candy since junior high."

"Sophie was so much trouble at school. Did I say fun? I meant to say fun. Ya, she was fun at school. You wouldn't believe some of the things she used to do and she always got away with them. I would just chew gum and get detention but Sophie had a gift when it came to trouble."

"That's not true. You were pretty good at it, as I remember. I turned to Bren. "I was just awful, maybe the worst kid at school."

"You weren't the worst but you may have been the most imaginative."

"Oh, ya? Tell us, Candy," Bren smiled at the others, "what kind of trouble did our Sophie get into during your high school years?"

"Remembah," Candy said in her Boston accent, "the time you put the Playboy pin-up on Mr. Sullivan's pull-down map in history class? He was lecturing on the Louisiana Purchase. I can heah him now, "...and this is what President Jefferson bought from France for fifteen million dollahs." He pulled down the map, and there was Miss July in all her glory."

Bren turned to Bellamy. "I like her already, don't you?"

"Well, I was bored in high school and I had a creative streak. I like to think I'm more mature now."

They laughed. "Yes, maturity is the first thing I think of whenever someone mentions Sophie!"

"It's an option," I stated.

"Then there was the time we spiked the oranges with vodka on our school trip. My Aunt Millie was diabetic. I took one of her syringes and we stayed up half the night injecting vodka from Sophie's parents bah into a whole bag of oranges. We could only get about a teaspoon in each of them, but we neahly peed our pants laughing at the thought of Old Lady Lockwood and all the chaperones getting drunk with the kids running around and howling at Old Sturbridge Village."

"Well, a good screwdriver can make anything palatable," I said. "I think we had sampled the vodka a little bit that night, hadn't we?"

"Then there was the squirt gun in Mr. Vitelli's class. He knew she had it. She had been squirting someone every time he turned his back. He searched her desk, her book bag, even her purse. He even made her stand up and paht her legs."

"Where did you hide it?" Misty asked.

"I stuck it to the bottom of the desk with my gum."

"That's brilliant," Annie said.

"Ha, and you say I'm not mature."

"Remembah the time you punched Nancy Zanelli in biology for calling you 'Pap smear'? She knocked her out in the middle of class and said she fell or something and she got away with it."

"Pap smear?" Bren did not need to have that information.

"Thanks, Candy." Yes, they called me Pap smear, but some kids have had to endure worse. I lived through it, became stronger and more thick-skinned because of it and *now* my closest friends knew about it.

Misty sympathized. "We all had to tolerate so much growing up. Kids are so cruel."

Candy began to tell another story about me in high school when Bellamy stood and marched off to the ladies' room. "Did I say anything wrong?" Candy asked.

"No," we said, "it's February."

"Oh, I totally get that. February is the most depressing month. It's so cold and the days ah so short. It's the worst month in Boston. Everybody gets depressed."

I followed her. "Hey, Bell, you okay?" She was admiring a small bit of jewelry.

"Ya."

"What's that, new earrings?"

"Not important," she said and slipped them back into her purse. "Candy's great, huh?"

"Yeah, refreshing, I can't remember when the last time we were talking about something other than men."

"Ya, but she'll get around to it. She's freshly divorced, and she is probably still in that 'men suck' stage."

"*I'm* still in the 'men suck' stage."

"Awe, Bell, you have the best chance of all of us to find love again. You believe in love. You told *me* to believe in love."

"I will never love again. Eddie was my last love, and I miss him so much." Her eyes watered. "I don't ever want to love again. They either divorce you or they die on you; it's too painful."

"I know it's painful but love is wonderful too. Remember when Misty said that we have to stay in the state of love in order to find love?"

"Oh, what the hell does that even mean? I'm so done with all of her judgment and the world according to Misty's rose-tinted life script."

"She's getting more spiritual. You know that." My nose wrinkled up. "You think she's judgmental?"

"Spiritual? Let me tell you what, I'm from California. I've seen and done every new age friggin' crazy belief thing. I'm sick to death of it. It's mostly just stylish bullshit, the guru-of-the-month club. Do you think Misty wouldn't be a little judgmental if she knew I have accepted a date with a Steve on Valentine's eve, one with Carl for Valentine's lunch and with some guy named Sammy for Valentine's dinner? They are all jerks, but if they are dumb enough to spring for meals, I am smart enough to eat them."

"I don't know what to say." It sounded reckless but Bellamy is a grown woman.

"It's easy for Misty to talk. She's found the love of her life."

"Well, ya, Eliot is great. But Misty is different. She lives love. She *is* love so she's got love."

"So what does that make me? I'm dating shits so am I a shit?"

"Well, I'm only finding shits; maybe I'm a shit too."

"So I'm a shit? Well, thanks a lot and screw you too." She stormed out of the ladies room with me following. She picked up her sweater jacket and bolted out the door. Stunned, gaping with my hands hovering, I appealed to Bren asking what I should do.

"Don't worry. She'll come back. She has to. I drove." Bren held her car keys up toward the window and beeped to unlock it. It was drizzling rain. Bellamy shivered with rage, frustration and probably-definitely she was cold. "I better take her home."

"Bren, let me go and help her."

"She doesn't need you now, Misty. You can't make her better when she gets depressed like this. I'll take her home." We left with drinks hardly touched. Only Candy's glass was empty.

March begins the beautiful spring, and it started to feel a little warmer around Bellamy too. Sammy seemed to be a nice man. He was a little bit younger than Bell but he was obviously taken with her. Bren said that he brought Bellamy a bouquet of pink tulips that didn't remind her of mourning and even though she'd been maudlin during their first dinner, Sammy liked her fine. We met him. He seemed nice. Bellamy had her semi-sparkle back and all would soon be right in the world.

Candy and I tried contra dancing and it was hilarious. It's a high-energy aerobic workout, much more so than I expected. At one point I thought they would have to call the paramedics but I found my old rescue inhaler in the bottom of my purse and sat out to watch a while. Ladies spun in long flowing skirts, lots of laughter, young and old. I watched Candy as her partners guided her through the steps; they directed her and redirected her as she learned the steps. We both *loved* it.

Candy went home after the first Tuesday in March with all the information about where the dances are in her area.

10.
More Boys

Most of the women at the gym don't shake their booties. Rita picks the most kick-ass motivating music imaginable and they step or kick with fairly little hip movement. They're too well-behaved to shake their butts in public. I don't mind being the boogie example, forging the way. I simply cannot stay still when good music is playing. I love to dance.

And you would be surprised how many grown people cannot throw a punch. Rita puts self-defense moves into the workout and most of these folks would break their wrist throwing a punch like that. How does one reach adulthood without knowing how to throw a punch? They wouldn't have made it past middle school in Boston.

A man named Barry who *could* throw a decent punch asked me out. I had admired his form while working out in the bag room and I thought this might be a good match. I knew we would at least be able to talk about boxing so I said yes till Lisa Fox told me that the man had been arrested for multiple counts of spousal abuse and had a prison record.

Date broken.

Misty had been on an animal rescue. A little bit of dog accident on her jeans led her to suggest coffee on the terrace in the sunshine at Starbucks. I held the leash of an old Labrador while she fed a skinny, one-eyed Shepherd mix. I told her about Barry.

"There are good guys out there. You don't have to attract the bad ones."

"So far I've met a nutcase, a guy with a thousand cuts and a woman's worst nightmare."

"Are you surprised that you attracted an ex-convict?"

"Well, ya, I am."

She gave me that wise look. "Why do you think you're attracting creeps?" she asked.

"I think it was my parents. They wrote the Sophie-World script. Mom said that men desert. Dad deserted. Jim supported the hypothesis and was a cheating liar too. Why wouldn't I believe that men desert, abuse or otherwise act the bad guy?"

"Who is abusing you now?"

"I wasn't really abused, more... neglected."

"And who is neglecting you now?"

"I think I'm supposed to say that I am."

"Are you?"

"I don't know."

"Sophie, if you keep running the same program over and over, then you *are* your own abuser. Believe that you are worthy of love, forgive and forget the past and move on. Be worthy."

"How do I start?"

"I have only told you about a thousand times. Be happy and joyful."

"How do I start that *now*?"

"By just enjoying the coffee, Sweetie, just enjoy the coffee."

"How does my life improve by enjoying this coffee?"

"By appreciating it, enjoy the warmth, the aroma. Think of the people who made that cup of coffee possible all the way back to the people who picked the beans. Imagine all of that was done for you so that *you* can drink it right here right now. So enjoy it completely, savor every sip. Drink in the richness and the flavor and value the boost the caffeine gives you."

"So you are telling me to live in the moment."

"I'm telling you to live in, appreciate and enjoy the moment."

Plan B, online dating, Bell helped make a profile. I chatted with a few and accepted dates with two, a Will and a Steve.

Will and I met in the late afternoon for coffee and I was attracted to him from the first moment. He was cute, slightly built with big brown eyes, a nice smile and overly-sure of himself. I could tell right away that this was a guy who knew his way around women.

"Will, you are an awful flirt."

"No, actually, I'm quite good at it." Witty, educated, polished and married twelve times, he made it known that he was currently searching for the new and improved Mrs. Anders. Well, twelve women couldn't be wrong. Will was adorably sexy.

He asked if he could buy me a beer and a sandwich and he

clearly expected me to ride with him. I thought about Albert and Mexico so I said that I'd rather drive my own car. He opened my door and dropped his voice. "Now if you had gotten into my car, you'd have been in my power."

I probably outweighed the guy by thirty pounds and, although the seniors kickboxing class at the Y couldn't really be called boxing, I used to fight when I was a kid before my breasts got too big. I met Jim at a karate school and he taught me how to kick. We would gear up and kick box at the Boston Public Gardens. I like to hit the bags at the Y because it's the only exercise that really makes me work up a sweat. I also like the bags because they don't hit back.

Some of the guys at the gym tease me about it. They'll pretend to take an overly wide arc to pass me by or duck and cover when I enter the bag area. And, yes, it has occurred to me that a reputation for boxing is not the way for me to get a date in the town of Kernersville. That just makes me want to hit things harder.

Steve was a wreck, about twenty years older and fifty pounds heavier than his profile picture and he was wearing bedroom slippers. This monotonous, boring man lulled me into oblivion by the unbearably dull details of his gallbladder surgery. I pretended I was in St. Croix… permanently.

"It was very nice to meet you, Steve, but I have to go."

"Why are you leaving? I like you. Don't you think this will work? Let me walk you to your car, at least."

The poor man was shuffling in slipper-clad feet, stooped over like he was scanning the floor for quarters. Just opening the restaurant door was a struggle. I thanked him but I was firm about not seeing him again. He gasped for air and probably had a prostate the size of Cuba.

Will lived an hour away and worked long hours so I didn't see him often, but we kept in touch online and by phone.

We met for a light dinner a few weeks later.

"So what do you think about a man who has been married twelve times?" Will asked.

"Well, I'd say you like women and you're not afraid of commitment."

"Most women have a strong reaction to hearing it."

"What type of reaction?"

"Across-the-board reactions, you can imagine."

"Well, I had at least that many boyfriends before I got married. What If I had married all of them? It wouldn't make me a bad person. So what really happened? Were all of them just too flawed, or did you have a problem with monogamy?"

"Monogamy only works if you cheat." It was an old Woody Allen line, but a good one. I still thought it was funny.

I never thought I'd get married. I certainly didn't feel an overwhelming desire to have children. I'd had several proposals but never felt that I could promise before God and all my family to be with someone for the rest of my life. Mom put such pressure on me that I may have married Jim just to shut her up.

Okay, what was he asking me? "Excuse me?"

"What kinds of movies do you like?"

"Well, let me think." He was asking about my taste. "*Dr. Zhivago* is an old favorite."

"Oh, ya with Julie Christie."

"And Omar Sharif."

"Of course."

"I like Ang Lee's version of *Pride and Prejudice*."

"Ya, I love Jane Austin."

"Ya, right."

"I do!"

What endless chick flicks had this man felt obliged to endure through twelve wives and the wooing stage which preceded each marriage. And then there were probably an untold number of women who had pursued or had been pursued by this charming man of amazing tolerance. How many pink frilly bathrooms had he shat in?

"My favorite movie of all times is *Shakespeare in Love*."

"Really?" I bet he likes long walks on the beach and a glass of wine at sunset. "Do you also enjoy long walks on the beach and a glass of wine at sunset?"

"Yes, I do."

"That wasn't on your profile."

11.
April in K'ville

Bellamy's home is beautiful, feminine, relaxed and homey. The sun set pinkly outside west-facing windows. The sky seemed to match the décor, or maybe the light was coloring my perception. Then again how can you clash with beige?

I love her sofa. It's a soft plush that somehow never gets dirty with mountains of creamy pillows edged in short, lush fringe. This could be the perfect balance of elegance and comfort. Of course, she has had it professionally decorated, Feng Shuied, space cleared, periodically smudged with sage. Bell was adamant in making sure that the *energy* was right because of Eddie's illness. When a neighbor said there was an ancient Indian burial site close by, she had tobacco offerings made by a Shaman. Not just any Shaman, one from a local tribe, Cherokee, I think.

I wondered why she stayed here after all the bad memories of Eddie's passing. I think I would have moved downsized maybe. She sure doesn't need all this space, no kids' rooms to preserve.

Her kitchen has a huge island in the center of it. I would have sex in this kitchen, right on that cold marble countertop! That's probably why she stayed here, sex in this friggin' kitchen. I got wet just thinking about it.

The days were warmer and her garden was lush with flowers. Sammy hung a rope swing from a tall bough in the center of her backyard. "Your garden is so beautiful." I said as I plopped the bag of fruit on the counter by the sink. I reached for a colander to wash the apples in. "That swing looks like it has been there for a hundred years. It's like a children's storybook cover."

Bren said that Bellamy's whole life sounded like a storybook.

"Miguel has done wonders with my garden. You should ask him to work on your yard, Sophie."

"I could not afford Miguel. He is surely an artist with plants.

59

I'm happy to let Alice's kid mow my yard."

Bren whispered to me, "Call him anyway. They say Spanish men do what white men can't."

"Shhh."

"He's a nice-looking man. I'm just saying."

I brought my DVD of *Shakespeare in Love*, a visually stunning film for the gals to watch. I set up the video while Bellamy made screwdrivers with juice from freshly-squeezed tangerines.

"Oh, guess who came over today, Joey Vecchia. He was all man-scaped, his beard all trimmed and even the eyebrows short and tidy. He even looked like he had lost a little weight."

"Oh, Sophie," Bellamy warned, "the fat man is after you!"

"No, listen. It was kind of cute. I said to him, "Joey, what's different about you?" He said it was his eyebrows. Natural attrition he called it. Natural attrition, how about that? Joey's got a brain and a sense of humor. He's going up to New Jersey weekend after next. Some niece is getting married. He hasn't seen his family in a long time and he wants to look good, so he asked me to help him pick out a suit for the wedding and to watch his dogs while he's away."

"So you said you would?" Misty, champion of all domestic beasts, anticipated my answer

"Sure I would. That will be fun to get old Joey all dressed up for his family. The dogs will be a blast. Chica will love the company, and they'll all get some exercise." Joey didn't look like he walked his dogs much and neither did they.

"So when and where are you taking him?"

"Well, Misty, I'll have to start right away in case he needs an alteration, which he will. I'm not sure what he's willing to spend on a suit but I think I'll just take him to the mall. They do quick alterations and he can get an idea of what suits cost this century. God only knows when the last time Joey Vecchia was wearing a suit."

"Well, good luck with that," said Bren. We settled in for another drink and started the movie.

Let me take a minute to tell you about Joey Vecchia. If looks told the story of every man's life, Joey would have been a professional leg breaker for the mob who had to relocate to Kernersville. He then put on an extra couple hundred pounds and grew his eyebrows long as part of his disguise. But the truth is that he's a little excitable, maybe slightly effeminate. He would be the first person to tell you to lock your doors because there had been a murder in Ohio or lecture you ad nauseam about climate change. I know there is climate change. I know that my congressmen know that there is climate change but there isn't much I can do about it, besides recycle and car pool. I just don't think it's right to run on about runaway CO^2 unless there is a plan and I don't see him putting up solar panels or trading in his minivan for a Prius. Joey acts like he's someone's elderly aunt who got excited about something she learned on the weather channel. I wouldn't be surprised if he had plastic covers on his matching sofa and armchairs with starched white doilies under his knickknacks. I think even his name means "old woman" in Italian. Joey Vecchia was definitely not on my list.

No one was on my list.

"Are you sure Will's not gay?" Bellamy asked.

"Surely he's not. If a man can take the amount of ridicule he gets from his friends and family for being married twelve times he would certainly be brave enough to come out of a mere closet," I reasoned. "He may just be a sensitive man but I'm taking the safer bet that he's a liar. Divorced twelve times would be the clue. But he is cute."

"You could become lucky number thirteen."

"He's either lying or he's had a sex change cuz this is a chick flick if I've ever seen one," Bren said. Neither Bren nor Bellamy had seen *Shakespeare in Love*. "If this man has convinced that many women to marry him, he has devised a set of lines that works for him and he is sticking with the script. Man's got kingfisher magic. He's a collector." She had the bird cards out again.

"Bren!"

"What?"

"Stop it," Bellamy started. "I told you to be more respectful of this."

"I'm not offended. I think it's funny," Annie said. "What about you, Misty?"

"If Bren's amused then I'm fine with it. I'm actually impressed that she is learning about the bird cards."

"Well, then why don't you just keep the cards? You certainly use them more than I do."

"Thanks, Bell, I will. Is this movie based on truth?" Bren asked.

"Oh gosh, no, we know very little about Shakespeare's life, almost nothing," Annie told us.

"Damn, I wish it was true." Bellamy's intertwined hands tucked under her cheek. "It's like they are so perfect together, and she gets all that poetry written for her."

"Poetry," Bren humphed. "What do you know about poetry?"

"Absolutely nothing."

"Oh, I like poetry. Some of my first boyfriends were poets."

"Really?"

"Ya, Bren, it was my Irish poet phase. I was always attracted to a blue-eyed magnet, but if he could recite poetry, oh ya, that took my heart. Of course, that was mostly before I lost my virginity. Then other things took on greater importance."

Bellamy hit the pause key. "So, this is a little off-subject, but I want your opinion. If you could only have one or the other, either great sex or a perfect friend that you could deeply connect with at a soul level, which would you choose?" She picked at the cuff of her sleeve.

"Which is Sammy?"

"Shut up, Bren. Don't answer that. Which would you choose?" I asked her.

"I'd choose the soul friend. I think I had that with Eddie."

"I'd go for the lover," Bren said. "I like to keep my life simple."

"At this point I'd take the sex," Annie said, "but I reserve the right to change at a later date. What about you, Misty?"

"I'd choose the soul connection but I'd sure rather have both. They are both so important."

They stared toward me waiting for my answer.

"I want sex," I stated.

"Just a short while ago, you were completely unready to get naked; now you want sex?"

"Honestly, Misty, I'm still not sure I'm ready for nakedness or a relationship but I am ready for a lover. I want to have raw wild sex, the kind that takes you away so that nothing else exists. Where the fire of passion is hard to control and we fall into each other's arms at every opportunity," I said and pointed at the paused screen, "like Viola and Will Shakespeare. I'll settle for passion now, and maybe love can grow out of that passion."

"So are you going to do the dirty with Will?"

"Maybe I should."

Misty reasoned. "You are supposed to fall in love and then have passionate sex."

"I'm old. I don't have time to fall in love. I want sex."

"You have all the time you want." Misty wasn't helping. My fuse was lit. Actually many fuses were currently lit and presently bottlenecked. The pipeline was dry except for an adorable womanizer who I could never trust so lift-off was still stuck in development. In hindsight I'd have to admit that it was probably fear that prevented me from sleeping with Will.

I better get a dildo. But I'd feel a lot less self-conscious buying a bag of carrots. Who has to know?

WANT AD: Old Yankee hippie chick with tons of baggage and skin to match, seeks equally old, preferably kind, honest man with parts in good working order for wild time with lights out and most clothing on.

The next morning Joey and I were in his mini-van and heading west towards Hanes Mall. "Thanks for-coming wit-me, Sophie. I appreciate this." With his accent, Joey was never going to pass as a Southerner.

"No problem, Joey. I'm happy to help."

"I probably should go to-that store that specializes-in tall and fat-guys, but-they never have a-good selection."

"The mall has everything. I think you'll find something you'll like. If not, I know a specialty store in Greensboro."

"Ya I-think I-know the place. Jesus, you believe-that guy's driving? He's gonna-kill somebody!"

"Ya, huh?"

"Fuckin' NASCAR drivers! Oh, sorry, Sophie."

"For what?"

"For swearing."

"I don't give a shit if you swear."

"Good. It's good to be-able to-relax in-front of someone. So what the-fuck is wrong with these drivers?"

"We have aggressive drivers up North. I've been on the Jersey

Turnpike. If you don't drive aggressively in Jersey you'd never get through the state."

"Ya but we-know what we're doing. I mean in Jersey, if you can't steer with-your knee while-you're lighting a cigarette, loading a thirty-eight and flipping the finger to the guy next-to ya at the same time, you'd fail-the state driving-test."

I laughed. Boston is like that too.

At home in the Mall, shopping for suits, even searching the clearance racks, shopping with Joey was just like shopping with a chick. After looking at about a billion suits he found handsome light wool in grey. It was more than I expected him to pay for a one time wear. Certainly I'd never seen him wear anything but extreme casual or work-in-the-yard clothes. I found a teal shirt that I thought would fit him and I picked out a tie to match, purple and teal with a touch of magenta. He took them to the dressing room. A few seconds later he walked out in his undershirt to ask me to get him the next larger size. The sight of Joey up close in his undershirt was something I'd rather forget about.

"So, Joey, you didn't need any help with this. Why did you ask me to come along?" I asked on the way home.

"You-always-look kind-a good, and I-wanted-ta be sure that I look good for-this wedding. This-is kind-a important to me. I haven't-seen anyone in my family in a-pretty-long time, ya-know? I wanted ya ta-come with me to tell me if I was making-a bad, ah, choice. Jesus Christ, did you see that fuckin-moron? Learn to drive, ya idiot!" He gestured at him. "I-think-you would-a told-me. Am-I-right?"

"Sure I'd have told you, Joey. You got a great suit."

"I used-ta dress pretty-good when I was living up-in-Jersey, but I put-on a-few pounds since then." He patted his belly. "A nice-suit can hide-a-few extra pounds, ya-know?"

Joey had extra kilos.

"I used-ta be a thin-guy. I could-eat anything I wanted. I used ta-cook a lot. Now I got-nobody to-cook for and it's no-fun ta-cook alone. I eat-out too much. I blame it on Amalfi's. He makes a fuckin' good pizza. Speakin'-of-which, lemme take you to-lunch for helping-me, okay?"

"You don't have to do that, Joey. I didn't really help much at all."

"You picked out that shirt-and tie, come-on."

Okay, I shouldn't say this. Imagine if Shrek had married Jabba the Hutt's momma. Think of what that offspring would look like. Joey is almost that bad. And yes, I was being shallow and hoping that no one I knew would see me out eating with this big ugly guy.

"Okay, maybe coffee."

"Forget-about just coffee. I-know-a-good Italian place up ahead. You-gotta eat. I shouldn't," he admitted, "but I'm-gonna eat too."

We stepped down a brick walkway into a darling little grotto. Wrought iron and Sangria bottles lined the walls and a craggy grapevine sought high garden windows. The waiter led us to a starched white table cloth and set seasoned oil and homemade bread. I must have passed this place a hundred times and I hoped the food matched the ambiance. We split an antipasto. He ordered the veal but I just wanted soup with that warm and crusty Italian bread. It was delicious and pleasant. Even Joey was good company.

He'd been a high school biology teacher for most of his working career. That was my favorite subject in high school. I loved my teacher, Mr. Andropoulos (who covered for me after I knocked Nancy Zanelli out in class) but he made me promise that I would never major in biology. He said I was a "people person" and that if I got a degree in biology, I would be stuck working in a laboratory. I always regretted keeping that promise. I remain a mediocre science geek and I often think people suck.

Joey said that what Mr. A said was true, and that was the reason why he went into teaching also. "But it-was a-mistake. I should-a gone on in-school. A-lot-a great things-happened in-biology in the-past forty, fit-ty years, I could-a been a part-a that."

After he yelled at about twenty more drivers Joey and I arrived back home. I suggested that he bring his dogs over to visit with Chica. She is a bit territorial so I thought it would be wise to have them acclimate as much as possible before he left for New Jersey.

"That's-Smokey, the-male, she's Gladys and this-one here is Vandella, Della for-short."

"Really. Smoky, Gladys and Vandella? So you love Motown."

"I'm an old Italian guy. Of course I love Motown. I love

any-music as long-as it's-good."

"How about opera? Do you like opera?"

"I like opera. I grew-up wit-it at home." Old lady Vecchia and I had some things in common.

12.
It Started Off Good

Bren's birthday, usually we just picked up dinner and drinks, but this time I had a little gift.

"I couldn't resist this. It's from all of us." I handed her the bag.

"Hey no gifts!" Her dimples puckered. "Thank you, Sophie." Bren peeked through the puffs of yellow tissue paper, tilting her head back and forth to her own inner beat. As her eyes widened from almond to round she cried, "Oh, this is so cool!" then displayed the decks of animal and insect totem cards in front of her. "Ya'll are in big trouble now, animals, bugs, no fish cards? I gotta get fish cards too. Do you think they make them?" She reached for a butter knife to open them.

"Why are you encouraging her?"

"Well, I dunno, Bellamy. "Why did you give her the bird cards from your coffee table in the first place?"

"I didn't think she'd actually memorize them."

"I didn't memorize them. But I've been listening to you and Misty run on about all that new age stuff and just when I think I've heard it all, I found these cards and they're… interesting."

"That is not new age; it's ancient and indigenous, ancient peoples on different sides of the world often had the same meaning for animals. Did you know that?"

"All I know is that I pay much more attention to birds since you gave that deck to me. I even got a book on identifying them so I can look them up later in the deck."

"Bren's bird watching. She's getting geeky." Bell finished her drink.

"Could we change the subject, please?" Misty asked.

"Bellamy is trying to ruin my birthday," Bren said unaffectedly. "Hey, Sophie, how did it go with Joey?"

"Pretty good, we found him a suit and then we had lunch." I gave some details.

"Sophie and Joey Vecchia," Bell started.

"Shut up."

"The Italian and the Greek."

"Shut up."

"Sounds like passion to me."

"Shut the fah, okay? He's got big icky moles all over his body," I shuttered.

"And how do you know that, Sophie?" I was dying here, and Sunday night was beginning to suck.

"What's with you, Bell? There is *nothing* between me and Joey, not in your wildest imagination."

"I didn't know you liked opera, Sophie," Misty changed direction.

"I hate opera." She hailed Carlos and held her empty glass.

"Have you ever listened to any? Ever been to an opera, Bell?"

"Hell, no. No opera for me, I'm with Bell on this," Bren added.

"In the famous words of Dr. Hannibal Lecter, "It's important always to try new things." and he's right." Those were the only scary movies I ever liked. Dr. Lecter was so brilliant and cultured. And he didn't eat just anyone. He was selective, like asshole flutists and defective FBI brains.

"Try new things like Joey Vecchia?"

"You are my friend, and you are being gross and disgusting."

"I'm gross? You are the one quoting a cannibal," Bell laughed.

"You're gross if you are suggesting I start a thing with Joey. I'm not even going to talk about it."

"At least you wouldn't have to be ashamed to undress in front of the man."

"What the fuck is with you, Bell?"

"Ya, Joey's got that *orca* energy thing going on," Bren said, just to pee in the sewer.

"Thank you. Joey happens to be a nice person and you are all being very hypocritical. Have we all been saying that we should not judge a person by their appearance? Have we, all of us, been judged because of our looks *and* our age? Are we being the superficial jerks now?" I indignantly walked to the rest room, judging her for judging. Misty followed.

"She's been drinking more than usual, Honey. Don't mind her."

"She's been acting weird for months. Remember how much fun she used to be?"

"I know."

I decided to cut her some slack because, believe it or not, I have acted like an asshole before.

We walked back to the table; Stella and Letta Steele were pulling up chairs to join us.

Shit.

After a round of greetings, Letta's eyes focused on me.

"Hey, I heard you lost a ton of weight. How much more are you planning to lose?"

"I think I'll stay around where I am."

She started at my hair and lowered eyes filled with judgment and disdain, slashed me in a slow sinking sweep, the full length of my body and ended somewhere near the gum under one of my shoes. Her blue eyes met mine. "Ya?" she said with a half-lip smile.

See, this is why I like boxing. But, much as I'd sometimes like to, I cannot go around punching people. I needed to express the anger I felt, and maybe someday I will learn to relay negative feelings in a kinder and more tactful way... but it will not be tonight.

"So you got a perm? You're beginning to look more like Aunt Pitty Pat from Atlanta every day."

Badda Bing.

"*Gone with the Wind* jokes don't fly here in the South. Do you know that we here in the South refer to the Civil War as the War of Northern Aggression?"

"Really, Letta? We refer to it as The War of the Southern Superiority Complex because you thought it was okay to own human beings to pick your cotton and empty your damned chamber pots."

Badda Boom.

"We are calling a time-out here. One of these two women is drinking at the bar." It was clear whom Bren meant.

"I was just leaving," Letta said. She turned toward me. "You gonna burn in hell." She spun on her heels. Stella gave us an apologetic smile and an ain't-it-a-shame little head tilt.

"And the Mason-Dixon Line is alive and livin' in Kernersville." Bren almost high-fived me. "That was a great comeback, Sophie. It made my birthday so special." She faked a sentimental tear and pretended to wipe it away.

"Sophie, you know she has issues."

"Oh ya, spider energy, that's her issue. And I meant that in a sticky, dead fly, entrapment kind of way," Bren read the back of the card.

"I know she has issues, Misty, but she deserved that. She *totally* deserved it. Bren, let me see that card."

"You do understand how hard it is for Southern women, don't you? They have been told their whole lives to be nice, act pretty, taught to listen to and obey their men."

"That's the truth," Stella added.

"So have Greek women, Italian women, Japanese and Iranian; it's not an excuse to be nasty to each other. Woman everywhere should stick together, support each other and not steal each other's husbands. And I am sick to death of all this passive-aggressive bullshit. It is both cowardly and dishonest. If she has something to say to me... let her say it and we'll deal with it without all this sweeping crap and war of aggression shit. I'm sick to death of it."

"Sophie, she can only push your buttons because you let her." Misty was usually right. "Nobody can make you feel anything unless you let them."

"Passive-aggressive behavior, it's like the Southern woman's arsenal." I ignored her. "And no one calls these behaviors what they are. Then if someone *did* point out that they've been insulted, she would make the victim look bad by saying, 'What did I do?' or 'You must have misunderstood me.' And they get away with treating each other like this time and again."

"I'll admit that I do it too," Stella confessed, "but we aren't direct like y'all are, and that is how we deal with conflict."

"I think "You gonna burn in hell" is pretty damned direct," Bren pointed out.

Annie said that after the Civil War was over, the man shortage was really severe. "No, seriously, maybe three-quarters of a million men died in that war. That would be like eight or ten million today, and who knows how many died during the reconstruction era. Some states spent up to a fifth of their budget just to supply artificial limbs to the survivors. There was such a shortage of men that your average Southern woman was willing to settle for, even *compete for* any nasty tempered, butt-ugly amputee who was three times her age and had bad breath just in order to gain respectability, status and have babies."

"Honestly, Sophie, I don't think half of these women even know when they are doing it. It's their only means of attack and defense," Misty said and paused to take a sip.

"That's probably how this all started," Bell said to Bren, "you know, how most women here do all the cooking, cleaning and child rearing after putting in a full day's work."

"And *how* would you know anything about that, Bell?"

"Ya, good point, Bren," she slurred as they high-fived each other. "Hey, next movie night let's watch *Gone with the Wind*."

"I love that movie. I have a copy," I volunteered. "I've watched it maybe a hundred times."

"Hey, Letta is leaving with Tommy Schull!"

"Oh gosh, and he is knee-walking drunk again, bless his heart," Stella voiced.

"I thought she was all in love will that Al Fredo guy," Bren said.

"She is. She says she is."

I pointed to the parking lot and sure enough, Letta was getting into Tom's truck. Before he turned the ignition she was kissing him like she meant it.

"Shit, that old boozer?" Bellamy frowned. "I bet he hasn't had a hard-on in years."

"I hope they make it home safely," Stella said.

"Nonetheless, it's nice to know that she's not stuck in that indigenous Southern-Anglo repression thing I've heard about," Bren enunciated.

"Ya," I agreed, "downright refreshing, ain't it?"

Damn.

We mouthed the word "slut".

Bell tottered into the foyer, hooked her keys onto her purse and tossed her sweater by the closet door. She knew she shouldn't have driven home that drunk. She stepped out of her Jimmy Choo's and paused in front of the door to the downstairs den. She took in a deep breath and walked in.

If none of it had happened, this room would look exactly the same. She stared towards the window where Eddie's bed had been placed. He loved the outdoors and the den had large sunny windows and a view of the garden and sky. She remembered the cold framed bed and the little padded chair she sat in, just like it was yesterday. Over there stood the IV pole, that table beside it covered with medicines. The book shelves across held fluids, diapers, syringes and gloves.

The room looked like this on the day the doctor told them that Eddie's cancer was terminal, and this is where they held each other and cried.

How he gazed at the majesty of the evergreens, as if this would be the last of this beautiful earth he would see. "Bellamy, take me to the beach. I want to see the ocean before I die," he whispered.

"Oh, Eddie, I miss you so much." Her eyes watered. The only man she ever truly loved declined from strong and solid to a weak, bony invalid, frail and incapacitated.

An invalid, invalid, in valid, she thought. *How could anyone ever think of Eddie as not valid?* But that is what the nurses had called him, during the illness that invaded their lives, no options, no alternatives. She sat and waited, powerless as he wasted away to nothingness amidst the smell of latex, urine and impending death.

Another drink would not be a good idea. She poured another glass, half sparkling water and half white wine then she climbed the steps to the bedroom. She undressed and eased into bed. She reached for a pain killer and followed that with a sleeper.

13.
Born Button Pusher

Misty is probably-definitely right about this. I allow Letta to make me fuming mad but I don't know how to stop myself from letting her. She makes me furious; the anger eats at me, burrows deep through the layers of my being. She was the first woman who slept with Jim and represents, to me, the beginning of the most vulnerable and painful time of my life. *Why do I spend so much of mine letting her?*

We feed each other in some kind of bizarre anger/rudeness game and, chemically speaking, I understand. I know that our bodies make anger molecules that keep the tinder burning, information molecules. They are why people get addicted to playing the victim, being afraid, watching the news, needing to be in love all the time, running, boxing, yes, and even contra dancing. Healthy things can be addictive too.

Anger information molecules are damaging and aging to the body. I know this, understand it but that does not necessarily make it easier for me to control or manage. I try to forgive myself for allowing myself to get sucked in to Letta's drama. *She to mine?* I suppose that I have to admit that I'm addicted to anger or else this woman, who is basically insignificant, could not enrage me so. I wondered how long an anger detox program would take.

Letta has called me a heathen, has told me that I'm going to burn in hell many, many times. That's her belief. She is entitled to it and I respect that belief. It's rooted in her. To her it is the absolute truth. I actually think my life would be easier if I had that kind of solid, immutable faith but I don't.

I *think* that I am open to wisdom of any sort. I *think* I believe that people are all the same with one Spirit, one God with many Paths toward it, many ways to say the same thing. I mean, I love Jesus but I don't *know* that He is the only way. I *think* churches mostly divide people, and that is another reason why people don't necessarily like me here in the South where the churches seem to define who you are. I've actually heard ladies introduce themselves as, "Hi, I'm Laura, First Church of Christ" or "I'm Betty, Main Street Baptist."

All of us have discussed religion at one time or another and have come to agree that having respect for others' beliefs is imperative. So if there are so many belief systems and they all contain wisdom who am I to say that spirit and totem animals are too strange? I read Bren's spider energy card. I have to admit that I also have spider energy, but the good kind—no, seriously, not just because it's me. Spider energy is cool. It's feminine, creative and fragile yet possesses tensile strength. That's one side. The darker side of spider magic, according to the card, lists three types. There's the sticky, dead fly sort that Bren used to describe Letta, there's the play-with-your-prey sort and a bite-the-head-off-your-mate-after-sex-and-eat him sort.

I'm the creative and strong part, except for the time I played with Jim as prey in the divorce battle and he's probably extremely lucky that he still has a head.

Joey's orca-self returned home with tons of pictures and stories which he shared. I listened and nodded while I was mentally in St Bart's. He got his dogs, and I was relieved when he left.

End of Joey story.

I had another idea for a product that I was thinking about marketing. This item was a little more man-friendly. I called it 'A Man's Can'. It was a quart paint can that had a label on the lid that said "hardwear", purposely misspelled. The can contained a bottle of wonderfully sensuous, all-natural massage oil that was safe for *all* body parts and directions for a sensual massage (which I know nothing about now, but I can imagine and learn). It would include a garment for the penis. Yes, that's right, an actual costume for the dick because, let's face it ladies, if we had penises we'd dress them up. So you had the choice to don your man's penis with a cowboy hat, if he is a rough rider; a bow tie, if he's the romantic sort; a hard hat, for the hardworking man or a superhero's cape in case, well, in case he deserved a superhero cape (and what man would turn down a superhero cape?). I decided that it would be responsible to supply condoms. I got prices and ordered quantities of paint cans and all the rest of the supplies. I planned to put these together and sell them online.

So I had a case of 500 condoms.

"We are definitely *not* spying on her. It's none of our business what she's doing with other consenting adults."

"Come on, Bellamy, you have to be curious," Bren said. I grabbed two cans of Food Lion brand coffee.

"Being curious is one thing; spying on her is another matter entirely. I'm not doing it."

"It would be much smarter to follow Mounty because we'd never fool Annie," I said.

Bren stopped and investigated me. "Damn, Sophie, you'd have made one hell of a good cop."

"Thank you, Bren, from you I consider that the highest compliment."

"I can't believe you are going to join in on this."

"That sounds like judgment, Bell. We aren't judging me, are we? I haven't decided one way or another," I said nonchalantly and I glanced away as if the matter was closed. Actually I had decided, promised even, but let this go on record—*I was against it when I promised and I still thought it was the wrong thing to do.*

Bellamy sighed, turned and walked up the personal care aisle. Bren examined some products on the end cap and I spotted Stella with Betty Lou Easter in baking. "Hey, Stella, *Stelllllla!*" I turned to Bren. "I love yelling her name."

Stella trotted over and said, "I can't stay too long. I'm with Betty Lou. She's all upset. Yesterday morning after church, Billy Ray confessed to Linda about him and Betty Lou having an affair. You know Linda, Miss Sally's granddaughter. It's true, Betty Lou did sleep with Billy Ray, but she's so upset cuz, ya know she wouldn't want to hurt Linda for the world, bless her heart."

"Wouldn't want to hurt her, but she slept with her husband; am I getting this right?" Bren asked.

"It was over a year ago."

"Oh, that makes a difference. So why did he decide to tell her now?"

"That's what I said, why scrape all that old mess up now?"

"And his reason to tell her was... "

"Billy Ray said he was moved by the Lord to be honest about it. Everyone is talking about it. I really have to run. Good to see ya."

"People are crazy. I don't understand their train of thought." Bren shook her head.

"Crap, I wonder how Miss Sally is. Maybe we should stop by to see her later," I suggested.

"You stop by and see her; she's *your* neighbor. I don't give a rat's ass about Billy Ray and Betty Lou or Billy Jean or Peggy Sue. I need to get cereal for the grandbabies." She walked off.

A kiss of forsythia greets early spring. Bright yellow jonquils pop among grape purple hyacinths and Bradford pears burst with tiny white blossom. Deciduous trees hide winter bareness; their branches grow tipped with reds and soft green. Azaleas abound like the sticky sweet frosting on birthday cakes and saucer magnolias present fist-sized petals reach gracefully, like fingers, up to the sky. Then the cherries bloom, and oh, the cherries! Weeping cherries of pale pink tickle the ground, then a myriad of showy ornamentals hail forth in every shade of pink from the whitest pale to deepest magenta. Everywhere are the dogwoods' crooked trunks with four petal crosses but my favorite, the redbuds, boast brilliant lilac. All is received by pastel puffs of light spring green then dotted with the muted rust-burgundy of an occasional red maple. I welcome the spring in Kernersville.

Sally was working out in her garden. I pulled the Camry over the swale and stopped to talk.

"No matter how bad I feel, it helps to get my hands in the soil."

"I saw Betty Lou and Stella at Food Lion."

"Whole town is talkin' about it. The phone hasn't stopped ringing. Oh they mean well, but people got nothing better to do than to gossip."

"Why do you think he told her?"

"Same reason Billy Ray does anything, to be mean."

"How is Linda?"

"She's talking about leaving him this time and takin' the kids."

"He's the one who should leave. Where is Linda gonna go?"

"She wants to move in here with me. I can't say I'm sad about it. I never thought Billy Ray deserved Linda. Of all my grandbabies, she's always been closest to me. She's the most like me. I hope she does leave him this time. I'd like having the young'uns around and Linda would be a big help. She's a nurse and it's a comfort to have family around at my age. Don't you worry, it'll all work out. It always does, besides, you know I love to have company."

"That doesn't mean you can stop having parties, Miss Sally, because we all love to be your company."

14.
Fecundity

Sally and Linda were out planting flowers and vegetables like most of my neighbors. I had decided not make any apologies for the condition of my yard. Gardening is not my skill. I am going to confess to you now that I have never started a lawnmower and I'm actually a little proud of that fact. But it was a beautiful day. Everything smelled green and I love the mounds of freshly-turned clay with the sight of hands appreciating the earth. I walked up to socialize, content to observe the expert gardeners in their element.

"Linda, go ask Joey now if he wants any more of this fertilizer."

"Granny, I was telling you about Billy Ray."

"Well, quit it. Linda, listen to me. Do you think God gave us them big heavy cast iron skillets just for makin' corn bread? You have told me enough about Billy Ray. You best decide not to talk about him anymore because I have decided that I have heard enough about him for a lifetime. So forgive him, forget him or go hit him in the head with a skillet. I'll lend ya mine."

"Hey, Joey," I yelled, "you want any more of this?" He grabbed a shovel and walked toward us.

"Now don't anyone bring up the pothole," Linda reminded us.

"Have you-seen that fuckin' pothole?"

"I've more than seen it. I may need new struts on the Camry."

"That's-what I'm-saying."

"Joey, you got to quit that cussing or I'll take a switch to you."

"I-got whipped as a-kid, a-lot; and it-never worked, not one time. It ain't-gonna start working-now. And besides, Sally, I've-been your neighbor for-a long time and I've-heard a few cuss words from out-ta this house too."

"And that's enough talk about potholes too. If you don't like the roads then go run for public office."

"Maybe I-will. Sophie wants to-talk about the pothole, don't ya?"

"It's Miss Sally's yard so she gets to decide. If she doesn't want to talk about the pothole then I am not willing to discuss it."

My first spring here, I had raised beds built in the yard. I filled them with soil, amended the soil, fertilized and planted well-established plants which I purchased at the local hardware stores. Tomatoes, green peppers, zucchini, eggplant and cucumbers and corn that I lovingly raised, followed the directions exactly like it said to in the book.

The peppers died first. Baby bells just fell off the plant. Corn grew high. I was about to claim myself, officially, as 'Corn Woman' when the blight showed up. The book said I could not plant any corn in that soil for seven years. I couldn't give the zucchini away because everyone had too much zucchini. I got a bit of eggplant and a few good cucumbers. When I counted the tomatoes and considered my overall yield, I realized that I could have bought about eighty-five times the vegetables for the money I spent if I had just gone to the farmers' market, like the frugal New Englander that I am.

I appreciate real gardeners and I know I am not one of them. I spend this time of year taking long drives with Chica on the old curvy back roads, admiring the quiet order of endless rows of plowed clay soil fringed with promising new growth. We spy an occasional herd of cows, sheep or goats, even llama. Chica barks at them. She thinks no animal has the right to be larger than she is.

There are over sixty different species of mosquitoes in North Carolina. The one thing that they all have in common with other life forms is that they need water to complete their life cycle. Mosquitoes lay their eggs in stale water that collects in containers. Old pots discarded by humans are claimed by these annoying little beasts for their breeding ground. Once laid, mosquito eggs attach to each other in groups on the water's surface like little life rafts, floating patiently and waiting for up to two years for the perfect conditions to hatch. Just a gentle drizzle or a torrential rainstorm can settle a drop in a slight indentation on the side of tree, or in a small depression in the middle of your lawn, maybe an innocent doll shoe stepped on, ground into the dirt and overtaken by lawn. That dirty, cracked shoe is now harboring tiny irritating creatures that suck your blood and leave red raised welts that itch like a demon.

I met a good-looking man named at the pet super store. Mick

was a bit younger than I. He petted his beautiful Lab and we talked while waiting for Chica's groomer. He was recently divorced. I vaguely remembered that our kids played together in school. We walked to Starbucks and took turns watching the dogs while we bought our own coffees then sat at the outside tables to enjoy them, to enjoy each other.

Chica's fur felt neat and smooth but my hair was near frizz. It was hot and humid in Kernersville, where the bad hair days start in May and end in October. He had curly hair too, ultra-curly and maybe he was too aware of his own frizz to consider mine.

We spent the better part of the afternoon together and I was entertaining… ideas. I noticed him checking out my boobs a few times so I assumed he had ideas too. He walked me to the car and I thought he was about to kiss me. I smiled at the idea of an intimate moment about to happen then he boldly reached over and fondled my left breast. It was the hottest moment of my life. Oh my God! This man was going home with me right now. I was exactly that excited! My lips parted, maybe I was panting a little and my heart thumped like tumbling boulders.

"You like that? See if you like this." He grabbed me forcefully and put his mouth on mine. I swear to you, I almost retched. He may have held an award for the longest tongue on record and he jutted it into my mouth like a larynx-seeking weapon. It was the worst kiss since Billy Gagnon gagged me behind the church at the eighth grade CYO dance. If I had had a better imagination or was thinking more clearly I could have found a better use for Mick's rock hard missile-shaped projectile, maybe a little bit of war-head. As nice as that thought is now, at the time, I knew there could be no future for us. Sadly he'd never learned to kiss and for me to like a man; he has to be a good kisser. He *has* to be a good kisser. Mick asked if he could see me later that night. I declined.

A man just has to be a good kisser.

Chica had behaved so well for her grooming that I thought she deserved a reward so we drove to Triad Park. I braved the heat and walked her into the cooler shade of the forest and downward towards the stream. That's where I met him. He was a skinny old guy with a long birdlike neck, as if Ichabod Crane had lived into his eighties just to grow liver spots. Tall, hunched shoulders and a long hooked nose, if anyone ever seemed like they didn't belong in the woods it was this man, near the muddy creek in street shoes, black socks and saggy shorts. He hissed and sputtered with eyes glued to the path and obsessed about exactly where he stepped.

He gawped at me. "He who is stupid enough to walk down this path must walk all the fucking way back up it." He was definitely the last person who belonged in the woods. "What's that sound?"

"Frogs."

"Frogs? What's next? Locusts? Boils?"

"Sir, do you want help getting back up the hill?"

"I don't need help but I'd appreciate the company. I could have a heart attack or get eaten by coyotes in here. God damn it. I'm in the fucking wilderness."

"You could hardly call this the wilderness. You're in the middle of Triad Park."

"I know this is Triad Park and I shouldn't even be here. Jesus P. Christ. Get me the hell back to my car, will ya?"

"Sure, I'm Sophie." I extended my hand. "Sophie Chase."

He stopped, took a deep breath and shook my hand. "Aloysius Dupree," he said. "They call me Hook."

"Hook?"

"Ya, cuz I have this nose. They call me Hook."

"So, I take it you are not a nature buff."

"Honestly, I'd rather be whipped. Seriously, I'd rather be tied up and whipped."

"Then what are you doing out here?"

"My doctor said that a walk in nature would lower my blood pressure. I hate this shit. I'm afraid I'll get a tick bite and end up with malaria or yellow mountain tick flu or some fucking thing. This can't be good for me."

"City boy, huh?"

"You might say that."

"Where are you from?"

"You name the place, I'm from there."

"Where originally?"

"Born in the Bronx, grew up in Philadelphia. I moved to Manhattan, lived there for a few years. I got to experience the ass-end of the beat generation in The Village. Then I moved back to

Philly because my mother was sick. I lived in Dallas for a while and the list goes on."

"Why did you move around so much? Work?"

"Eh, a long story and you don't want to hear it."

"You might feel more comfortable walking at the mall in the air-conditioning, no bugs or frogs, people all around you."

"I can't walk at the mall."

"Why not?"

"Too many young girls. Give me just five minutes alone with one of them, and I'd be in jail for the rest of my life."

I had to laugh.

"Ya, you laugh. Do yourself a favor and run away now fast.

"And leave you to the coyotes?"

I saw the old perv back to civilization, which in his mind was the firm asphalt of the parking lot with the comfort of cars and vending machines around him. Chica and I continued on to the dryer dirt path of higher ground, smelling pines and inhaling the fresh warm air of the woods. Chica sniffed and peed, peed and sniffed. Triad Park is a place of dog bliss, a place where all her senses become enlivened. Birds tittered in the trees and she searched upward to spy them. Distracted by another scent she tracked another critter that had crossed this path before her. Her tail wagged and I wished I could allow her to run free and hunt.

Freedom. Hmmm. I took a moment to ponder. What does freedom mean to me?

Travel came to mind. There are more than a few places that I'd love to visit, but travel is pricy and Chica is my responsibility. Security is freedom. If I live modestly I have that. I could use more money. I'd really like to have more money but would that necessarily equate to more freedom? What about a man in my life? Would that give me more freedom or less? My inner mind immediately seized the skeptical view. Jim had represented imprisonment for me. Could I ever get over that feeling? My situation is completely different now, I told myself. I now reside in a peaceful intermission, that interval between no kids at home and no grandchildren in the near future. This is *my* time, my time to expand, to stretch the breath of my wings. Now, this was my time of freedom.

So where are my chains? What walls confine me? What in me needs to be released?

My thoughts turned to the experience of Mick fondling my breast in front of Starbucks. Why was that such a turn on? Was it because it was in broad daylight with people all around the place? It was a little humiliating, risky and public. Did I like a little risk? Was it the surprise aspect or was it the novelty of it? Was it the freedom to express myself sexually in public? I was getting turned on again just thinking about it. My God, he had a nerve to do that in the parking lot in front of Starbucks. Had it been on camera? Did some geek review a recorded tape at the end of the day and edit it down to weird behavior and show his friends? Naw, no way, nobody would care if my breast was fondled in front of Starbucks, surely.

Synchronicity, I had met two perverts, back to back, Mick and Hook on the same afternoon. Misty would ask how I attracted them. Maybe I should explore my most private thoughts and fantasies and unleash the hideous beast that seems to lie within. Maybe I should just get a tee shirt that says, "I attract weirdos".

15.
K'ville when it Sizzles

Summer in Kernersville is like walking down streets piped for radiant heat as the sun boils saturated air into a slow deep steam. Your car is like a solar oven and there never seems to be a shady parking spot. I would go to the beach but I don't care for crowds or traffic. I'd rather enjoy the shore when it is cooler and less packed. Bell has a beach house that the gals visit throughout the summer and I sometimes enjoy it before the season starts and again after it closes. But I still spend the heat of the day with my needle and thread and puddles of color playing with light and hue of the tiny glass beads.

Bren's grandkids were out of school and she was spending lots of time with them. Misty and Eliot were frequently at his cabin and riding his motorcycle through the Smokey Mountains, escaping the heat and communing with nature. They were probably fucking in the woods by a rushing stream right now, I thought.

Annie and Miss Sally spend the summers gardening in spite of the heat, and I don't know how they manage to. There are more flower beds in Sally's yard than grassy areas. Her roses and peonies are award-winning, as are Annie's. They are adversary friends in the garden club and compete in the county fair. Between them they have enough blue ribbons to tie up Martha Stewart and swat her with a spade.

Annie, Bellamy and I frequent the farmers market in the mornings while the temperatures are still cool. Bell showed us the lovely gold pendant Sam had given her.

"He must be in love, Bell."

"I don't know if you can call this love but he sure spends his money generously."

"Do you think you could love him?" I asked.

"I really like the guy, but he's more like a comfortable old shoe. He's a sweetheart, helps me around the house and cooks like a dream. He bought me a new oven last month. I haven't even turned the damn thing on yet and he's taking me on a sales trip to Florida this November. I enjoy his company," she explained as we tasted samples of delicious sweet pink watermelon.

"Oh my God! Bell, check out that guy."

"What guy?"

"That man over there in the green shirt. Is he gorgeous or what?" Talk about sweet and juicy.

"Oh, he is luscious."

"Gosh, I can feel the sex appeal from here!"

"Go stand next to him, Sophie, and see if you get sucked into his force field," she said, laughing at me.

"The guy, Bellamy, *the guy;* how can I meet him?"

"Go over there and bump into him, ask him a question about produce, have him thump a watermelon, tell him you like his jeans. Rip your top off. God, Sophie, how do you *not* know how to meet people?" I turned to attempt to meet him.

"Wait," Annie said and she unbuttoned two more buttons on my shirt.

"Really?"

"Really," they said in unison.

I sighed and walked past him in hopes that he would stop at the next vendor, maybe fondle my boob. He did stop. Actually I think I felt him before I saw him. Damn if he didn't have a force field. I turned to see this man's gorgeous face. Nervously I dropped my bag of cherries. Then I knocked my hat off stooping to retrieve the bag. I made the snap decision to ditch the cherries because underneath my hat there was *hat hair* and I didn't want him to see that. With calm and an ease that bordered on elegance he bent down to pick up my bag. His lips were moving. He was saying something, smiling even; but I was paralyzed, my mouth frozen open.

It's not so much that he was handsome; he was — well, breathtaking. Rugged and manly and he oozed sex appeal. His front teeth were a little crooked, his nose too. It had probably been broken once or twice. I realized he had spoken but I had no idea what he said.

"Excuse me?"

"I said, here's your bag of… " He peeked inside and smiled. "Cherries?" His eyes sparkled and they were blue, blue as the

85

Carolina sky, and he had lush silver waves. I think he was aware of the effect he was having on me. I might have been drooling.

I thanked him and walked away. I, stupid, stupid woman that I am, I walked away. I am, without doubt, the most socially inept person on earth.

"Bell, I blew it."

"Ya, you did. He watched you walk away and it looked like he liked what he saw."

"I didn't even notice if he were wearing a ring."

"I noticed. He was not."

"Damn. Why didn't I ask him to coffee or something?"

"You are just out of practice, that's all."

"He had a nice deep voice."

"That's what you noticed, his voice?"

"I noticed his eyes. He had eyes like the sky. And now he's gone. Is there any way to find him again?"

"Not without looking foolish."

"I could look foolish. I wouldn't mind looking foolish."

"Sophie, there will be other opportunities."

"But what if I always think of him as the one that got away?"

"You don't even know him. Don't worry, the next time you will do better."

"But I want *him*!" I imitated a baby crying. Bellamy took my hand and dragged me away like she was my mom and I was her errant child who didn't get the favorite treat.

Did I mention that I have 500 condoms?

16.
MILFs on the Fourth of July

Misty, at any point in time, has about a thousand rescue dogs so she bought a house across from the dog park which is named Fourth of July Park and it is, oddly enough, where they set off the fireworks display. Kernersville loves fireworks, and they do them well. I'm not saying they are Gandalf the Grey but for a small town they are impressive, and why not?

She has a party every year. The entire yard is fenced for the dogs, but the back is gated into separate kennels and she only lets them in the front yard after her Fourth of July party so her guests don't sit in fresh dog bombs. We bring extra chairs just in case.

A cousin from Vermont was visiting. "We call her 'don't-believe-anything-she-says' Andrea. I know that sounds bad, but I have to tell you. Do not let her scam you out of money or anything."

"You've got to be kidding. You've taken in another stray?" Bren said what the rest of us were thinking, and it may have been the only time in history that I heard Misty say anything negative about anyone so this Andrea must be a piece of work.

Apparently Andrea, a recovering alcoholic, came here from Vermont with her son Jackson for a change of scene. This is ridiculous because Kernersville in the summer can make you awfully thirsty and this is a national holiday requiring beer.

Jackson was a nice-looking young man but his friend was as handsome as the Archangel Michael. Annie whispered in my ear, "No young man should be that handsome. It should be against the law."

"Watch, he's checking Bellamy out. What is he, twenty-four, twenty-five?"

"That's legal." Bren looked amused. "Oh, he's going to make a move." He engaged Bellamy in conversation.

"Misty, who is that kid hitting on Bellamy?"

"That's Jackson's friend, Michael." No shit, his name was really Michael.

Bellamy let him down gently and gave him a little kiss on the cheek. Unfazed, he began scanning the crowd for a first runner-up to the 'win-an-archangel-for the-night' contest. He turned his gaze to Bren, considered her and then regarded me. Of course, I was looking at him so he smiled at me and walked forward.

Oh shit.

Michael dragged a chair over and set it next to mine. "You know, my last girlfriend was forty-nine. What are you, thirty-seven?"

Bren and Annie left me alone with him, giggling like a couple of adolescent girls. "Ya, when I get that old, I'll let you know."

"No, seriously, you are a beautiful woman. You married?"

"Divorced."

"Good. Ever dated a younger guy?"

"As young as you? No."

"Want to get together later, after the fireworks?"

"How old are you?"

"Twenty-six, does it matter?"

"What year did you graduate high school?"

"East Forsyth class of '05." Jesus, he went to school with my kid. "So what about it?"

"You need a mom or what?"

"My mother died when I was a baby. It's just me and my dad now."

Oh crap. "I'm sorry, I didn't know. I'm really sorry."

"Not really, I was only kidding. So you want to get together later?"

"You are really an asshole, you know that?"

"Ya, I know. So you want to hook up or not?"

"Not."

Not a problem. Michael went off to find another play partner.

At least at a covered dish, the leftovers never go to waste. It's a pretty sensible thing to do actually. You make what you like; and if others don't eat it you get to take home your own food, which you must like or you wouldn't have prepared it.

"But you'll keep this shrimp and broccoli, won't you?"

"Oh yes, Eliot loves that."

"To heck with Eliot; I'll split it with you," Bren got a plate and another for Bellamy. "So how do you know that Michael kid, Miss Misty Lou?" she sassed.

"I told you, he's Jackson's friend."

"You know what they call him, don't you?"

"Yes," Misty backed up a step, sipped her water and quietly observed.

"What? What do they call him?" I asked.

"The Pizza Angel," Bren said with a smirk.

"The what?"

"He's the Pizza Angel. He used to deliver pizza at Mario's, and soon the pizza orders doubled on his shift. Apparently the older female customers used to tip him really well!" She grinned salaciously.

"Scandalous," Bellamy pretended shock.

"So now he's the MILF King."

"What is a milf?"

"It stands for *mothers I'd like to fuck*," Annie told us, "and he has turned it into a profitable business from what I have heard."

"No kidding?" I was solicited. That was a first for me.

"Oh big deal, they are all consenting adults," Annie said.

"Ya, but Bellamy kissed him."

"It was only on the check!" she defended.

"He even does bondage and S&M," Misty added.

"That must be how Annie knows him."

"Shut up, Bren!"

"How do you know everything, Bren?" I felt like a newcomer to earth.

"For your information," Misty said, "BDSM is considered just another life choice."

"What? Are there kinksters in Kernersville?" She feigned shock. "Any more wine left?"

Misty poured the last of it into Bren's glass. "You realize that you cannot help what it is that turns you on, don't you?"

Bellamy jumped up. "Oh, speaking of BDSM, I forgot to tell you, I was on my way in to the library and Betty Lou Easter was coming out with a black hardcover book. She was holding it by the binder with the cover facing down. So I said, 'Betty Lou, are you reading *Fifty Shades of Grey?*'"

"Oh Jaysus, what did she say?"

"Busted."

"She turned all red and said, "I knew I should have driven to the Walkertown Library." She was so embarrassed."

"Sophie. How much have you had to drink? Are you going to be alright to drive?" Bren asked.

"No, my eyes are red and itchy. It's the cats. I better go soon; I certainly don't need any more to drink nor do I need any more graphic images to keep me up at night like Pizza Angels." *Yeah, Pizza Angels — me with beautiful young men all over me feeding me pizza ... with maybe ... some pirates, yeah, handsome pirates with pizza.* "Thank you, Misty, it was wonderful as usual. Good night everyone, and Happy what's left of the Fourth."

"Bren and I are leaving too. This was great, Misty, thanks a lot." Annie kissed Misty goodbye. "You staying, Bellamy?"

"Just till the traffic's thinned out a little more."

"I'm going to put on some tea. Would you like some?"

"What kind?"

"What kind would you like?" Misty filled the kettle.

"Chamomile is fine."

"Chamomile it is."

"Okay, that's good."

Misty watched under blond bangs, assessing Bell. "You want to talk about something, Bellamy?"

"How could you tell?"

"I've been, sort of, expecting it."

"Misty, I don't know what to do. I'm turning to shit. And I really need help." Bellamy held a napkin under an eyelash. "I'm short-tempered and obnoxious. I make snarky comments, even to people I like. I'm drinking too much, and Sammy says he thinks I need mood stabilizers."

"Well, before you start medicating the symptoms, why don't we try to find the underlying problem?"

"When can we start?"

"Any day after work, I'm usually here."

"I'd rather come to your office some morning and see you in a professional setting."

"Really, Bell, I love you. You're family. I'm happy to see you after hours, before hours if you want mornings."

"Better in the office."

"Okay, do you want me to set something up?"

"You better call me. I'm queen of avoidance these days."

She left her chair and walked down the hall to the bathroom. Bellamy shut the door, flipped on the fan and sat down on the john. She gathered up a length of toilet tissue, folded it neatly and began to cry.

Misty waited for the water to boil and the tea to steep. She arranged the tea on a serving tray, knocked softly on the bathroom door and entered.

"You okay, Bellamy?"

"Yes, I just needed to have a good cry. Maybe I'm having a second menopause," she said as she dabbed under her eyes, "or a nervous breakdown."

"You sure you don't want to start now, Bell?" Misty sat on the edge on the tub.

"No, not now, definitely not now." She took a few deep breaths as she gazed around Misty's bathroom then her eyes filled again and she broke down and sobbed. She reached for more tissue. Misty lifted her to a stand and held her close and let her cry.

"It's going to be okay, Bell. Whatever we have to do, we'll make it so."

17.
Now We Arrive at Chuck

I said I'd never date a contra dancer.

When Chuck asked me out, I pretended I thought he was teasing me. I wanted to think about it, and make some discrete inquiries.

He was single, people seemed to have only nice things to say about him and he made artisan furniture for a living. Somebody showed me Chuck's business card with a table on it. The table was art, primitive board with free-formed metal legs. I liked the idea that he created it with his hands. He was a big man around my age, still handsome and I had been dancing with him for almost half a year. I sat out a dance and watched him. He had wonderful style.

Maybe a more appropriate word for describing a contra dancer's style would be their personality. Some dancers are orderly, very precise. They want their lines to be straight and the movements perfectly synchronized. They don't laugh when a dancer messes up or isn't on time with their count (unless it's a really funny mistake). Flair matters more for those on the opposite end of the spectrum. Creative flourishes and dips abound and have led to an occasional contra-related injury — a knocked head here, an elbow where it shouldn't have landed, maybe a stamped toe.

Chuck's style was graceful for his size, yet playful. He seemed to have individual gestures for every person he met as new couples traveled up or down the line. Just enough flourish to show that he was a creative soul but with a kind man's character. Certainly he treated everyone with dignity and respect.

I maneuvered myself to be near him when one dance ended, and I extended my hand to ask him for the next dance.

In and out of the calls, I had brief exchanges with him. "So were you serious?"

"About what?"

"About going out some time?" Ladies allemande right, a courtesy turn, and back to Chuck.

"Should I have been serious with you?" I gypsied and swung my neighbor.

"Are you being serious right now?"

He suppressed his smile. "I'm a very serious man. I hardly ever joke."

"I know that's a joke," I gave him my sweetest and most flirty smile.

We bantered till the end of the dance then he took my shoulders in his massive hands. "I would very much like for you to have dinner with me sometime and maybe a few beers. You do drink, don't you?" he asked.

"A little."

Friday night there was a wait for the tables so we ambled up to the bar. Chuck asked for a dark beer and I ordered a Jameson's, neat with a water back, no ice. The bartender appeared somewhat amused by my order and looked to Chuck as if to confirm that I wasn't joking. Chuck was definitely amused.

"Well, if that's what the lady wants… " He gestured to serve me. "So you drink a little?"

"The place is called Finnegan's Wake. I picked my poison." My smile grew. "Besides, good whiskey is a beautiful thing."

"That it is; however, I'll just stick to beer. One of us needs to keep our wits," he picked up the menu. "We better order because I don't want you to drink that on an empty stomach. And do you always drink your whisky straight?"

"Yes, I have always loved the taste of whiskey." When the bartender set the whiskey before me I guessed that there were at least two shots in the glass, probably two and a half.

"I hope you like it a lot," he nodded.

"Good whiskey needs to be savored and it will take most of tonight to savor this much," I said, toasted him and took a small sip.

"So Sophie has a dangerous streak." He half-smiled.

"I've been known to enjoy myself."

Gee, he was cute. He had an impish smile, mischievous and a little crooked with eyes like a wild grey sea. They say that Irishmen are either poets or fighters. He knew the words to all the Irish tunes and his nose was straight so I guessed poet. He could certainly sing. It was warm, romantic and sweet but it began to feel more like the Chuck Show. It could have been nerves. Was he a show-off, maybe a narcissist? *Stop looking for flaws.*

When our dinner arrived his singing stopped, and we settled into conversation that felt comfortable, flowed easily. He was smart but not pedantically, funny without being obnoxious or deprecatory. We had a wonderful time, chuckles even.

After dinner, we held hands along Trade Street, laughing at silly stories about the amusing personalities within the contra community. The night was warm and balmy. He pulled the pins from my hair and fluffed it out. I knew it looked ridiculous but I let him. He pulled me close and... hmmm. I noticed that his junk was in good working order. Chuck had some *wood*. He smiled at me. I smiled back as I knew I was about to be kissed. I momentarily flashed back to the unpleasant sensation of Mick's torpedo tongue, then quickly tried to drop that thought. Rewind, playback. *Stop that!* And I brought my mind back to Chuck's gaze. Chuck's lovely, romantic...

First kisses should be sweet. His had not the gentle quality of Will's first kiss or the warmth of Kenny's. To tell you the truth, it was possessive in a damp suction kind of way, and almost a little scary, like I could have been sucked through a wormhole to another dimension. I pulled back. I think my mouth hung open a little.

"What?" He appeared puzzled.

My face must have tattled and I was committed to some type of explanation. "Chuck, that was a bit ... umm, emphatic."

"Emphatic?"

"Assertive."

"Assertive?"

"Wet, it was wet," I sounded like *Rainman.*

"Are you saying that I'm a lousy kisser?" He was obviously insulted.

"It wasn't a bad kiss *per se.*" I'm really blowing this. "I, I didn't mean... "

"I'll walk you to your car."

Maybe I am too picky.

So two steps ahead of me and without one word, he saw me back to my car. Gee, I'm sorry to have insulted you, buddy, but how do you get to be an old cute Irish guy who sings like an angel without learning how to give a tender first kiss? It's unnatural and quite the temper on you too. Look at that.

Chuck him.

It was a balmy ninety degrees with not the slightest breeze, and winter was too far into the distance to matter. I didn't even want to venture out of the air-conditioning to get the mail.

The phone rang and it was Annie. "Hey, Sophie, Bellamy and I are going to see an action movie. You are welcome to join us or meet up with us after the show to have a quick dinner before we go to the funeral home tonight."

"What do you mean? Who died?"

"Oh darn, didn't anyone tell you? Stella's older sister, Vicki."

Everyone knows I don't like funerals or wakes. I want to be cremated with no fuss and if friends or family want to take the time to commemorate my life in some way let them choose. I'd just as soon have my ashes left on the Boston subway or mixed with some joint compound by Norm from *This Old House* and spackled onto someone's drywall. Maybe I could have them spread around the floor at Costco so that my essence is firmly imbedded in the air as a silent memorial to my love of bulk purchasing and recycled cardboard boxes.

Sometimes this life feels like I'm at a very geeky cookware party, and I wouldn't want my real friends to find out that I was there eating tortilla chip casserole and microwaved bunt cake. Feels best to leave quietly from earth's back door, and maybe nobody will remember that I actually participated in using all these Styrofoam containers and disposable plastic bottles.

We met at Smitty's for fish tacos. Bren asked how long we thought it would take for Letta to start flirting with Rob, her best friend's newly widowed brother-in-law.

"It should be good for a few laughs!"

"It's really not even funny anymore. I'd hate to have her reputation, honestly," Bellamy said.

"Sophie, you need to downgrade your reputation a little. Why don't you be the first woman to make a play for Robert?" Bren suggested.

"Not gonna happen, Bren. Hey, there's Hook."

"Who the hell is Hook?"

"See that old guy sitting by himself over there? Hey, Hook, *Hook!*" I got his attention and waved him over.

"Hi, I remember you, Sophie, right?"

"Yes, we met in the park," I told the others.

"She rescued me."

"Oh, stop it. Hook, these are my friends." I introduced them. "Are you eating alone? You are welcome to join us. Pull up a chair."

"No, you don't want to be seen with me. It will ruin your reputation."

"Nonsense, Hook. Eat with us."

"Sit with Sophie. She needs some bad press," Bren said.

"Sophie, you seem like a nice person. But according to the State of North Carolina, I am not one."

"What do you mean?"

"I'm a registered sex offender. It's not a secret and nobody wants to know me. Even my family doesn't want to know me."

"Then you need to go back to your table and leave us alone." Bren pointed the way.

"Bren, you don't even know him."

"And I don't want to know him, either."

"It's okay, Sophie, I'm used to it." Hook walked back to his table and sipped his drink.

"Damn, Bren," I said, "you know what some of these laws are like. Stuff like fellatio is illegal in some states."

"Hey, I got grandchildren. When you have grandchildren, you'll feel the same way, believe me."

"Eddie and I used to make love on the beach in California, and it was no big deal. If we had done that on the Outer Banks, we both would have been jailed and I'd be a registered sex offender right now."

"You don't even want to know what I have done in public," said Little Annie.

"Actually, I really do want to know," Bren laughed.

"I think we owe it to Hook to give him a chance to explain," I said.

"I owe him nothing. And what the hell kind of name is Hook anyway?"

"Think of how lonely he must be."

"I think making a person register like that is a gross invasion of privacy. Murderers don't have a registry. Violent criminals don't. *High on crack and maimed an elderly person for life* doesn't have a registry."

"But we're talking about children here, people who molest children."

"Not necessarily, consensual anal sex can get you locked up in some places," Bell added.

"Not since 2003. The Supreme Court ruled that all consensual sex—anal, oral, any kind of sex as long as it is private—is no one's business." Annie told us. The states haven't caught up with changing their laws but they know that Federal Law makes these things impossible to prosecute.

My phone chirped. I reached into my purse to find a text from Chuck. "Oh my God, you won't believe this." I had already told them about Chuck and the kiss. "Are you ready for this and a drum roll, please? It says, 'I'd like to request another chance to kiss you.' Wow, what do you think about that? Now he wants to kiss me."

"I think this is better than the action movie!" Bellamy answered.

"Squid magic."

"Ignore her. I don't think you should go with him," Annie said. "If it was that unpleasant, you will never be able to forget it. It was your first kiss."

"It wasn't unpleasant. I overreacted. I like Chuck, liked the kiss. I thought that I blew it with him."

Bren thought it showed character. "Hey, he is willing to admit that there's room for improvement. I think he shows promise. Besides, I think you are being kind of picky. What is wrong with a wet kiss?"

"Nothing, not one thing; when you think about it, it's bound to get messy eventually. I want to sleep with this guy and sex is wet sticky business. I can't wait to get some of it." I smiled indecently and covered my lips with balm.

Bellamy agreed. "Technique can be taught; I think it's time for you to have some excitement in your life."

So I accepted another date with Chuck, my mind full of wicked thoughts and high expectations. He does have many of the qualities

I like in a man; he is very attractive, fit *and* he can dance.

So we met for beer and snacks at a Foothills Micro-brewery. It was a bit awkward at first; but after a beer or two, we both loosened up. He even gave me a little nibble kiss preview at the bar. It was a nice little kiss. When he walked me back to my car, he took me into his arms and gave me a warm, respectable kiss with a tiny taste of tongue. I was definitely interested in sampling some more of that tasty Chuck Roast.

Sunday night at El Mejor, the girls were anxious to hear about my date.

"This might be it, Sophie, your big chance to see if your cooch has completely rusted out or not." Bren went right to the down dirty.

"You think I should? It will be the third date, you know."

"You should do it. You owe it to yourself; besides, you have known him for a while, and you both have loads of friends in common. You know he's not a creep. I think it's time you take the leap and get over your, ah, reservations." That's easy for Bellamy to say with her long, lean yoga body free of the wear and tear of my two pregnancies.

"Ya, but it's because we know so many people in common. What if it turns into a disaster? And how do I get over being so self-conscious of my body?"

"Candle light!" They echoed.

"If it's a disaster, then you will know he's not the one. As long as you are strong enough to dance with him afterward, then go for it. But if you think it will chase you off the contra floor then don't do it." It was great to have Annie perfectly articulating the issue. "But you better get some lube."

"Lube?"

"You haven't done it in a long time and you say he's a large man. You better have lube. I suggest coconut oil."

Either I have sex with a cute guy that I like and get over my fear, or I say "no" to the cute guy and give in to the fear. Either choice would lead to an awkward situation whenever we danced together.

"So, where do you buy coconut oil?"

Misty fumbled to find her cell in her new bag. "Hey, Bell, I've been waiting to hear back from you."

"Misty, I'm sorry I haven't returned your calls. When are you and Eliot going back to the mountains?"

"I'm tied up with rescues, but he's going up this week for a 'men's week'. He's going to spend some time with his sons and grandsons. Isn't that a wonderful idea?"

"I guess. I think I'm ready to start seeing you."

"Oh, Bellamy." She raised her eyes upward with gratitude. "I'm proud of you. You've seen a therapist before?"

"Briefly. It was a joke; I was a joke."

"What do you mean a joke?"

"This one fell asleep. I didn't realize I was that boring."

"You are not boring. When do you want to see me?"

"I'll call you."

"We can set something up now."

"No, no, I'll call you."

"Whenever you're ready, Bellamy, I'm here for you."

"I know that. Misty, thanks."

18.
The Beef

An action film, probably the same one Annie and Bell saw. To tell you the truth, except for the kiss at the end, I couldn't tell you one detail about it. I sat next to this large attractive man in a dimly lit theatre, his thigh against mine and my hand palm to palm in his. This felt nice, comfortable but distracting enough to keep my mind from following the plot. When the guy finally kissed the girl I thought of Chucks kiss, that crazy Chuck Sucking kiss, a kiss you would follow into battle or outer space or deep into the jungles of Peru, but better than that because unlike every fabulous cinematic kiss, Chuck's was real.

We exited the theatre with my arm tucked under his. "I have a bottle of single malt in my kitchen. Would you like to... um, taste some of it?"

He stopped to face me. His grey-sea eyes shown in the parking lot lights and he bit his bottom lip. "I'd love to," he said as he ran his enormous hands up my arms and held my shoulders. "Wait... I just want to remember this... this moment... you inviting me." He breathed in heavily and in spite of the warm night, chills raced down my back.

We settled outside on the porch and listened to the sounds of the night. Chica skeptically eyed him. He sang a few notes of a song I'd never heard and scratched her head and back till she decided that he could be trusted. He then leaned back and began to play with my hair... I could have purred when he moved closer and cradled my chin in his hand... almost painfully slow... he guided my face to his. Sweetly, tenderly he kissed me. If first kisses could have second chances, this was it. It was perfect.

"That was beautiful," I whispered.

"You're beautiful," he said and we walked to my room. I lit a scented candle and began to unbutton my blouse. His mouth nibbled my neck and he touched my breast as I peeled the fabric from my body. My skirt fell to the floor. He watched as I unfasten my bra and dropped that too. I stepped from the puddle of clothing and sank to the bed. He stripped to the skin within seconds and his mouth found mine. This was it, Chuck's kiss, mind altering and thrilling like a Tilt-a-Wheel on dope. I would have willingly consented to being sucked on into his face, down through his guts and full on down to China.

His flesh on mine, I was ready for this, all my senses livened like neurons on fire. I opened my thighs and moistened my bits to receive him. Here it comes, the 100% beef Chuck…then he stood and said, "Oh my, look at the time. I better get going."

"What?"

"Ya, it's getting pretty late." He continued to insert legs into pants.

"Chuck, what are you doing?"

He smiled evilly, zipped his jeans up over his erection, picked up his shirt and began to walk away.

"What are you doing?" He walked out of my room. "You *asshole!*" I screamed. "You vindictive son of a bitch!"

He walked out of my house singing a lively tune. *'And he left her wanting more. Yes, he left her wanting more."*

I heard the front door shut and I ran to the front window where I incredulously watched his Jeep creep up the drive and his tail lights disappear around the bend.

"Fucking Chuck!"

"How could he do that? Have you ever known a man to just walk away from sure sex just like that? Has anything like that ever happened to you?"

"Not to me," Bellamy said.

"Me neither," Bren added.

"I don't think it's ever happened before," Annie said.

"What are you saying? You think I'm the only woman in the history of the world that this has ever happened to?"

"No, this could happen, but there would have to be outstanding circumstances involved; maybe it would have to be preceded by an appropriate statement," Annie said.

"Like what kind of appropriate statement?"

"Like someone yelling *Fire!* You know?"

"Oh great.'"

"Or 'Sire, the Huns are storming the north gate.'" She pressed her lips together and suppressed a giggle.

"How about, 'Holy shit! The boat is sinking, bail, baby, bail!'" Bellamy outright laughed.

"I'm hopeless."

"Oh, this isn't helping. Sophie, you're not hopeless," Misty consoled.

Bren said, "I told you not to be cruel. 'Vindictive son of a bitch' might have been a wee bit overly critical." She actually lilted a good Irish accent.

"Do you think he was, ah, unable to… ya know?" Misty asked.

"He had an erection and left me. He was friggin' laughing about it, singing a song about it, that no-good, stinking swamp sliming, slice of shit!"

"Face it, girl. You were punked," Bren said.

"I'll punk him till the middle of next Tuesday. Okay, I'm not a gorgeous woman; but I have *never* had a man just walk out on me like that. What is that supposed to do to my confidence?"

"Actually, I think it should boost it," Bellamy offered.

"Boost it. Just how do you figure?"

"He had to have taken the kiss insult really hard. He had to have put a lot of thought and planning into this retaliation. It takes a ton of fortitude for a man to walk out of a woman's bedroom with an erection. Are you sure he had an erection?"

"Positive."

"That's premeditative, proves he put a great deal of thought into this. He actually went to the trouble to write a poem about it and *then* he set it to music."

"I know, such a compliment, huh?"

"How about, 'Shit, my wife's home! Get in the closet!'" Bren re-started.

"'Stampede! Damn them cattle!'" Annie continued. "Or 'Holy smokes, there's a snake in the tent!'"

"Not helping!" Misty said sternly.

"Ya, not helpful at all," I agreed.

Then Bren cupped her hands in front of her mouth, "This is J. Edgar Hoover. Come out with your hands up."

They bit their lips; put hands to their faces trying so hard not to even look at each other. Then Bren burst out laughing, reached for her napkin and the rest of them followed. Even Misty couldn't resist. Bellamy excused herself to the ladies' room, and Bren almost beat her there.

"Oh, cheer up, Sophie, maybe we'll find some guys at the beach next week."

"Sure, Annie, we'll find guys. We'll find them watching younger women!"

19.
The Outer Banks after Labor Day

Annie and I arrived at Bell's beach house in time to spend just the weekend. The fall trip to the Outer Banks is a little piece of heaven that I look forward to each year. Her home is comfy and beachy, stacked with porches of every shape and size and it overlooks the waterway from atop a high bluff, boasting wispy pink sunsets beyond an array of private piers. They are mostly empty, useless to all but johnboats, kayaks and canoes because Currituck Sound, though miles wide at this point, is only a few feet deep most of the way across. A family of deer lives in the natural area at the base of the property. You can walk down the boardwalk to Bell's dock and watch them in the evening as they eat vegetation by the water. This is all part of Bellamy's perfect life. Damn, I want her life! I want her life!

The end of the season party is a huge clam/fish bake, a celebration for the year-round residents who have worked their businesses all summer and can now relax and enjoy the beach. It's also a welcome home for all the property owners who rented their homes for the summer and are returning home to spend fall and the rest of the year with uncrowded shore and nearly-paid mortgages.

The party was at a house in Corolla, north of Duck, where the wild horses from old Spanish ships still roam the dunes. Corolla is pronounced *corralla*, like a corral rather than like the Toyota. The highway ends and those who are lucky enough to live in homes beyond the end of the road simply let the air out of their tires and drive on the beach.

Sammy decided to join us for the end of the season party at the last minute because his golfing doctor friend would be there. Sammy has a sales personality; he's never known a stranger and gets extremely excited about pharmaceuticals. Whoopee!

One thing I am very sensible about is good skin care so I was completely tan-free from staying inside most of the summer, *always* wearing a hat and applying copious amounts of SPF 40.

We piled into the SUVs, picked up a neighbor named Harold and drove to the end of the road. Then we shuttled in jeeps and rovers to the party house. I rode in the back seat with Harold while Bren got cute with the driver. I liked Harold. He had keen wit and nice eyes and good eyes for spotting horses. He pointed out a few packs, five or six together, a stallion with his harem and a colt or two.

"This, the evening, is when they are most active, like deer," he yelled above the engine and wind. "It's kind of unusual to see them this close to the gate."

"Aren't they frightened by the vehicles?"

"No, they're used to them."

It was a fairly large house but extremely rustic, shack-ish even. The place appeared to be a ramshackle assortment of unrelated driftwood held together with wire and paint then accessorized with discarded rusty signage of various sizes and styles.

"I know it looks like a gumbo joint, but they did this on purpose. This is a good party, and they build the homes solid here. How many hurricanes you think this place has stood through?"

I'd guess about seven hundred and eighty.

We walked up two flights to the entrance and then paused to rest on rockers. Harold was right; this top deck was solid. Bren waited with us, unwrapped the scarf she had tied around her hair art creation. I could not believe what she was wearing.

"That was a stimulating ride," she said. She was revving up to party-mode. Annie arrived with Bell and Sammy, and we all moved in to the great room.

There were definitely some well-weathered characters in this crowd but most of the guys seemed like young Kennedy boys with their khakis, collared shirts and sweaters casually slung over one shoulder. Many of the women wore their end of season tans and any outfit that would show off their brownness. I bet they freeze their butts off and thank goodness that all those rich, sensible Kennedy boys have nice warm sweaters to lend them.

I expected that Harold would introduce us around. I turned about to ask him but he was already gone. He went off to find the cooler women, the ones with less clothing on.

I wore a blue top with flattering diagonally crossed lines and a pair of navy linen slacks. Annie had on brown slacks and a burgundy sweater that hung to mid-thigh. It was fall and night does get a little cool this time of year. These were timeless and practical outfits. Bellamy was covered in black linen head to toe, sexy but understated.

Bren, on the other hand, wore aqua tennis shorts and a matching sports top. Her hair was braided back into a high elaborate pony tail with extensions trailing down to her shoulders. This was a dramatic statement, even for Bren. What her top lacked in fabric, it more than made up for in breast top, a chocolate-flavored Barbara Eden, straight from *I Dream of Jeannie.*

Surrounded by men, Bren was in her element. Old leathered ones, young Kennedy-looking ones, mostly wealthy men were hanging on her every word, spellbound by exotic glamour, fascinated by the gold NYPD pendant flanked by ample cleavage. These fools made socializing with Bren a contact sport, competing for her attention, vying to get her drinks or snacks. I almost expected cricket bats and polo mallets to start flying as she over-smiled and over-flirted, a caricature of self. Bren was by nature entertaining and these men were completely captured by her natural authority. I watched her command control of the crowd with the kind of confidence that might only be learned in the New York Police Academy. They were ready to devour her and she was doling out her tasty sweets one tiny flavor at a time.

"Can I get anything else for you, Miss Bren?" One of those Kennedy-looking guys asked her.

"Just another one of your beautiful smiles," she replied, tilting her head. He cast his eyes shyly downward, maybe even blushed a little.

One older and obviously very wealthy man, perhaps the silverback of these hominids, plowed forward and pressed his dominance, getting all Darwin on the others. He turned, not to Bren, but to the other men surrounding her and said, "I'm going to escort this lovely Negress to the buffet." There was an uncomfortable pause. Most everyone was stunned by his obvious lack of awareness which only he seemed unaware of.

Bren's lips curled upward in her evil smile. She peered up at him through her long thick eyelashes and said, "Why, that's very…

white of you." She took his arm as he led her to the buffet leaving half of them hiding their amusement, the other half rubbernecking to check out Bren from the back.

Bell and Sammy were seated with several couples, probably doctors and their wives. I couldn't hear what Bellamy whispered in Sam's ear but he turned the color of raspberry sherbet and remarked, "I love it when a beautiful woman makes me blush." He laughed loudly.

Later on I observed one of the men in deep conversation with Sammy and I was not above eavesdropping. He wanted to know about Bell. Who was she? Where and how did he and Bellamy meet? How long had they been together? Were they getting serious?

"Why, Andrew," Sam laughed, "do you seriously think I'd let an old hound dog like you steal that gem away from me? You'd be mistaken."

"She is a gem, finely cut and flawless, like Sharon Stone. She reminds me of my first wife. I shouldn't have let that one get away." Andrew replied.

"Your new wife is a very beautiful woman."

"Ya, hmmm."

"What's the matter, Andrew?"

"She wants to have a baby. I'm fucking sixty years old. My youngest two are in college, and *she* wants me to have another baby. I mean, I love kids but…"

Sammy raised his eyes.

"I'm getting a vasectomy. I've been thinking about it, but, Jesus, she'd leave me for sure. We talked about this. It was spelled out in the pre-nup. She knew I didn't want more kids, but now that we're married she says she has changed her mind. Maybe she'll stay with me and maybe not. It's better to know now rather than later. I don't want to go through all that again."

"Your choice, Buddy, whatever you decide, I'm behind you all the way. She is a beauty."

"Now why can't I find a mature woman who is as elegant as your Bellamy?"

"Her friend Sophie is available."

"Which one is she?"

"She's the busty brunette in blue. She's around here somewhere. I'll introduce you."

"No, I have to have a blond."

I had heard enough of that conversation and went off to be a wallflower with Annie. "Have you ever heard a woman say that she would not consider dating a man because he had the wrong color of hair?"

"No, that's stupid."

"But men say that shit all the time."

"Men are usually more concerned about how a woman makes *them* look, how she looks on his arm."

"Like a prop, an accessory? That's disrespectful *and* dumb."

"Men are dumb. Haven't you been watching Bren work the room?" she asked. "What a bunch of dummies! Could they act any more stupid?"

"She's something."

"She sure makes a statement. Bren knows a lot of these folks. You know she comes up here pretty often with the grandchildren. And she loves people. That's Bren."

We had a bite to eat. The food was fresh and tasty, and there was plenty to drink but we wanted to leave. We were both tired from the trip and the music was not great. We stopped to tell Bell we were leaving and asked for the keys to Big Red. It was already given that Bren wouldn't be driving home tonight. We caught a shuttle vehicle back to the parking lot and the drive back was cool and lovely.

"Want to go down to the pier?"

"Sure," she said and we proceeded down the catwalk. We settled on a bench until we noticed the smell of cut bait and moved to the railing.

"When did you know?" I asked her.

"When did I know what?"

"That you had, you know, different taste in sex?"

"Did Bren put you up to this?"

"No, I'm not asking particulars. It's just that I have unusual fantasies sometimes, and this guy grabbed my breast in public and I thought I'd Krispy Kreme in my jeans."

"Exhibitionism, Sophie, really?"

"Annie, you're the only person I can talk to about this."

"It's nothing to be ashamed of, honey. Remember when Misty said that you can't help what turns you on?"

"Ya, I believe that but I always thought I was sort of normal, not that I think your abnormal. I didn't mean that."

She laughed. "Vanilla, the word is vanilla."

"Well, when did you know?"

"I worked as a secretary in the automobile industry, Generous Motors." She cleared her throat. "The way you got ahead was by how pretty you were, how big your tits were and how many men you slept with. I was pretty, I had huge breasts… "

"*You* had huge breasts?"

"I had a breast reduction just before I retired."

"Ya?"

"Well, after Vern disappeared, I decided to take the fast track and started sleeping with my boss. Word got around, and I began to climb the ladder."

"Really?"

"Well, I had three kids to feed."

"No judgment here." I held my hands up to emphasize.

"Eventually I was offered a much higher-paying job to work on the jets, the private jets. It paid really well, but you had to be willing to do *whatever* the passengers wanted. That meant anything from serving drinks topless to having kinky sex, even with multiple partners. I was always a horny little so-and-so, so I went for it."

"Wow."

"Service with a smile!" She showed her teeth.

"That's unbelievable."

"Early retirement with mega benefits."

"Mega unbelievable!"

"So I was actually a well-paid call girl for half of my career. But I had a fraction of the hours and an expense account for hair and make-up and stuff like that."

"I can't believe you did that, Annie."

"It wasn't so bad. I liked the attention, the power of it, being desired by all those men."

"Having sex with multiple partners, strangers. I can't even wrap my mind around Bren's Leroy."

"I was a grown woman, thirty-two and approaching my sexual

peak. As far as jobs go, for women in Detroit, this was a really good one."

"But wasn't it demeaning?"

"I didn't think it was any more demeaning than sleeping with my creepy boss for a raise. Believe it or not, half the guys just wanted to be dominated. They would want to massage and kiss my feet or be degraded in some way. At least I got paid a lot. I have to admit that I enjoyed it, well, most of it. So do you want to try some exhibitionism? I can set you up with a guy I know."

"Oh God no, I mean it sounds hot but I couldn't do that, no way. With my luck I'd end up on a sex offenders list like Hook."

Annie smiled. "You think about it. I'm going to get some rest."

"I'm going to get some whiskey."

With a shot and a blanket I sat on the stairs where the pier meets the sand and laid back on the dock. I thought about Annie, imagined some of the things she got to do on the jet. Soon I was squirming in my slacks. So I unzipped them and put my hand down inside. I imagined that I was being watched by men with binoculars and telescopes. I imagined their arousal and pictured them unzipping their trousers, fondling their members and that they were jerking it as they watched me. I cupped my breast and flicked at my hardened nipple over my shirt and my orgasm came quicker and stronger than I had ever remembered.

Damn! My heart beat riotously as my breath normalized; when I finally opened my eyes, I was rewarded by the sight of so many brilliant stars, the thousands that are visible from this dock in Duck on the Outer Banks of North Carolina.

I spotted a few constellations but I am awed by the Milky Way. I tried to remember the last time I saw the curve of the galaxy this clearly. Salt air filled my lungs and wafts of bayberry spiced the breeze. This was a nearly perfect night. This was a perfect place to enjoy this night and probably nobody saw me touch myself but the deer.

Don't think, I thought. *Just be here now.*

I usually walk to the beach in the early morning before everyone else is awake. As the magnificent peachy pink of the sky appeared I moved quickly hoping to get there in time for the sun's first peek at the day. I arrived as it ascended then sat on the stairway that crowned these delicate dunes. Bundled up in thick sweaters I marveled at the morning light before me, another Atlantic sunrise.

I slipped off my shoes and walked through a layer of stiff sea grass to the cool grit and the softer sand beyond. I dug in with my toes as I watched a little crab burrow a hole to safety and hide from the morning's hungry gulls. I tottered through a barrier of course pebbles to the fine wet sand near the water's edge as a remnant of a wave kissed the tips of my feet with a gentle but tickling chill.

The beach brings peace to me, yet possesses such awesome power and strength. Water meeting land, wind cooling as the sun warms. I stood staring off to the horizon as if I could see on to forever. A tiny solitary boat in the distance aided perspective. I felt completely connected and yet all alone.

So what if I am alone? What if I'm alone for the rest of my life? It's entirely possible, but how bad would that be really? I need to face the fact that, blond, brunette, red or silver, I may not ever find anyone. I wished it had turned out better with Chuck.

I often hear women say that all the good ones are taken, but I don't believe that it's true. I think there are lots of good guys out there that I would like. I just don't really believe, deep in my heart that they would like me. I have too many faults, I'm too outspoken, I have a temper, a big butt and I swear.

Maybe it's just as well. I don't fit into this generation of Southerners and I'll never be patient and submissive enough. And I don't think that the kink scene is for me either. Good God, what if people found out? What if my kids found out?

I am lucky in so many other ways. I have travelled, had an interesting career and I have my health. I have a decent home; my kids are doing well and I have good friends. One of them has a great beach house and has invited me here. There is a lot to be grateful for.

Let me just live in this moment. It is so beautiful here and now.

Coffee was brewing. Bell and Sammy were making a frittata for breakfast. It smelled wonderful. The kitchen and great room were on the top floor with a wall of glass doors open to the balcony and the blue of the sound… and the dock that I masturbated on last night. Oh my God, I masturbated out in the open on Bellamy's dock! If I had been caught I could have been arrested and *I* would be on a sex offenders list. I doubly washed my hands and began setting the table mostly to hide my face. Within a few minutes Bren stumbled up the steps, a bit blurry-eyed and in search of a coffee cup. Her timing perfectly diverted my mind and those shameful thoughts were neatly tucked away for later.

"Weren't you the Miss Popularity last night?" I teased as she sipped and slowly came awake.

"I've been showing white people how to party since 1957," she yawned.

"It seemed more like 1857 to me," Annie said and smirked.

"Huh?"

"Why, Miss Bren, you were acting like Scarlet O'Hara at the Twelve Oaks picnic with the Tarleton twins." Annie's eyes met mine and I jumped on board.

"Were you eating barbeque with all the boys in the county, Miss Scarlett? I think that Ashley Wilkes is a dream, don't you?"

The corner of Bren's lips turned up, and she began batting her eyelashes. "Well, fiddle de fucking dee," she grinned. "Wasn't that a hoot? The woman didn't like me *nearly* as much as dem men folk did."

"And how was the whitest man alive?" I asked. "Was he just Caucasian or a cock occasion?"

"Oh Jaysus, was he trip-pin' or what? Have you been to the beach already?"

"You know me, up before dawn. At least here I have something to do when the sun comes up."

"Annie, you want to walk to the water with me after breakfast?"

"Sure, but you best wear your shawl. I won't have you freckling like white trash."

Ain't fittin'.

I dragged a beach chair to the boardwalk and spent the remainder of the morning under my favorite trees. I brought a book. I always bring a book but the view of the sound is so stunning in this spot that I hardly ever open it, preferring to enjoy the beauty of the oak trees. These are the same variety that I found so captivating on the high ground hammocks of inland Florida and on the coastlines nearer to Vero Beach: Southern Oak, the small-leafed, gnarly-limbed variety that you often see draped with moss. Three of these trees form a canopy of shade, and the dark twisty curves of the limbs are contrasted by the light blue of the sky and the soft teal of the sound. They are the survivors of storms, have endured persistent, ever-changing winds and gales, and the surges of the sea. No moss gathers on these for long. It settles around their bases like mounds of raffia cradling a precious gift. I have a special attraction to this spot and for these particular trees, a respect, perhaps even empathy or kinship, for theirs was a life of a thousand gusts.

By noon we had a rudimentary outline of a plan to get even with Chuck. "He likes to sing. Maybe Sammy could pretend to be a talent scout or an agent. We could make him think he's being *discovered.*"

"Sophie, you are positively devious. Sammy, you'd do that, help Sophie?" Bell asked sweetly.

"Sure, I'll help. It'll be like my old fraternity days. We had fun playing pranks. We even had a prank quota my sophomore year. I'm excited about doing it."

After lunch, we shopped. Bren nearly bought out the autumn sales racks of shirts and hoodies, kitschy stocking stuffers and artsy gifts as she thought forward to her family and the holidays. We tagged after her like we were fans, her entourage, the people known to have accompanied Bren on her beach trip. And she would verge on the brink of a Scarlett imitation or edge into a famous line, "I'll think about that… when we get home." She even began calling Annie Miss Melly.

I wished that I had her joy and her nerve. But then I did at one time. I used to be fearless, the girl who would do anything for a laugh, take on any challenge or dare. I wanted to tap into the young person I used to be before I got beaten down by a bad marriage combined with the gentle but inexorable force they call North Carolina.

The next morning I built a sand castle. It had high outer walls and a mote.

20.
The Bellamy Hour

"Thanks for seeing me, Misty. Do I lie down or sit?"

"Just get comfortable. Take a few deep breaths, and I'll get you a bottle of water."

"Misty, I've probably needed to talk to someone forever, and I'm sorry I put you off for so long."

"I'm glad you're here. What do you want to talk about?" Bell took a seat beside her.

"Misty, I'm so depressed. It's like I'm just going through the motions of life rather than living it. I don't want to live like this, and I don't know why or how to shake this feeling."

"Go on."

Bell bit her lip. "I don't know where to start."

"Where you want to."

"Well, to begin with, I can't seem to work through all the grief. Every day I'm so depressed and I wish I could remember what I used to be like, but I can't."

"When did you stop enjoying life? Can you put this feeling to a specific event?"

"This past February, I never bounced back from this past February. I used to have fun, you know, like Sophie does. I used to be funny like Sophie is. Now I'm just miserable."

"Does Sophie have anything to do with this?"

"I don't know."

"Are you saying you want to be more like her?"

"Maybe."

"Why?"

"She's smart and funny, she had kids and she has such enthusiasm for life."

"Let's back up to kids."

"Why kids?"

"You said smart, funny, kids and enthusiasm. Which one jumps out of that list?"

"Kids."

"What is the issue here?"

"Kids?" Bellamy stared out the window and her eyes filled. "I wish I'd had them. Sophie has kids and she never even sees them. It's like she doesn't even appreciate what she has. I love kids. Christmas at Bren's was so much fun, so alive. And when she brings the grandkids down to the beach house, I'm in heaven. I love them so much it hurts." She wiped her eyes.

Misty handed her a box of tissues. "I didn't know that about you, Bell. Why did you never have them?"

"I guess I should start with my mother."

"Your mother."

"Ya, bet you haven't heard that before. My mother," she said and took a deep breath. "She worked out constantly but she was never satisfied with her results. She was never able to get rid of that last little pooch around her middle and she acted like it was a deformity or something. She was obsessed. She walked into my room practically naked one day to yell at me and show me what I did to her body when she was pregnant with me. She pointed out every stretch mark and the tiny drape of skin on her belly, complain about her sagging breasts; she even made me promise to never get pregnant, never have any children so my body wouldn't look like hers did."

"Is that why you never had kids, Bellamy?"

"No, not exactly."

"Then?"

Bellamy took a long drink and began. "When I was eighteen, I married my first husband, Larry. He was a young lawyer at my father's firm. In hindsight, I think he may have married me to make partner, ya know? I was so young, and he was so handsome."

"Hmmm."

"And charming, I fell for him bad, and so we eloped."

"Mhhmm?"

She swallowed. "I got pregnant right away. When Mother found out, she went berserk. She marched me right down to the … abortion doctor." She paused and sniffed. "I was just a kid, and you know what it was like to get abortions back then. We could afford a decent doctor, but still."

"Yes, I know."

"It was horrible." She blew her nose and resumed. "I guess I was torn between wanting a baby and pleasing my mother. The recovery room... I remember it like it happened yesterday. There was a girl next to me who was loud-mouthed and crude. She was saying how glad she was that that *thing* was finally out of her. I burst into tears. I was practically hysterical and the staff surrounded me, wrapped me in blankets, wiped my face with damp cloths and made me drink juice."

"And?"

"And then I told Larry. Oh God, Misty, when Larry heard what I did he beat the living shit out of me. He punched me in the face, blackened both of my eyes and then he... "

"He?"

"He repeatedly punched me in the stomach yelling, "You killed my baby? You killed my baby?" Then he..." Bellamy broke into uncontrollable sobs.

Misty gave her time to collect herself. Bell took a few deep breaths and another minute to gain control. "He ruptured my uterus," her voice was lower. "I started hemorrhaging and had to be rushed to the hospital, blood everywhere. I had an emergency hysterectomy at nineteen."

"Oh, Bellamy."

"I love kids, Misty," she sniffed, "and I wish I could have had them. Look at Bren's big family. I could have grandchildren by now. I can't help but feel jealous when I watch her building sand castles and collecting shells with her grandkids all summer."

"And?"

"My mother said that a hysterectomy was a small price to pay for beauty and that she had saved me from the terrible fate that motherhood was. It felt like she hated me. I hated myself. I felt such guilt for having ruined her body and for being the reason she was so miserable."

"Were you the reason she was miserable?"

"No, but it seemed that way at the time."

"I'm glad that you understand that. She was most likely projecting her lack of self-esteem onto you."

"Ya, I get that, kind of."

"And?"

"Well, Sammy and I took a trip up to Virginia last spring. On the way up, I saw one of these signs outside a church. It said, "Women regret their abortions". I think I started to cry then, and I haven't stopped since. I'm even having dreams about a son. How would I even know it would have been a son?"

"So you are mourning your loss and regretting a decision that you really had no choice in making?"

"Well, did I have a choice? Couldn't I have stood up to my mother and refused?"

"You were just a child; you said so yourself."

"I was eighteen, a married woman. I should have had a sense of self enough to refuse her."

"She was your mother. It's not always that easy to stand up to your mother."

"She was a self-absorbed bitch. I should have stood up to her. I had a husband," she yelled.

"A child's brain is not even fully formed until around age twenty-eight. You were a child. You could forgive a child, couldn't you?"

"Yes, but I wanted to have that baby, maybe several. My grandbabies could be playing with Bren's right now."

"All of our lives are made up of successes and failures, things we did and things we didn't. You can't change the past. You can only decide where you want to take the future."

"I heard somebody say that we are all "victims of victims." My mother had no idea how to be a parent and probably her mother was clueless too."

"I've heard that expression also. I'd rather see it as we are all children of children. All of us are learning as we go."

"Do I have to come here every week for the next three years and cry into tissues?"

"No, we're on the fast track now, cutting-edge. Three or four sessions, and you will have the tools you need to move past this. We just need to identify what the real issues are. You started this by saying you wish you were more like Sophie."

"Sophie has kids, grown children whom she hardly ever sees and no grandbabies yet. But she will have them."

"Not necessarily."

"I guess, but she seems so unconcerned about it."

"Why do you say that?"

"I don't know. She never talks about her kids, never talks about wanting grandkids."

"Well, I can't speak to that. I want you to think about why you wish you were more like her for the next session. It may be important to get in touch with your feelings about her." She reached up on the shelf. "This is a book about forgiveness. It's different, one that speaks to us spiritually. This will help because I believe, with your background; you would be open to forgiving in a softer way. Read it, do the exercises. I want you to work on forgiving your mother and your first husband; then we can work on you forgiving yourself."

"Forgive myself?"

Right, but that's for another time. Right now I'm going to show you a tapping procedure called EFT. Let me get you another bottle of water."

21.
Flood of Tears

Chica stressed her harness as she zig-zagged the paths at the dog park chasing curious wildlife aromas and trickling pee on everything that could possibly be suspicious. It was a clear cool morning. I adjusted my ball cap and wondered if I could actually do something with my hair today. There was a definite hint of autumn so maybe I'd get some product and try. We did an extra lap then headed back to the car.

My cell rang. It was Mother's nursing home, not good news. She was apparently declining rapidly and not expected to last the night. I called Candy.

Candy had me booked on a mid-afternoon flight out of Charlotte. She said she'd secure a car rental for me so I could rush to catch the flight. I packed a few things and charged out the door with Chica's dog food and bowls in hand. I stopped at Joey's. He said he would watch her for however long I needed, and he also offered to drive me to the airport. I accepted willingly. No one should drive in the state I was in. I hugged my little dog and kissed her on top of her head.

You know, I never liked my mother; but when the big event is imminent, I found myself rushing to her bedside in a dramatically emotional state. I was fighting to hold back tears as we sped toward the airport with Joey cussing at the other motorists all the way. My mother, gosh, who ever thought she'd die? This should not have been a shock, and yet it was. I was not thinking clearly and was grateful not to be driving in Charlotte traffic. She can't die before I get there. Surely she will wait for me.

Candy met me at Logan Airport. She drove me to an East Boston car rental and handed me her GPS. I had been in Boston since the Big Dig, but someone else always drove. Thank God for satellite guidance because I found Mother's nursing home with no trouble.

My brother Nick and his wife met me in the hall. Nick was the first born and male. In a Greek family the first born boy (and in our family the only boy) gets all the perks. Nick got law school. Nick got Dad's business. There was also the added tension of knowing that most of Dad's assets were bequeathed to only Nick. Ours was not a bad father. He was a Greek father. Kathryn and I were married, and Dad felt that we were well taken care of. I doubt that he would ever have imagined that I'd be living alone and so modestly.

Before Mom went into the nursing home, she deeded the family townhouse to Nick. That was a blow to Kath and me. A townhouse in Back Bay was worth half a fortune today. Even split three ways it would have made a huge difference to our lives. We reasoned that she was already suffering dementia but I think she would have done the same even if she weren't.

Kathryn seemed tired and worn as she stroked Mom's brow. She was, we both were, surprisingly tender toward this woman who was so neglectful one minute and verbally abusive the next. Somehow none of that mattered anymore.

Nurses who had tended to her through the years came in to visit briefly, to say their good-byes, pay their respects and pray for her, love on her. They hugged us and told us a touching story or two. Every one of them remarked on the quality of Mom's skin, how there was not a wrinkle, how they wished they had such good skin, even at their age. My eyes and Kathryn's met momentarily with each remark. Hers mirrored mine. None of the bad memories mattered now. She was our mother, the only one we had ever had and she was dying.

Kathryn said that it would be a long night and went out for a cup of coffee or maybe just to stretch her legs. *How long had she been here?* I wondered. Since morning, I guessed. I sat up close to Mom. I laid my hand on her cheek and told her I loved her. I told her it was time to go home, that she could go back and get a brand new body now. "But, for God's sake," I added, "keep the face."

I've heard it said that people choose their time to die, that they will hang on until the prodigal son returns or for the first great grandchild to be born. I never expected a patient with end stage dementia to do something like that, but I believe it now. I think Mother waited until I got there and she waited for Kathryn to be out of the room. Then I watched her pupils get really big. Her mouth opened a little wider, eagerly, as though she were about to speak;

and then my mother, Maria Helen Pappas, emptied her lungs of her last breath.

Our family was not a large one, but people found their way to her wake. I didn't know many of them, probably Nick's clients or employees. There were faces that I found familiar but could not place the names and I was much too embarrassed to ask. My cousin Tina, always thoughtful and observant came to my rescue. She'd whisper a name and tell me how they knew Mother so I could receive them. People were kind. They told me how beautiful Mother was or how much they admired her. Nobody loved her. These people hardly knew her. Most of her contemporaries were dead. No one ever visited her. Hell, Kathryn and I never visited her and we were her daughters. Nick was her favorite but did I think that he or his wife ever spent any time at the nursing home? Probably-definitely not.

She'd picked out her casket and made her own arrangements. This was a woman who thought nothing of buying a two thousand dollar hat and her casket probably cost less than that. I was surprised at how modest her choices were. I would have expected more grandeur. Maybe Kathryn was thinking the same thing but it didn't need to be said. So with very little fuss and a few deep sighs, I gazed upon my mother's face for the very last time. She was the most beautiful corpse I had ever seen. Then they closed her casket and took it away to the crematory. There would be no graveside last scene for Maria.

I stayed with Candy for a few days which gave me extra time to visit the last few relatives who I loved dearly. Cousins invited me for Greek food. We drank Retsina wine. We ate lamb. I saw grown adults who I last saw as babies and they showed me the babies who now belonged to them. Everyone asked about my children, and I didn't even have a picture with me.

These were the people I grew up with. We ate together, splashed each other at the beach. We snuck out of the house together, argued together, got in trouble together and punished for it together. How did I lose touch with them?

I took a long walk along Boylston St. and then up Newbury and down Commonwealth. I stood in front of the home I grew up in, counting the windows and spying the roof that I used to climb out onto when I snuck out at night. I never got caught. I laughed to myself at the memory and wondered who lived there now. I walked on, trying to de-numb my brain.

Candy's condo is on Marlborough St. in the heart of Back Bay. She bought it in 1975 for forty-three thousand dollars when she got her first job with the airlines. That seemed so much money back then for a tired old flat. It had been updated through the years but had retained its character.

We returned the car on the last night. Candy planned to take me to the airport in the morning to save time. I was so tired I could hardly stand. It had only been four days, and my mind was a blur. She poured a small glass of whiskey for me and I was out, sleeping to the sounds of my city, Boston, my home.

Mid-morning while waiting for a stand-by flight at Logan International my cell phone rang. It was Joey calling. "Hi, Joey, Is everything okay?"

"Sophie, something happened. Not too-bad, okay? So don't get-too upset."

"What? Is it Chica?"

"Chica is fine. This-morning, early, I-went to your house to-get her some-more food. There was a-flood at your-house. A small flood, just-in your kitchen."

"A flood in my kitchen?"

Holy crap!

The small flood covered a much larger area than Joey originally thought. He'd discovered a leak in the supply line to my ice maker. The water had spread out under the laminate flooring. Joey pulled the oven out to show me the wall behind it full of black mold. We took pictures for my insurance agency. And then I called Bellamy to ask her if I could stay with her for a while. My bags were already packed with my mourning clothing and any essentials that I might need. I grabbed a few things from my closet and left.

By the time the adjuster got there to see the damage, there was so much mold in my house that I could barely breathe. I had to wait outside while he met with the disaster team, and they edged into a crawl space which was puddled in water. He determined that there could have been a slow leak before the water line split so the insurance company would not pay for the damage.

The disaster company gave me an estimate of almost fifteen thousand dollars to demolish the kitchen, most of the dining room and part of the living area and hall. Then they would treat the area for mold. After they finished, I would have to build an entirely new kitchen without any insurance compensation whatsoever.

Really?

I felt like I had been kicked in the chest, like I had fallen off a cliff, like I was watching my life's savings pour out the door. It was doubly mind-numbing.

I told the disaster team to start right away because I had to get the mold out. I was sure that I could fight this. Surely the insurance company would listen to reason.

They would not.

I spoke to three lawyers. Two said it would cost more to litigate than to fix the kitchen and the third told me to buy a new house and let the mortgage company foreclose on this one.

Nice.

I tried the insurance commissioner. There was no help there either. I was screwed.

A few days later I donned a particle mask and entered a property which no longer resembled my home. The sound hit me first and then the heat. I had been told that blowers, heaters and huge dehumidifiers would run around the clock in the affected area. The entrance to the living room and ahead to the kitchen/dining room was obscured by a plastic bubble zippered from top to bottom which bulged convexly. I was curious but decided that a trip into the bubble would not serve me in any good way so I walked past it and headed back towards the bedrooms.

I packed some more clothing into a plastic garbage bag so I could launder them before I took them to Bellamy's. I was ultra-cautious about spreading the mold so I had a pair of old Crocs that I left on the front steps near the stack of particle masks.

I stopped to visit Chica at Joey's. He wasn't home, but the dogs were out in the yard. I sat on the back steps, holding Chica and scratching Smokey's back. Della and Gladys expected treats. These comforting creatures distracted me for a few minutes with a much-needed love break.

It is funny how attached we get to our homes. Mortar and brick, wood and glass but ingrained with the memory of a third of my life. Would it ever be the same? If I fixed it up I would use up most of my savings. If I walked away from it, I'd ruin my credit. Neither made good sound financial sense. But this was my *home*. This is where I raised my children and sentimentality won.

Joey met the disaster guys every day for the week it took them to gut, dry and treat, then seal the damage to my house. Then it had to be tested to be sure there was no mold and safe for me to live in.

The mold was gone. Now it was time to rebuild.

After a few deep breaths, I walked into my half-demolished home. I had no floor from the center of the living room to the end of the dining area. There were no cabinets, no sink or counter top, no dry wall. Even the insulation was gone. My appliances were in another room, and half of my furniture was stacked on top of the other half. Nails stuck up from the subfloor and I walked with care. *Where do I even begin?* I wondered.

Joey appeared on the threshold with Chica in his arms. "I saw your-car go by."

She jumped out of his arm and ran to great me. I picked her up and scratched her head. Not wanting her to walk on this danger-floor I held her tightly. I sank into my sofa, awkwardly pushed up against other piles, and surveyed the bulk of the damage. This was mentally shattering: a triple mind-numbing. Joey looked like I felt, a couple of beat-up dogs in one of those Sarah McLachlan commercials.

"What else? What else could possibly go wrong?" I said, as the UPS guy appeared at the door with a package.

I signed a slip for a box of Mother's ashes. That was the drop of rain that started my tears, every emotion I held back, every posture of fake courage and every perceived denial of my Mother's love flooded through and I sobbed like a wounded child.

Joey sat next to me and put his big old arm around me. "I'm

Toggle

so-sorry, Sophie. I should-a come down-and checked every day."

"It's not your fault," I sobbed. "When it rains, it… pours." I let my head drop to his shoulder and sniffled into his big fat belly-chest… I just plain heaved.

I can't say how long I wailed, my brain and body felt like limp spaghetti but at some point and I became aware that he was stroking my hair then he began to kiss the top of my head. He felt so warm and strong, supportive; and I was such a pile of mush, and all that tenderness felt so comfortable, so good — I don't know how else to describe it — somehow like I was home. Like I was loved.

He was kissing my temple, then my cheek, my lips — the perfect warm-soft kiss. I was responding to his touch. It felt so safe and natural to me. Then I don't know how it happened but he had hold of my bare breast and I might have been moaning. Next clothing was flying and I was on his lap and, holy shit, I was about to make love with the grossest guy on the planet. And I didn't care.

"Sophie," he said, "I don't have a condom."

"I got some." I took his hand and led him down the hall to my bedroom.

My art tables were stacked high with unfinished projects, boxes of beads and other jewelry-making supplies. Next to them were cartons full of everything that would be in a kitchen if I had one. My desk, computer and office supplies were in the middle of the floor because all available wall space was taken with makeshift book cases. I had crossed into the surreal. I was making love with Joey Fucking Vecchia surrounded by a pile of shit.

Remember in the movie, *Don Juan DeMarco*, the scene where the aging Brando is about to make love with his wife, Faye Dunaway. She turned out the light, and the screen is completely black. All the audience hears is something like: *Ouch … my hair! Bad hip! Damn it! Shoulder, shoulder … oops!*

That is exactly what it was like, the sounds of two old people trying to screw. Like either of us could die at any second. There was such urgency and a *knowing* that both of us needed each other at this particular moment in time. This was a chance return into the primal need for contact. But Jesus, this man was homely.

I shut my eyes.

I going to tell you the truth here, Joey's penis was just about the best looking part of Joey. It was thick and straight, not too long and, most importantly, it was erect. I grabbed the jar of coconut oil from the bedside drawer and smacked a goodly amount on my twat like I'd been doing it for the last thirty years. I asked him to lie on his side. I lay back with our legs scissored groin to groin... almost touching and feeling the heat. I edged closer.

He slipped a finger, testing, feeling and I gasped, holy shit that's my G-spot.

"My God, you're tight," he said. He licked his thumb and placed it smack dab on my clit. *How does this guy know how to do this shit?* How in the hell and I'll be damned if I know why, but Joey Fucking Vecchia knew his way around a woman's body.

"I-gotta have you-now."

"Ready."

He ripped open the condom, slide it on and he broached my neglected vagina. Damn, that felt lovely and complete. I positioned his top leg over my pubes to feel the friction of his thigh on my clit. I crammed it deeper, still... fuller and he brushed one nipple with the back of his rough knuckles then pinched it just enough.

He pulled me closer to his left side. Oh, that was a good angle and it freed his right hand to mess with my tits, honest to God that was nice... and honest to God... I fucked this man with all my might till I floated, till my insides rushed and exploded into billions of rippling atomic particles, rearranged and re-rearranged into a new-old quantum event, orgasmic and singular. It was bliss and damnit if that old man didn't cum too.

We basked, chests heaved.

"You are so beautiful, Sophie," Joey said when he caught his breath and he curling me into his chest.

I listened to his breathing as it slowed and Joey fell asleep with a deep, but resonant, snore. I cuddled in and inhaled his essence just happy to be naked and satisfied, skin to skin with a man.

Bellamy's ringtone woke us. I didn't lie... exactly. I said I had a much needed cry and I told her I was going to spend the night with Chica. When she was satisfied that I was okay, Joey and I nuzzled up and kissed.

"Sophie, that was so-wonderful," he whispered as he nestled in and breathed into the folds of my ear. "This time let's take our time."

He kissed down the length of my neck, a nibble here and a tiny bite there. I allowed every cell in my body to unwind, open to receive this affection. Downward and he sucked my hard-berry nipples, tweaking and twisting. Downward, teasing with nips and nibbles around my belly and then my inner thigh, he slipped a flattened tongue between my folds, and did some kind of magical exotic tongue push-ups which maxed out my moan.

How does he know how to do this shit?

Two hours, one nap and three orgasms later, it was finally dark so we walked two doors up to his house, in through the gate and up the old cracked back steps. He bent over and picked up a small, flat, broken stone revealing the edge of a key. We entered his kitchen and he led me to a soft leather sofa that embraced me in comfort then Joey covered me with a thick cotton throw. I rested there in his den and nodded to the sounds of a competent Italian cook. He prepared our first meal together and an excellent meal it was.

I don't remember what he made. I just remember that there was lots of red wine and it was delicious and I sucked it in like a starved animal. Then I fell asleep in Joey's bed, wrapped safely in his big arms.

I woke the next morning to reverberating snores. It took a few seconds to remember where I was. I turned over and saw the big gray-haired chest with moles and a blubber belly like a giant squid with a membrane disorder. I sat up, pulled the sheet and experienced a wave of full-on nausea. Oh ... my God! I slept with fucking *Joey!* What the fuck was I thinking? How will I ever explain this? Wait ... wait ... I don't have to explain this to anybody. And I lay back down, settled into that thought and into the lovely contented and slightly sore feeling that a woman has after she's been made love to by a man who took great care to satisfy her. I sighed.

Joey gathered me into his arms. "I thought it was a dream."

"It wasn't."

"It was a dream come true."

I was never the kind of woman who fantasized about or pictured other men while I was making love so I was not pretending to be with Brad Pitt or Bond, James Bond; I just enjoyed feeling completely like a woman. The sex was *wonderful*. I simply closed my eyes and reveled in the touch of an extremely accomplished lover. I allowed Joey to touch and stroke and kiss and lick and oh … my God! He was giving me every bit of demonstrative loving that I had longed for, and I fully intended to milk this for everything it was worth.

He made love to *me*, made the whole experience about *my* pleasure. More than a few times I felt that this was specifically happening in order for me to learn and understand what true tenderness and nurturing from a man felt like, about me learning to receive, allow and enjoy the touch of another. I had no inhibitions with him. Never once did I fret about my body because he made me my body feel adored. Everything flowed freely and I was transformed, beautiful, young and vital once more. It was Joey-Jabba-Shrek sex and I liked it.

22.
Bell Told

"Good morning, Bellamy. How are you today?"

"Better."

"Did you do your homework?"

"Gosh, Misty, I should have come to see you years ago."

"So you *have* been doing your homework," she smiled.

"I've read up to page eighty-six and tapped on every bad memory that I can think of that has bothered me through the years. I'm surprised that I am not bruised with all the tapping I've done!"

"So do you feel like you can forgive her?"

"Well, I feel more like I can be willing to forgive her. For me that is a huge step, Larry too."

"It's like peeling away the layers of an onion, isn't it? What about Eddie? Did you work on forgiving him?"

"Well, he had no control over his cancer so I guess I have to."

"Well, the door to forgiveness is open and you can ask your higher self to help you with the whole process. Do you have a visual for what your higher self might be like?"

"Ya, she's kind of lavender and angelic."

"That makes it easier. Now ask her to help you heal the part of your being that has been injured." They breathed deeply for a half a minute.

"I feel almost normal. Will it last?"

"These are tools. It's up to you to use them. Have you given any thought to your feelings about Sophie?"

"Yes."

"And?"

"I guess I do wish I was more like her."

"Because?"

"Well, she's so smart and funny."

"You're smart and funny."

"Not like her; she has about ten years of college behind her."

129

"She'd laugh if she heard you say that, Bell."

"Why would she laugh?"

"Because she lived near a community college in Florida and took science and math classes on a part-time basis for eight or ten years."

"You're kidding. All this time I thought she was brilliant."

"There's a difference between being educated and being brilliant. In some ways you are smarter."

"How so?"

"I think you have better social skills."

"I still wish I was more like her."

"In what way?"

"I'm not really sure what it is, but can we put it on the back burner for now?"

"There is something else you want to address?"

"This is hard for me to admit." Bell took a drink of coconut water and wished there was vodka in it. "But if I don't do it now, I may never. Okay, here goes, she breathed heavily. Just after Eddie's death I started having back pain and headaches. Dr. Miles referred me to a pain clinic. Seven years, seven years I've been on pain medications and they keep increasing the dose. These are the ones I'm on now." She handed Misty the list.

"And these are the current dosages?"

"Yes, mostly."

"Have you asked your doctor to decrease the dosages?"

"They are kind of discouraging it."

"Did they tell you why?"

"They didn't give me a real answer. It almost feels like they want me to be on these medications for the rest of my life."

She read the list of medications. "Let me pick the brain of a friend in pharmacy. And you add alcohol to this mix? Are we trying to die?" She considered Bell. "I guess you've chosen to live."

"I want to get off these drugs, but I can't do it right now. I have to find a better time, maybe in the spring."

"You know that you will not get out of this without some pain, Bellamy."

"Misty… "

"It's not insurmountable; but understand me, this will not be easy or comfortable."

"I'm so afraid of withdrawal, Misty."

"The thought of it, the fear of it is sometimes worse than actually doing it. We can do it gradually. Maybe it won't be that bad."

"From your mouth to God's ears."

"Bellamy, we are vessels. Life comes at us and we get filled up with all these feelings because we are humans… humans with feelings. What we do with the feelings is our choice."

Her voice got strong. "Eddie dying and my mourning were not a choice, Misty."

"Mourning is like suffering with a big hole in your heart. You allow yourself to feel it for a reasonable time; slowly you learn to lighten those feelings. Then you fill the hole with something healthy, nature maybe or let's say … rocking babies at the hospital."

"My husband had just died."

"And you chose to medicate those feelings. I'm not judging you. I'm suggesting that you had a choice how you dealt with what life threw at you."

"I really don't see how I did."

"Bell, your thoughts, your emotions will rule you until you realize that you can be the ruler of them. Where you are in that process is entirely up to you, but I will be here for you and help you all the way through this."

23.
Telling

I showered at Joey's with a clean face, frizzy hair and in the clothes I was wearing the day before. I walked into Bell's kitchen and poured myself an afternoon coffee. There was no way I was going to even try to lie to Bellamy about this so I told her; I confessed that I had slept with Joey. And a confession is exactly what it felt like, like I had done something heinous, something awful and base. And I *was* ashamed, ashamed of *feeling* ashamed. I had made love with a man, a very nice man but a really unattractive one. Had he been a handsome man, would I not be elated and eager to share the marvel and beauty of last night? Hell, yes, I'd be shouting it from roof tops and frightening more than the dogs.

Bellamy listened quietly until I finished. Her eyes didn't meet mine. "Maybe we shouldn't tell the others," she said.

"Not telling doesn't feel right but neither does telling. I think they will know as soon as they see me."

"I'm not telling them and maybe if we're lucky no one will ever need to know." I hung my head. "Sophie, did Bren tell you about Leroy as soon as she could? And who knows what the fuck Annie is doing?" She had a point. "You don't have to tell. Let's just sit on this a while and see how it goes." And that's what I did.

The next few weeks I spent most afternoons with Joey, and more than a few of those ran into overnights. I enjoyed every minute. He was creative and experimental, tender one moment and forceful the next but always great, always supremely orgasmic. I was a happy, malleable, brainless post coital jellyfish.

We cooked together in his marvelous kitchen. He chopped last summer's garlic and I sliced the basil. We inhaled the sweet, delectable aroma of his red gravy simmering while we made love yet again. Later we enjoyed a glass of wine and had dinner by candlelight. Needless to say, my Joey had a romantic flair and I was in sensory heaven.

Did you just hear me say "my Joey"? Funny, he didn't seem

ugly to me anymore and I found his absolute lack of concern for his appearance cute and somewhat endearing.

One evening he lifted me up on the kitchen counter and like I was a piece of shortcake he covered my parts in chocolate syrup. He lavished the folds of my labia as I stroked the smooth skin on the top of his head and the soft thin curls like lambs hair behind his ears. We kissed in chocolate, made love in chocolate then continued in the shower, his old knees cradled on a folded towel, my foot glued to the soap dish.

Another night we fed each other bits of shish-kebab which were hot and juicy from the grill. We licked our fingers and then licked each other's fingers. He took my hand and kissed it in the palm, like you see in old movies. He massaged the sensitive skin between my pulse and my thumb. Kisses gave way to licks as he made love to my hand in a way that almost brought me to climax. My fucking word! Was it the esoteric knowledge of the biology teacher, or is this just how they roll in Jersey? We left the food to get cold while he sucked on my clit till I convulsed in a peak of pure pleasure.

So I asked him. "Joey," I said, "how is it that you are so good at this? I mean, where did you learn all this?"

"I pay-attention, that's-all," he replied.

"Were you ever married?"

"Oh-ya, it didn't work-out."

"What happened? Do you mind me asking?"

"She left-me for the-roofer. It's-okay. We-were too young and didn't know ourselves."

"She left you for a roofer? Was she upgrading? Sorry, I shouldn't joke, I mean, you were a teacher."

"Not at the time. We-dated in high-school, got-married after we graduated. If she-hadn't left-me, I-wouldn't have-been able to-go on to-college."

"You never told me."

"Hey, I'm-from-Jersey. We don't-ask too many-questions, and-we don't volunteer-much information. That's just how-it-is."

Of course, the girls noticed something different about me. I told them that I was going to the tanning bed; but they are pretty sharp and I am still pretty white so I just smiled and told them I was *really* enjoying the tanning bed and let them think what they wanted. Not volunteering information, like I was from Jersey, and my girls left me alone about it. Soon "tanning bed " became our euphemism for getting laid.

Joey took care with my reputation. It was old-fashioned and sweet, the way he worried what the neighbors were saying.

"Ya-know-that Sally knows everything that-goes-on. We-ain't foolin' her one-bit," he said as he peeked through the blinds.

"Probably, but Miss Sally minds her own business; and anyway, I think she'd approve. What about Rod and Alice or Bill Fields? Do you think they know?"

"It's hard to say. I think most-people are just-payin' attention to-their own-lives. Maybe-they do. I dunno. We could be more descrete." Again he stared out the front window at Miss Sally's house. "I wonder-where she goes at-night."

"Who?"

"Sally. Every Tuesday and Saturday night she leaves and doesn't come-home until-morning."

"You're kidding." Those were my dance nights so I never noticed. "Have you ever asked her?"

"Hell-no. I couldn't ask-her that. It's her business."

"Wouldn't it be nice to know that she's had a lifelong lover that she spends treasured stolen time with? I think that's an exquisite thought."

"It would-be an embarrassing thought for Sally." I supposed he was right, but one can't help wondering.

Joey and I made no declarations of love, no plans for the future; and I certainly wasn't picking out china. I was — I think we both were — simply living in and loving the moments.

We laughed a lot about Kernersville and what it was like as a Northerner living in the South. His railing issue was the roads. "I hadda-get my license renewed; and they-handed-me this card, told-me-to memorize the road signs. I never saw half-a these fuckin'-signs before, and-then-I realized that I-stopped-looking at-the-signs long-ago. There's too-many of-them. It's more than the-brain can process. So I started paying better attention. Like you go-to Greensboro and there's-a-sign saying, 'Welcome to Greensboro Citywide Speed Limit 35'. Then twenty feet down the road is another-sign that-says, 'Speed limit 35'. What a waste of tax dollars! Take I-40. This-is-a-road that-goes across the-whole fuckin' country; but to-stay on it going east, you-gotta exit to the-right or you end up south, at the zoo in Asheboro. If you're-going west, you-gotta exit left or you-end-up on route 421 north to Boone. What's-that-about? It's-all complicated. You never know how they will screw it up next. It makes me-crazy. You-got a sign to tell-you there's-a stop sign-ahead. You got-one for farm-equipment. Do-you not notice when-you are driving behind-a tractor?"

"They're warning that a tractor could turn onto the road in front of you."

"Then that's even-worse. It's insulting to-the farmer because-I guarantee-you that anyone driving a-tractor is going to-look both ways. I saw a-sign the-other day with a see-saw on it. I have never seen a see-saw in the road, have you?"

"That's telling you to watch for children!"

"There's already one wit-children on-it and another-one-for children crossing. That's three different signs-for-children. Someone must be making a fortune on kickbacks. All along West Mountain Street, ya-know, along the-tracks, there are these crazy-signs to tell-you that if you turn there is a railroad track there. Like in-case you miss the-closing gate and four sets of red-flashing lights and-you don't-hear the roar of an oncoming train or-the earsplitting whistle blowing, then-you will probably-remember, 'Hey, that fuckin' sign back-there said there might be-a train track nearby. Maybe-I should look around to-see if there-is one.' I-saw one sign the-other day: it was two arrows pointing diagonally." He pointed his index fingers downward and toward each other. "I-can-only assume it-means to cross your eyes."

We watched Woody Allen movies, *Annie Hall* and *Manhattan* with all the dogs cuddled up. Chica, dominant even in his household, claimed the prime Joey-lap-top property.

"I-can't-believe how spoiled your-dog is," he said and scratched her head.

"I think she's spoiling you." She licked his chin.

He held me close, kept me warm with our stockinged feet on his sleek red coffee table. I admired the art on his walls, paintings from local artists and I imagined the two of us browsing fairs and strolling along the street in the art districts.

He was fastidious in some ways and lax in others. You always needed a coaster under your drink and his table was always set with a cloth and chargers. He preferred that you removed your shoes if you walked on the carpet. His baseboards were vacuumed daily. Yet he wore shorts that looked as if they had been splattered with battery acid and shirts that appeared to have lost their battle with giant fire-eating lizards. He was uniquely Joey.

24.
Re-Chuck

It had been over two months since I danced. I needed to go, at least to show Chuck that I would not be intimidated by him and be chased off the floor. I put on my favorite twirling skirt and went to the hall in order to show and to *save* face.

I saw him almost as soon as I entered the hall. Fortunately, since many friends approached me, I'd already been asked for the first and second dance so I didn't think he would be an issue. Maybe I wouldn't have to talk to him to for the rest of the night. Unfortunately, when I met him in the contra line the big brat taunted me.

"Last time I saw you, you were naked," he said as we swung. "We should do that again." Ya, that was funny.

"It would take a lot more whiskey."

"How much more?"

"Decades, decades of it."

That jerk was going to get punked; he *deserved* to and it was going to be good. I had done what I needed to do; I'd faced him. And there was no awkwardness on my part because I knew that he was going to be completely humiliated by the mischievous mind of Sophie Chase.

I called Candy to discuss a few more ideas for punking Chuck, and she was a wealth of help. She had become friendly with a touring contra band. They had slept on blow-up mattresses on the floor of her condo a few times on their way through Boston and she said they were a mischievous, fun-loving group of guys. They would be in Winston-Salem on the Tuesday before Thanksgiving. She was sure she could count on them to be willing accomplices.

We agreed on one point. Nakedness had to factor into this. How to accomplish said nakedness was a problem that we had yet to surmount. It is not that easy to get a man to relinquish his clothing unless there is a naked woman in the near vicinity. In Chuck's case even that was not a reliable inducement.

We needed more planning and the window of opportunity was approaching but I was preoccupied. Showered in Joey's attentions, I had consigned too many of the details of our prank to Sammy.

Joey had a single-minded ability to concentrate on whatever he did — gardening, shopping, watching old movies, even cleaning the oven. But when that single-mindedness went to the act of lovemaking and the single purpose of that concentration was me — my pleasure — he became the sculptor and I was his art. His focus was the complete adoration of my body. This was *stupid passion*. And then I'd sink into the sensual bliss of orgasm recovery period. Whoa, baby.

I suggested that we eat out once or twice, but Joey insisted that he loved cooking for me. "Besides, where are-we gonna-find food this-fresh and this good?"

He had a point.

His nephew had moved to Kernersville fairly recently to start a business designing and building kitchens for restaurants. With the influx of un-Southern people, more diversified food choices were in demand. Although I had not met him personally, he was a wealth of information on how to put my home back together. Joey acted as my contractor and jobbed out to some of Allen's employees who were willing to moonlight. So far, things were getting done. I had insulation in my walls and crawl space; subfloor was in. Joey calculated that they could disassemble the intact laminate flooring from the living area and reuse the material to cover the damaged kitchen. We could lay carpet in the living room. They saved me half a fortune with good advice and reliable workers.

My birthday wasn't going to be a big deal that year. Bell was away with Sammy, and I figured the girls would buy me a drink on Sunday. Maybe Joey and I could split a bottle of wine and listen to *La Traviata*. He made it a celebration, baked an Italian wedding cake and presented a neatly wrapped package with a blue velvet bow. Inside the box was a new toothbrush. He took hold of my wrist and slipped on a silver cuff with a wide casted heart mounted to the center of it.

"Now you'll have your own toothbrush for my bathroom and you can wear my heart on your sleeve."

"Thank you, Joey. It's beautiful." I kissed him and excused myself to the bathroom. I actively tried to control my breathing. This felt... permanent... like losing freedom. *It's only a gift*, I told myself. I'm okay. I'm okay.

Listen, I *really* liked Joey. He was the comfortable shoe, just how Bellamy described her Sam. He provided the emotional support and listened as I droned on for hours working through mother issues, and it goes without saying that the sex was great. Joey had so many of the qualities that I wanted in a man. He listened to me, treated me with respect. He was *kind*. Did I not say that I could overlook a lot if I found a kind man?

But if there was one thing I loved, *loved* about him, it was the way he looked at me. He looked at me like I was the bicycle he never got for Christmas, like I was the girl he would have loved to take to the prom. He looked at me like I might be his last chance for love in this lifetime. I was extremely glad that I had opened my eyes to see Joey and I didn't want to give that up.

I drove to the Greensboro airport on the Monday before Thanksgiving. I was a little late and expected that she would already have her luggage and be waiting outside for me. I drove slowly and scanned the sidewalk when a blond woman tapped her hand on the hood of the Camry. I stopped short, pulled over and raced out to hug her. It was Candy from home. We screamed and jumped crazily like the demented high school girls we once were.

"I should have warned you about the hair."

"You are so cute as a blond and I love the cut!"

"My hairdresser couldn't cover the gray anymore so I finally just gave in to her advice." She appeared ten years younger; and I was pretty sure that Chuck would not remember her from her last visit.

Since I was still half staying with Bellamy, she generously opened her home to Candy. Sam cooked a great dinner of fish and shiitake mushrooms on the grill and we opened a nice Pinot Grigio. Then we got down to serious scamming.

"Okay, what are the plan's weak points?" I had paper to write on, but I had only small doodling. I needed a proper list.

"We don't know for sure he'll agree to sing," said Sammy.

"He'll sing. But he'll want to sing Irish songs."

"So we let him sing his song and then Sammy could say that he'd like to heah him sing in anathah style, and he could make suggestions," Candy said. "How about asking him to sing something from Woodstock?"

"I like the idea of a Woodstock song, but it had to be something he'd know. I think the Who's 'Pinball Wizard' would be funny but he might not know it."

"Oh, who doesn't know 'Pinball Wizard'?"

"This is Kernersville, Candy. I bet a lot of people don't know it."

"Joe Cocker sang 'With a Little Help from my Friends.' It's a Beatles song and I think most people would know it."

"How do you remember that?" I asked.

"I rented the movie last August."

"We should see if Netflix has it," I suggested and Candy nodded.

"I want to be there too. I could be with Sammy as his wife or part of his entourage."

"You could go, Bell, but we can't run the risk of you being recognized as a local pretending to be with an out-of-town talent agent."

"Chuck doesn't know me," Bell said.

"He may have seen you around. You *are* pretty memorable."

"Yes, my dear, you are *certainly* memorable." Sam nuzzled up and put his arms around Bellamy's middle. "By the way, I arranged for a cameraman to video Contra Crossing and the prank. We can get this whole thing down for posterity."

25.
Punkin' Chuck

Tuesday, contra night, one camera was set for a wide shot of the band and a second for close ups. With extra lighting and microphones it appeared very professional. Sammy seemed self-assured and Candy considered ways to approach Chuck. She'd always been an effective flirt and with her new blond hair style I was sure she'd convince him to sing.

People often shoot video at contra, but this was visible coverage. Barbara, from the Fiddle and Bow Society, agreed to help us with anything we needed to pull this off. Chuck was a beloved contra character and "A joke on him," she said, "would be a blast."

The band was fabulous and I danced most of the first set, then Barbara made her contra-related announcements. She used that time to introduce Sam Vargas and Candice Shields from Lost Wood Entertainment who had just signed Contra Crossing. The crowd applauded wildly and then she pointed at Sam. "So, if anyone feels that their talent needs to be discovered tonight he's the one to hound."

I asked my friend Leon to suggest this to Chuck. It could be his big chance at getting discovered. Chuck was thinking about it. I could tell from his body language and Candy picked exactly that second to approach him. "Excuse me, are you Chuck Loughlin? Mr. Vargas has been told that you are a wonderful vocal talent. Would you be interested in singing a song with the band? That tipped the balance and Chuck was on his way to the stage. He asked the band if they would play "Kilgara Mountain."

Chuck sang well. The crowd applauded and Sammy did exactly like we planned. He complemented him and asked if he would sing in a more commercial style. "How about a Beatles song, can you sing 'Do You Want to Know a Secret'?" The audience approved.

This was not 'With a Little Help from My Friends' from Woodstock like we planned. I wasn't sure but Chuck began to sing it. This might be our one chance to do this, one chance to get this right. I nodded at Candy. She walked over and opened the door to stage left then held up crossed fingers for me to see. Out came a line of what appeared to be a group of male backup singers. Chuck noticed them but continued to sing. They began to strip off breakaway costumes and by the time Chuck realized that the crowd's enthusiasm was for more than just his singing, they were wearing little green jewel bags… boulder holders, the male stripper equivalent of G-strings that there must be a name for.

Entertainers must be the ultimate extroverts. Maybe a show is a show is a show. It doesn't matter if it's a tragedy or a comedy. This well-loved Beatles tune digressed to an R-rated comedy and Chuck segued from a serious singer in to a near comedic genius. Sure, he was surprised by the strippers but he effortlessly adapted and I was truly impressed with how smoothly he made that switch. Obviously he realized he had just been punked but he was good enough of a sport to play along. He kicked in a chorus line with the male strippers then grabbed someone's sweaty yellow hand towel and wore it over his head and twirled the corner like it was the light blond hair of a bashful woman. He whispered a secret to one of the dancers then picked him up and carried him away for the Grand Finale! The crowd loved him, *loved* him. We had to admit that we could not have planned better entertainment. It just wasn't the *type* of entertainment we had planned.

"That was lame."

"It was hilarious!" Sammy said.

"They were supposed to undress him, and he was supposed to look ridiculous. Instead he danced and sang his way into the hahts of America," Candy said.

Sammy said that it was a fine line between prank and assault, and I understood his point but I don't think anyone expected that Chuck would enjoy the attention so much. He had a blast. He had laughed along as if he had planned the whole scene himself.

"I'm sorry. I must be getting old, losing my touch."

"Aw, hell, Soph. It's hahd to top the pull-down map with the pin-up on it."

"I hope he never finds out it was me."

Up-Chuck and die.

26.
Let the Holidays Begin

Misty handed Bellamy another bottle of water. "I still don't understand my feelings toward Sophie."

"If you are uncertain about your feelings for her, then why are you letting her stay at your home?"

"Well, she is a diversion. I mean, she keeps me from sliding back into depression, I guess. She lives so ... so out loud."

"What does that mean to you?"

"She has such deep feelings about everything. Next to her I feel sort of shallow."

"Are you shallow?"

"Well, I've never had to work for anything. I think that bothers Bren, and Sophie's a little judgmental."

"Of?"

"The way Sammy always buys me gifts."

"Has either of them said anything to you about having those feelings?"

"No."

"Then how do you know that's true?"

"Oh it's true. I know it is."

"Do you absolutely know it's true?"

"Don't you believe me?"

"I believe you believe it. But do you know that it's true ... for a fact?" Bell was noncommittal. "What matters here are your feelings, do you think you are shallow? Does it bother you that you have never had to work? Are you judging yourself for accepting Sammy's generosity?"

"Well, things come easily to me, and I see Sophie struggling with her house and I see other people struggling. I can't help them all."

"Is it your job to help everyone?"

"Well, no, but I feel guilty sometimes."

"Ah, so you feel guilty that you are beautiful and financially well-off and that things come easily to you?"

"I maybe do. I've never done anything to deserve all this."

"So go do something."

"Like what?"

"You love children. Volunteer at a pediatric floor or at a day care. Bellamy, the problem here is your sense of worthiness. Just feel worthy. You have been blessed in so many ways. Just be grateful for it all and fill your heart with love."

"I sure don't get any from Sammy."

"What about Sam?"

"Well, I haven't told anyone this but we don't sleep together."

"Because... "

"He's taking some medications that make him impotent and so he buys me all these gifts to compensate. I'm starting to not like him for it. It feels demeaning."

"Demeaning?"

"There's no real relationship. I thought there was but now I think I'm just there to impress clients."

"Why do you think that?"

"Do you know that he can make himself blush? If there's a client around, I could whisper "salt and pepper" in his ear; and he will spontaneously blush. I thought it was funny at first but it's so phony. It's almost humiliating."

"Have you talked to him about how you feel?"

"Yes."

"And?"

"He bought me a home entertainment system."

"You could have refused it."

"I feel like I'm a business expense, and it is the most derisive relationship I've ever been in."

"Then why are you with him?"

"He's safe."

"Safe?"

"I will never be hurt by him."

"You used the words derisive, humiliating and demeaning. Is that not hurting you?"

"Not like Eddie dying."

"So you are with someone you don't like to prevent yourself from being hurt by someone you do?"

"I don't know."

"Bellamy, life doesn't come with guarantees. You want to surround yourself with cotton batting to prevent yourself from getting bruised?"

"I just can't be hurt like that again."

"Tell me, do you wish that you had never met Eddie in the first place?"

"God no! He was the best thing that ever happened to me."

"Then would you say that the love you shared together was worth going through the hurt you felt after his death?"

"That I'm still feeling."

"Death is part of life. Be grateful for the time you had with him. Bellamy, live your life until you die your death."

"I don't know."

"Use the EFT to tap on your fear and ask that lavender angelic higher self to open the door to forgiving."

"Forgiving Eddie for dying? How could either of us have prevented that?"

"Yes, forgive him for dying and then forgive yourself for using his death to deny yourself love."

Bell's home smelled delicious as Sam carried the turkey to the table. He had been at Bell's since sun-up and he had supplied everything from apple pie to the wine.

Candy's friends in the band told her that one of the male strippers had recently joined a comedy team. He had been so impressed with Chuck's performance that had he set up an interview with the group's leader. One of the performers backed out for family reasons and Chuck happened to be at the right place at the right time. He had indeed joined the comedy troupe and he would be doing his first performance at a club in Asheville on Sunday night.

"Well, he can sing, he can dance and does comedy pretty well. Why don't I just pay for acting lessons and make him into a quadruple threat?"

"Too late for that, apparently he's a graduate of NC School of the Ahts and had extensive theatrical and improvisational experience, everything from musicals to Shakespeah so he fit right in," Candy explained the night's fiasco to the others.

"You'd think that something like that would have come up during conversation."

"Maybe you should have walked away from that one," Misty said. "Could someone pass the squash?"

"I don't know, Misty. Maybe we could spin this as the Sophie bump. In this case, it was lack of bump," Mounty laughed.

"You told Mounty?" Oh crap. I'm a living joke.

"Mounty, don't make it worse for her," said Annie.

"I'm sorry, Sophie. Hey, you are a healthy beautiful woman, and the man had to be crazy to do what he did."

"Thanks, now could we try to all find something to be thankful for on this holiday?"

"That's a great idea," Misty said. "Annie, you start."

"Okay, I'm thankful for Mounty and my best friends and for this beautiful turkey."

"I'm thankful for my precious Little Annie," said Mounty, and he kissed her.

Sammy was a little long winded, thankful for his health and his business and his gorgeous Bell, blah, blah. Then Bellamy thanked us for the great company, great food, and the wine which she toasted to Sammy.

Misty thanked the Great Spirit and for the love of a wonderful man and the best friends anyone could hope for. Eliot was thankful for his motorcycle and his motorcycle Mama. He smiled, slipped his arm around Misty and hugged her.

Candy thanked Bellamy and then said, "I'm happy to be in North Carolina with my new friends and old ones." She smiled at me. "And very thankful for contra dancing, I've lost twelve pounds since I started!"

It was my turn. "I'm thanking the tanning bed." The gals toasted me with a hoot as the fellas exchanged confused glances. At least I had one secret.

And I *was* thankful for Joey, my personal secret tanning bed. He was the man who put color back in my face and warmth back in my life. His passion, affection and loving kindness renewed my faith in men. He was the man who taught me to trust again. It was a very happy time.

27.
Anger Management 101

Allen's birthday fell just after Thanksgiving and I had so much to thank him for, I insisted that we take Allen and his date to that little grotto where we ate Italian food last spring.

The morning started out badly. I could feel a cold sore starting on my lip. I wet it and covered it with salt to stop it from getting worse. Whatever I had eaten last night hadn't agreed with me, so I was having my third bowel movement by ten o'clock. By eleven-thirty, my butt was on fire so I had to go to the pharmacy to get some Desitin ointment. And speaking of my butt, it was getting bigger. With all Joey's pasta and less time spent dancing or at the gym my clothing was markedly tighter.

I had so much to do before the dinner. A nail broke deep into the nail bed and I needed to get it fixed before it caught on something. I wanted to find a small cake for Allen; Joey needed razors. He was completely out of coffee and milk, I had a certified letter to pick up at the post office and I needed to buy bigger underpants.

Joey fussed about my second shower. I *had* to shower. I had shitty Desitin on my butt. I twisted my hair into a knot to save time but I noticed a makeup stain on my new white blouse. Then I needed to find another outfit that fit. After the wardrobe change, my hair wouldn't cooperate and then I could not find the silver earrings that I wanted to wear with my new bracelet. Joey tried to rush me because it was past time to leave. He got a healthy dose of my Scorpio temper.

We were late but they were later. We'd been seated in the back where we couldn't see anyone, and just as I was thinking that nothing else could possibly go wrong, I heard Joey say, "Sophie, this is my nephew, Allen Predo and his girlfriend, Loretta Steele."

Oh fuck.

"Oh, *I've* known Sophie for ages," Letta said, her voice several octaves above normalcy. "I'm so glad she has *finally* found someone. How long have you two been hooked up, Joe?" She smiled wickedly, eyeing Joey's homely face and checking out the expanse of belly hanging over his belt.

"No, Sophie and-I, we're-just-friends, neighbors and friends. That's-all."

"That's a shame. You'd make such a lovely couple."

Bitch.

I was struggling to keep a plain poker face, and I think I was succeeding. I did not want to embarrass Joey. I did not want to ruin Allen's birthday. Every fiber of my being told me to leave that table because I did not want to sit, break bread with and pretend to be cordial to a woman I despised, a woman who was sleeping with Jim while I was trying to preserve my home and family. This was an awful situation, and I didn't see any way out of it.

I reminded myself that I am a tough Boston woman. Hell, I'm a Spartan woman, and I can sit toe-to-toe with this Steele magnolia and I will act with the utmost assurance and cordiality because as a Bostonian I have a responsibility to *think* intelligently and *act* well-mannered.

"Nice to see you, Letta." My face turned to Allen with the friendliest smile and the most exaggerated praise. "It is such a pleasure to finally meet you. Thank you so much for all you have done to help me. I am sure that I could never have managed without your expertise."

"Glad to-help you, Sophie. Uncle Joe has told-me so much about-chou. Joe, this is-a very-beautiful woman. What's wrong wit-chou? Why aren't-you dating this-goddess?"

Letta wrinkled her nose and managed a teensy weensy annoying laugh. "Sophie a goddess?"

"Oh, Allen, that is so sweet of you to say." I beheld him through mascara-coated lashes. "What a nice compliment. Joey, you didn't tell me how charming Allen is." But I'm eye-to-eye with Letta, spider to spider, pincer to pincer, exoskeleton to exoskeleton, heart beating like Keith Moon on an acid trip, but I maintained a passive saint-like face that Maria Helen Pappas would be proud of.

"Could we get drinks?" Letta asked, and she snapped her fingers for the wait staff. "Sophie's paying, right?" My stomach gripped. I was sure she'd order the most expensive dish and then leave it uneaten just for spite.

Obviously she was jealous of my attention to Allen and was

struggling for a distraction tactic to maneuver back into the spotlight. Fluff, baby talk and cupid lips usually worked so she turned that game on, slipping her hand into the crook of his arm she started to coo. I let my lips turn up slightly as if I found her sweet but I knew it for the tightening adhesive of a spider's silk.

The more poise I maintained, the more she drank and the sillier she sounded. Her voice was approaching the frequency that soon only canines would hear. "Sophie used to be real fat, remember that, Sophie? How much weight did you lose?"

"Hey, don't-talk about fat when-I'm eating,-okay?" Joey saved me. "Guilt is not-good for the-digestion."

"I meant to say that she looks so good now."

Sure she did.

I slowly sipped my wine. I maintained that slight smile and pretended that I was riveted to Allen's story, Allen's work, Allen's plan for his company's growth and future. As long as I kept the focus on the Allen-Show, I could keep my anger smoldering in a slow and controlled burn. Bermuda was definitely not working. I had to remind myself that he was my guest and that she was his guest and that I could not just punch her in front of all these people.

We made it through dinner, sang "Happy Birthday" and ate cake.

"I-thought she was-a nice-girl, good for-Allen."

"Joey, she's the town tramp. She slept with my ex in our own bed while I was getting medical tests. You should tell Allen about her reputation."

"No, I shouldn't."

"Why not? He's your nephew. Maybe she's a sex addict. He should know that. She's also sleeping with another guy when she's not with Allen. She could be diseased."

"What happens between a man and a woman is none of my business and it's none of yours either."

This could have turned into a big argument. I needed to blow off steam and it would not be fair to take my anger out on Joey. I asked him to drop me off at home.

I paced between stacks of furniture and boxes. I seethed past rolls of new carpet and padding. *That bitch!* My rage was so strong that I had to punch something or go mad. The gym was closed at this time of night so I stripped off my clothes, donned shorts and boxing gloves and went down to the chilly basement half that had been flooded and did rigorous punching on Jim's old bag. I imagined that the bag was Loretta Steele and I beat the crap out of it, picturing her, picturing her body parts and me punching them. An elbow shot to her face, and I smashed in her front teeth; a back fist broke her jaw. Left, right, left and a right upper cut, both her eyes were blackened; her nose was a bloody pulp. Then I did repeated and merciless kidney shots till I imagined she was down on the ground in a moaning bloody heap.

I slept like a baby.

"Oh, Sophie, you really should never direct that kind of anger. It will come back to you in some way. What you do to another you do to yourself," said Bellamy. "It's Karma."

"I'm Greek. If I directed my anger at her, it would probably be like giving her the *mahti*." I pulled my lower lid slightly. "That's the evil eye." I demonstrated *the look*, that uber-Greek, all-knowing look that means something really bad is about to happen to you. "Maybe she'll get kidney disease." And I don't care.

"She's not going to get kidney disease from you punching a bag," Misty said calmly.

"She could. Take Jim. I directed thousands of punches at him, and he's sick."

"That's about the best example of 'what goes around, comes around' I have ever seen and Jim's getting his payback now," Bellamy added.

"You had nothing to do with Jim getting sick. His thoughts and his decisions directed his own life to what it is today."

"Or it could be Edie Marsh's cooking."

"Edith Chase. Her name is Edith Chase now, Bell. She writes my alimony checks so show some respect."

"Jim may feel a lot of guilt about what he did to you, and perhaps he believes that all guilt deserves punishment. Maybe being sick is just part of his life path. We can't ever really know what is in his life experience. Now let's backtrack to Edith Chase."

"Don't go there," Bell pleaded.

"We're going there. Just hear me out. You are showing respect to Jim's wife, right?"

"Right."

"And you have no major animosity toward her."

"Nope."

"You think and expect that Edie will write your checks and mail them on time. She doesn't mess with you or create big dramas in your life?"

"Right."

"And you see how messed up that is? You have no problem with Jim's wife, Edith, but Letta Steele brings this strong reaction to you. You attract the drama and she delivers it because drama is what you have come to expect from Letta."

"So that makes it all my fault? I just needed to get rid of that anger so I didn't stay up all night hating her. You know Letta makes me crazy."

"It's not about fault. It's about taking responsibility. No one can make you crazy. You let yourself feel crazy. You and *only* you are in charge of how you feel."

"Misty, you know what she does to me."

"Then you may as well admit that you have relinquished your personal power to her."

"How?"

"Well, if you say she *makes* you do or feel anything that you would not otherwise do or feel, then you must think she has power over you. You have to take responsibility for your own feelings. If you have anger then you need to release it yourself."

"Isn't that what I did?"

"I think it was a perfectly appropriate way to release your anger."

"Appropriate, what are you saying?" Bell's voice rose. "I'm surprised at you. It really was not appropriate, and you *know it*. She needed to release her anger in a less harmful way: meditate, pray for Grace or send the anger to the angels for transmutation. She needed to find a way that isn't destructive because it will come back to hurt her."

"I don't think so, Bell," Misty said.

"It's Karma, Misty!"

"And if meditation and prayer works for you, Bellamy, then great. Sophie, have you tried to forgive her?"

"You know I have."

"Have you meditated and prayed to release the anger?"

"You bet."

"Sophie is a more physical person. Punching a bag may be more appropriate for her."

"I was just having fun. I wouldn't really punch her. If it was so bad, then why did I feel so good after?"

"Ego," Bell said.

"Ego?"

"Ego. Disliking her, judging her behavior feeds your ego. It makes you feel like you're better than her."

"Pruff." Like that wasn't obvious.

"Combine that with the endorphin rush that beating the bag gave you, and I bet you felt great," she explained.

"I agree with you there; that was Sophie's ego but I don't agree about the Karma part. Karma is the old paradigm," Misty articulated.

"Old paradigm? What do you mean?"

"Old model or concept."

"Are you saying Karma does not exist?"

"It exists if you believe it. Belief is everything. At the risk of constantly repeating, you create your own life. That includes beliefs. They are a choice too."

"You talk about this like it's a fact and you can't prove it. Prove that the Law of Attraction is a fact."

"It does make scientific sense. It's how the earth was formed. Dust attracted enough dust to eventually become rocky planets like ours. Gases attracted other gases to create the outer gaseous planets. *Like* did attract *like, does* attract *like.*" Carl Sagan would be damn proud of me now

"So, okay, the Law of Attraction may work in the physical world; but what about the spirit and the soul? You can't prove that," Bellamy asked.

"*Prove* isn't a good word to use. Scientifically proof doesn't exist. Gravity is still just an accepted theory, so is evolution, but even gravity gets all wonky out in space."

"We're getting off-subject. Sophie, it's because of your anger that you attract the Letta's of this world. If it weren't Loretta Steele, it would be another woman or man."

"It's always a woman."

"Always a woman?"

"No, that's not true. I was pretty cranky during the George W. Bush years."

"We're off the subject," Bell stated, "and the subject is Karma. There is some sort of payback law in all the religions that I know about. There are Karmic sayings all through the bible, like 'an eye for an eye' and 'as you give, so shall you receive.'"

"And those can all be interpreted to support the Law of Attraction also. We create our own reality by our beliefs and our feelings and our emotions. Here is an example. How many times have you heard that the rich get richer and the poor get poorer?"

"Lots."

"Money, wealth is just energy and you are living proof of that. You were brought up with money. You know how it feels to be wealthy and you have always had money. You expect money."

"I always thought that the Law of Attraction was about getting rich. Isn't that the hook?" Bell snickered.

"The hook?" Misty appeared amused. "I think it's about getting happy, being joyful and seeing happiness as a choice."

"And being rich, of course, makes everyone happy."

"It wouldn't necessarily make me happy. What makes me happy is nature and animals. But I think many people believe that they need to have more money in order to be happy."

"Well, I was brought up with money. I know how to feel rich and I don't have much now. I didn't decide to be without. It just happened."

"Nothing *just happens*. Did you feel poorer when you married Jim?"

"Well, he was a good provider but he refused to invest. We had so many opportunities to make killings but he was a weeny when it came to speculation. When I think of all the property that we could have bought when we first moved here, it makes me want to wring his neck."

"So you fought about money?"

"Oh,ya."

"And you got poorer."

"We did."

"Funny how that just happened, isn't it? The Law is very simple, so *Peter Pan* simple that most people don't understand it. Think happy thoughts and you can fly. You get to decide whether to see the tree or the litter underneath it. See and appreciate the beauty of the tree and more good stuff follows. See and condemn the trash and all you get is more garbage."

"So a bad day is never just a bad day, it's because I looked at trash… under a tree?" Bell took a sip and thought how stupid that sounded.

"If you having a bad day it usually starts that way, right? Your hair looks awful, the store clerk is rude and the momentum gets going, the car doesn't start or you meet Letta in a restaurant. I'm just saying that you can turn it around to a good day…" She paused. "Say… wait a minute. What were you doing having dinner with Letta Steele, anyway?"

28.
And this took us to Christmas

"Joey Vecchia. You slept with Joey Vecchia? Tell me you didn't sleep with Joey Fucking Vecchia."

"I *am* sleeping with Joey. I will again tonight. Is that clear enough?"

El Major, lit up for the holidays. I was celebrating my coming-out-of-the-Joey closet. I had admitted the relationship to Misty and she was supportive. That gave me the confidence to tell Annie and Bren.

"Since when, how does something like that happen?"

"Bren. I have been with him since shortly after the flood. He is a very nice guy, he treats me like a queen and I like him. What more can I say?"

"Nah-ah. I want details."

I told them pretty-much-sort-of the whole story of how we got together and how good the chemistry was between us.

"Looks can sure be deceiving," she replied.

"That is exactly what you told me a year ago, right here at this table, that a homely man can have some sex appeal. Joey and I have some kind of... attraction."

"Fatal attraction, I'm like to die of embarrassment if anyone we know hears about this."

"Bren, that's not helping. It took a lot of courage for her to tell all of us, and that's an unkind thing to say about Joey." Misty had my back on this one.

Annie patted my arm. "Sophie, I'm glad you did it. You needed to do it with somebody sometime, and Joey's safe. You can feel certain that there is no chance of him breaking your heart and you, I'm sure, felt comfortable enough to undress in front of him. I know that was a big issue for you. I'm proud of you. It's about time; and if his appearance doesn't bother you, then good for you."

"He's butt ugly."

155

"If she can look beyond a person's appearance then that speaks volumes about her character, Bren. Give her some credit," Annie replied. "She had to start somewhere, and this will make it easier with the next man."

"Why does there have to be a next man? I really like him, and he's the best lover I have ever had; he's totally *unbelievable* in bed."

"Joey Vecchia is unbelievable in bed?"

"Oh, ya."

"And the devil shits ice cream."

"Shut up." Carlos came with fresh drinks. "Carlos, tell me again what *el major* means in Spanish."

"You know that, Amiga. I tell you many times. It means *the best*."

I eyed Bren, tapped my finger on the tip of my nose and said, "Yup."

"Sophie. You can do better than old Joey."

"Nope, I was ready and I'm happy. That should be the end of the story. He's a nice guy, Bren."

"Leave her alone, Bren. It's Sophie's life." Annie came to my defense again. "If she likes him and he treats her well, then who are they hurting? Besides, why do we have this obsession with youth and beauty?"

"It's an accident of birth for the most part. Pretty parents make pretty babies, big deal! It's not like it's an accomplishment to receive attractive DNA," I said. "If you are unattractive and you have developed enough character that shows your inner beauty, then that is an accomplishment, right there."

"Now you're sounding like Misty," Bellamy stated.

"It's just the picture of it," Bren shuddered. "You know, I have a very graphic mind; and this is traumatizing."

"Bren, quit it." Bellamy jumped on her.

"No, it's okay. I'll admit that I had to keep my own eyes closed the first few times." I chuckled a bit. "I understand and it's okay. I know."

"Well, I have to say that you seem contented and relaxed. At least you're not doing that annoying nail-flicking thing anymore," Bren said with another shudder.

29.
Last Tango in K'ville

"Close your eyes. We want this to be a surprise." Joey covered my face.

Like a child discovering a playhouse kitchen, I wore a half-goofy smile. Allen's workers had salvaged some of my original cabinets. They divided the new from the old with a corner wine rack and built a small pantry closet on the opposite wall for extra storage. All of it, a cool light grey with mid-century pulls and my walls were a warm creamy yellow. The old diner-style barstools fit perfectly. But the biggest surprise was the dark granite countertop. Allen said that he worked the cost of it into one of his construction jobs.

"It cost-you nothing but da-time it-took to attach-it."

With black appliances the speckled stone pulled the entire look together. It was beautiful, perfectly homey, better than it was before. The deal was dodgy but I was not about to pick a fight with two big guys from New Jersey over ethics. Nope, I was grateful. It was clean and pretty and it was my own working kitchen.

"Thank you, guys. I could never have done this, and it would have cost me twice as much."

"Sophie, it was my pleasure," Allen said and bowed graciously.

"Oh, you don't even know!" A tear trailed from my eye and I wiped it away with the back of my hand. I was getting my home back. I took a few seconds. "I just love you guys. Please let me make you dinner. Oh heck, it's Christmas. Let me make you Christmas dinner."

Allen declined. "Thanks, I gotta go to Loretta's family thing. I promised."

Joey was shuffling his feet.

"Well, another time then."

"Ya, Sophie, another time, we gotta-go now-anyway. Come-on, Uncle Joe," he said and Joey followed him out the door and back up the hill to his house.

A half hour later he returned to help me unpack and arrange the cabinets. "So why don't you want to come for Christmas dinner,

Joey? Do you have a better offer?"

"Did-I say I-didn't want to-have dinner-here?" he asked.

"No, but you seemed uncomfortable."

"Sally already invited-me and I-said I'd come."

"Miss Sally would understand and all my friends will be here."

"I have it every year with Sally."

"Joey."

"I don't-wanna be with-all your-girlfriends. I'd be in-the way. Your house isn't that-big."

"You won't be the only man. Eliot, Mounty and Sam will be there too. They're nice guys. You'll like them."

"You-know the carpet guy is coming in-the morning," he said. "We-gotta get-the small stuff out-of the-living room, they-can work around the sofa-and chairs. Hey, here's-that box."

"Oh shit, my mother's ashes; what do I do with those?"

"What did she say she wants done with them?"

"I haven't looked. Knowing her it probably involves a trip to Greece or some other big deal. Why me? Why not my brother?"

"A trip to Greece would be nice. Open the directive, Sophie."

"Maybe after the holidays, I'll put them in this drawer for now."

"Okay, whatever you-want. You comin'-up for dinner? I made spaghetti and meatballs."

"I'd love to but no pasta. I'll make a salad."

"Joey," I said, "No pasta, just meatballs, okay?"

"How can-you have meatballs with-no spaghetti?"

"Because my clothes don't fit, and I refuse to buy a bigger size. My ass is the size of Milwaukie."

"I like your ass. It's round and plump, soft." He reached around me and began to knead my bottom then dumped both plates back into the pot. "We-can fuckin' keep-it warm for-now because I want-to snuggle up to-your magnificent ass." He took my hand and led me to the bedroom.

Joey licked his lips as if he were forming a game plan. I lay knees slightly bent away and twisted at the waist with my arm out toward him. My right breast was miraculously, dreamily, almost magically balanced on the shelf of my rib cage in a near perfect mound. It looked flawless, the way they both used to look when they were firm and... beautiful... till Joey sat heavily on the bed.

My perfect tit slid off its shelf and lolled into a Dali-esque teardrop in the hollow of my pit.

I closed my eyes.

And Joey went into sex-art. He caressed and petted, stroked and fondled. He traced circles down the length of my body, around my breasts, my navel and lower to my pubic mound. He spread my thighs wide and touched the folds of my labia, separating them with his thumb then stroked… gently… teasing. He lifted one leg and brought my foot to his mouth and kissed my toes, sucked each one in time then licked his way up the back of my calf to the inside knee.

He found places on my own body that I never knew were erotic, trailed my inner thigh with soft lips and circled my button with the tip of his tongue, just enough to drive me crazy. I was in agony of need when he honed in on the clit with a fluttering tip then a full on tongue side to side

He inserted his middle and ring finger into my vagina, cupped his palm over my clitoris and began to move his hand up and down very quickly. This was a really good move because he got my G spot and entire clitoral area simultaneously. My mouth hung open. I wanted to ask him what the hell he was doing, but I couldn't possibly have formed the words. All the sounds that came from my mouth were absurd noises like whimpers, "Ahyowaha hawa, ama ga, ama ga."

He continued this until I didn't care what he was doing as long as he didn't stop doing it. Then I passed the threshold to the warm fluttery place your body goes when it's about to cum and I climaxed… unlike any orgasm I had ever experienced before. It was… more. More intense, more of a release and way more wet, like I climaxed and peed at the same time. Fluids shot out and wet everything — my legs, the sheets. He didn't seem to think this was a big deal. He rolled on a condom and lay on the dry side of the bed and directed me to straddle him facing away so he could watch my "magnificent ass" as it ground into his loins. With a slow, steady circular motion, I worked his perfect erection high into my body then I cupped my clit. It was still dripping wet, and I was wondering what the hell had just happened but I was also into fucking Joey. I set a pace. I was in complete control of the movement. Then he titillating my anus... just a tease then I heard a spitting sound.

Slowly, carefully he inserted his wetted finger up my ass and pressed against the wall of my vagina. I arched my back and filled my belly with everything he could give. It was the moment, the feeling, the pleasure, the moaning mounting need; and I exploded, shattered into billions and billions of breathtaking stars, exploded into another big bang as I jerked and quivered my way into outer space.

I ate meatballs, pasta, bread…everything.

30.
The Piss Off

As soon as the carpet installers left, I put up the tree. Both of my kids were spending Christmas with their significant others' families, but I was definitely having a big dinner here, with or without Joey.

"Why? Why would he not want to have Christmas dinner with us?" I asked the girls.

"Probably afraid to take up too much room."

"Bren," Bellamy admonished.

"Sophie, he may have his own personal reasons. People have lots of baggage surrounding holidays, especially Christmas," Misty comforted.

"He's willing to celebrate with Miss Sally. You don't think he's embarrassed that he's with me, do you?"

"Hell no," Bren said. "That is not possible. He should be thanking Jaysus for finding you."

"Well, he has never taken me out, not even to lunch or a movie. I insisted on that grotto dinner with Allen and … Letta," I shuddered.

"It sounds like he's married. That's how a married guy would act," Bell stated, "or a cheap guy, ha ha."

"No way Joey's married. He's been my neighbor for a hundred years and I've never even seen a woman over there. I thought he was gay."

"He introduced you to his nephew, didn't he? A guy would never let you meet his family unless he cared about you. A man of his age is more likely to be hiding a serious illness than a wife," Annie said. "I suggest that you put it out of your mind. Everything comes clear eventually."

"Shit, do you think he could be really sick? I'd hate to see him sick."

"Sophie, have another margarita and forget about Joey. I bet everything is fine. If there is something wrong, you will know it soon enough," Annie added.

"Hey, ladies," an itty-bitty, high-pitched voice interrupted.

"Hi, Letta. What's going on?" Bren smiled slightly.

"I just wanted you to know, Sophie, how much Al and I enjoyed double-dating with you and Joey Vecchia."

"It wasn't a date." I made a casual gesture.

"That's good to hear because Joey Vecchia is married. Allen told me."

Bren spit her drink. My jaw hung.

"So there *is* something between you and Joey, ha. Merry Christmas, Sophie... and to all of you." She turned away with a self-satisfied grin and sauntered back to the bar.

"We are all going to act like this is a normal Sunday night. Smile, Sophie." I plastered a stupid smirk on my face. "Bellamy, laugh or something." Thank God, Bren had the presence of mind to keep us acting nearly normal.

Bellamy laughed like crazy, and the rest of the girls covered for me by laughing along with her.

"Where is Carlos? Do you see him anywhere? There he is, hey, Carlos." Bren motioned for another round. "Okay, that is the meanest little slut that I ever knew. Isn't that funny?"

We laughed on cue. How am I ever going to get through this night? How could he lie to me like that? I could see Letta at the bar pointing at me, holding her arms out to demonstrate Joey's girth and laughing. Laughing at me and poking fun of Joey's appearance. It was good that I didn't carry a gun.

"Let's kick her skinny little ass. Isn't that funny?" Bren kept us going until Carlos arrived with our drinks, and she asked him to teach us the words to *Feliz Navidad*. We sang it over and over like we were happily celebrating the season until Bren decided we could leave without looking beaten.

Out in the parking lot, she said three words, "My house, now." We got in our cars and drove.

Bren bought a four-bedroom ranch with two acres of trees. When the rest of her relatives saw what she could afford in Kernersville compared to New York, many of them sold their homes and moved nearby.

"I've been getting the house ready for family. I got cousins and an elderly aunt coming for Christmas." She was in the midst of polishing her silver set on the kitchen table so we sat around her oversized dining room table as she put on a pot of decaf. I moved a huge floral centerpiece of poinsettias with sprigs of holly and pine to the sideboard, pausing to admire the beauty of her arrangement.

"Sophie, sit down."

"It's okay, Annie, I'm okay." I touched a tiny pine cone and bit my lip to hold back tears.

"I know this is a big shock, Honey. Sit."

"I'm okay, believe it or not." I wasn't. "I'm just trying to decide who to kill first."

"First Joey, then Letta," Bren said as she brought out plates with forks and napkins. She had a sliced Sara Lee pound cake on a serving plate. "It's still a little frozen so wait for the coffee."

"Letta's just the messenger. You can't shoot the messenger," Misty said.

"In this case I could. Someone should put her out of my misery. Bren, you have a gun. Loan it to me for an hour or so," I said too calmly.

"Nobody is shooting anybody with my gun. Let's just have some cake and coffee, and we'll talk about this rationally."

"I know you're hurting, Sophie, but…"

I held up my hand to stop Misty from consoling any further. "I'm not in love with Joey. I loved the affection. I loved the companionship, and I loved the sex; but I never loved *Joey*." I was still sorting out my feelings. I didn't honestly know where Joey was in my heart.

"You more than liked him."

"Yes, I liked him a lot." My lip trembled a bit. "I think what hurts the most is that I trusted him."

"Which was huge for you, I know," Annie said.

"See, that's why I got Leroy — no complication and that's the way I like it." She brought the cups, sugar and creamer.

"Ya, trust is huge," said Bellamy.

Misty began, "Yes, but trust is a good thing. He just wasn't the right guy. You did rush into this."

"Yes, and I got passion, exactly what I asked for. I didn't ask for a man with principles, remember? I added that as an afterthought." I hurt and they knew it.

"That is true. You got what you asked for," Misty said.

"How could I have been so wrong about him? And how am I ever going to trust a guy again? How will I ever trust my own judgment again?" Bren poured the coffee. I took a sip, welcoming the warmth.

Bren was done serving. She pulled out her chair and slowly sat. "Listen to me." She waited until we were quiet, and she was sure that she had our attention. "I think that Joey Vecchia is a vulture."

"This isn't the time for birds, Bren."

"I'm dead serious. Listen, back in high school there were these boys. We called them the "vultures". When any girl had a crisis, heartbreak, a family problem, even a bad grade on a test, the vultures would circle around and then swoop in, ready to comfort. If you fell for his lines, it usually led to having sex with him."

"We had a boy like that, Arthur Thompson. Then his friend started doing it too. I forgot his name, Pat something," Annie said.

"Billy Thorndike and Tommy Freeman in my school, we called them the "pity patrol". One of them got Jenny Goode pregnant and the other one was there to console her. He screwed her too." Bellamy remembered.

"Think about it. First your mother died and then that flood in your house. You were vulnerable and Joey was there to soothe you, comfort you in your time of need." Bren's voice dropped an octave. "I think he knew exactly what he was doing. It would explain why you slept with him and why you to trusted him."

"And there's the extended hug phenomenon. If you hug for more than seven or eight seconds, the body makes oxytocin, the bonding chemical between mother and baby. It leads to trust. He's a biology teacher and might know that. That supports your theory."

"You could just ask him," Misty suggested.

"Hell no, you can't ask him. I vote we move straight to torture." Bellamy raised her right hand.

"The *Queen* of Karma votes for torture," Misty teased.

"I'm with Bell on this."

"Just ask him," Misty said.

"And he'll give you another load of crap," Bren voiced loudly.

"It may not even be true, you know. Letta may have lied about it just to see your reaction. I wouldn't put it past her," said Annie.

"She is a bitch."

"Sophie. The man is a cheater. There is no excuse for withholding that kind of information, none at all! You better proceed carefully," Bellamy exclaimed.

"Let's be fair to Joey. We don't know for a fact that this is true. Tell him what Letta said and ask him," Misty reiterated.

"It's true. He's married, so why should she trust anything that man says?"

"I can give you three reasons," I said. "They're flimsy, I'll admit. First, Letta may, in fact, be lying. Second, I've never, in all the years he has been my neighbor, seen him with a woman." I paused.

"And what's the third?"

"Well, Joey didn't have a condom with him when he consoled me that day. I think a vulture would have been prepared for sex, and he would have had a condom."

"That's a point," Annie agreed. "Sleep on it. You can't do anything about it now anyway."

"Yes, she can. She can go wake him up right now and blindside him. If you take him by surprise, he will be less able to lie about it convincingly."

"Bren, you are determined to think the worse of this man. Why is that?" Misty wanted to know.

"Cuz I know men, and very few of them will volunteer that kind of information when they are getting some."

"I'm kind of tired, and I think I want to be alone."

"This isn't like you, Sophie. You usually shoot from the hip. Should we worry about you?"

"What do you think I'll do, jump off a cliff over Joey Vecchia? I'm fine; don't worry. Have another piece of cake. Bren, get some chocolate sauce for my girls." I picked up my purse and drove home.

You know, there is a certain kind of humiliation involved when one gets duped by someone of Joey's stature and appearance. I was torn between embarrassment and sadness. Embarrassed because most everyone I knew *knew* that I had been played by a homely fat guy and sadness because there would be no more homely fat guy and no more homely fat guy sex. Just think of all those potential orgasms. Now they were forever lost in the ethers. And I felt cheated for only having a meager few months of it. Was it really only that long? That, in itself, was tragic.

I liked Joey. Maybe I even loved him. The friendship was very important to me but I couldn't imagine the friendship without the sex, not after knowing the height of the orgasms I'd experienced with him. But the very idea that I may have been vulturized by Shrek was absolutely nauseating.

Too restless to sleep, I took a Benadryl somewhere around three a.m.

It was a damp chilly morning and I awoke with a stiff hip. *Joey's married* I remembered and began the decent into Mordor. I took a couple folic acids, some vitamin D and mentally listed my known tools for combatting depression, my favorite two being animals and communing with nature. I decided to take Chica for a walk in the dog park. It was almost empty at that hour, bare trees surrounded by light fog… eerie. I should have worn a hat, no gloves either, so as cold and stiff as I was, there would be no clearing of the mind in the woods. Chica sniffed and peed on a few bushes and barked at a large mixed breed dog that, in her opinion, had no right to be carrying on so, running freely and untethered. She seemed pretty satisfied with herself. I patted her head and told her that she was a big dog.

Miss Sally was out getting the paper. I pulled the Camry over and stopped to talk with her.

"Come on in out of this damp." She poured me a coffee, and I absorbed the warmth with both hands in silence. "So what's wrong, Sophie? I can see worry in you."

"You know I've been seeing a lot of Joey lately."

"I had noticed, but I assumed it was about your house."

"Well, it is. It *was*."

"So it's like that, is it? I didn't think so because you are much younger than he is. You're a good-looking woman. Joey is, well …"

"Yes, I know but he's very nice, and we found that we had lots in common. One thing led to another, and..."

"I was going to say Joey's married, Sophie," she declared. "I hope he told you he is married."

166

"No, he didn't tell me. I heard *that* last night from Letta Steele."

"And I bet she said it none too kindly."

"You might say that."

"That's another one. She hasn't changed much over the years. Still scared and mean. And yes, Joe is married. He got married just out of school to the wrong woman, and he never divorced her."

"Why ever not?"

"Well that's something you need to ask him about, Darlin'. I can't say. But I can say this, she is coming down here to live with him and pretty soon too."

"When?"

"April, I think."

I stewed for a while, and then I called Annie.

"Well, Bren was right. He is a shit. He is married, and his wife is moving down here to live with him in April."

"That shit. So you spoke to him?"

"Nope, I asked Sally. Joey saw me coming out of her house. He tried to flag me down. I couldn't face him. I drove right by."

"Well, that's it then. Are you okay?"

"Confused, I don't know. I thought he was different."

"He is a guy. It is what it is."

"Hold on, someone's at the door. It's Joey. Call ya back."

Joey walked in soberly, shuffled. "I just got-a tongue lashing from-Sally."

"So what, you want another one from me?"

"Sophie, I'm-sorry, real sorry. I-never meant for-this to happen; I never-meant to hurt you like-this."

"You are married?"

"Let-me explain, please."

"Explain what?"

"We were only together-for-less than a-year. That was fifty-three years-ago, Sophie."

"And you stayed married to her?"

"I did."

"Why?"

"Well we're-both Catholic, and… "

167

"Don't you *dare*. Don't you dare shit on my sandwich and tell me it's Jesus. Jesus, Joey, you don't even go to mass. Don't shit me." I was so pissed!

"I never expected this-to happen between-us, Sophie. I never expected to-find anyone like you, who would wanna be wit-me. Hell, all these years of being-alone and-now I found-you... on the same street?" He tried to take hold of my shoulders, but I blocked him... hard.

"And you didn't think I'd find out until a wife magically appeared out of nowhere? Did you think I wouldn't notice?"

"I should-have told-you, I know."

"You had plenty of opportunities."

"Okay, from the start, last spring when-I went-up for the-wedding, I saw Viviane, that's her name. I heard-that her lover had passed-on, and I-thought, since she's-alone and has no-one to-care for-her that we-could, well, take care of each-other. We're old now. It's good to-have someone to be old-with, and we've always been good friends. So I said she should come-down and try living here with-me. I didn't know I'd get wit-chou."

"You knew she'd be at the wedding?"

"I-did."

"And that's why you had me help you buy that suit, to impress Viviane?"

"Sort-a, and-now I screwed up everything."

"I even asked you if you were ever married."

"Well, it's not so-easy to tell a-woman that you have just slept-with that you have-a-wife. I-didn't plan this. It just happened."

"So can't you tell her that you have found someone now and that you've changed your mind?"

"Sophie, she-don't have any-family, no kids to-care for her, nobody. She's all-alone, and the-house belonged to the-lover. She doesn't have any-place to-go now. She sold all-her stuff, but everything-else went into fuckin' probate. She is my-wife legally, and I do care for her. I don't want-her to be-homeless in Jersey or anything. I don't want that-on my head."

"Hmmph."

"I think if-I explain-it to-her, she'll let us keep-seeing each-other. I don't-think she'll mind. She's a really good friend."

"That is never going to happen."

"Sophie, listen."

"You lied to me."

"I didn't lie. But I should-a told-you."

"You lied by omission. And I do not date married men, period. You should leave."

"Even if Viviane gives us her blessing?"

"No."

"See, that's why I didn't-tell-you right-there. Sophie, we are so good together. I think maybe she'd-be happy for-me, for us."

"How come she never married him, anyway?"

"It's not something I want to talk about."

"Then there's the door, bye."

"You gotta promise to-keep this-a secret."

"I'm not promising anything, Joey. Tell me or don't tell me. It makes no difference."

He hung his head and shuffled. "It's true she left-me for-a roofer, but it was a woman roofer. She left me for a woman."

"He got caught and has had time to think about it."

"What kind of person would make something like that up? She insulted his manhood by running off with a woman fifty-three years ago. Can you imagine what that must have been like for a Guido from Jersey? His friends probably laughed him out of Jersey and straight down to Kernersville and he has been alone ever since."

"But he lied, so how do you know this is true?"

"Why would he say something that unflattering about himself if it was not the truth?"

"Well, then answer me this. If you are the only woman in his life, how did he get so good in bed?"

"Good question," I said. She was my Butch Cassidy. "But he never actually said I was the *only* woman."

"Did you ever ask him how he got so good?"

"How he knows a woman's body so well? Yes, I did."

"What did he say?"

"He said he paid attention."

To what, some hooker? Soph, don't be a fool. Wait. Don't sleep with him until you know it all. Wait until she moves here; and if she wants to give you her blessing, which I doubt, then you can work it out with them. Women have to get creative these days if they want a sex life. There are too many women and not enough men who have dicks that work. They either have to learn to share the men or go bisexual. Hey, one of these days, why don't I send Leroy over to your house?"

"I don't want Leroy. He's your friend with betterfits."

"Did you just say 'betterfits'?"

"Did I?" We burst out laughing, ran to separate bathrooms, holding our bladders. It took a few minutes before we got our breath back and were able to talk like semi-normal adults.

"So you want to meet Leroy or what? He's got several women he services. And I highly recommend him."

"That sounds like he's tuning up your car or something."

"Something like that."

"I don't want just sex, Bren. I want a heart connection."

"You wanted just sex."

"Well, I didn't know what I wanted but now that I've had both, I want both."

"You think that you had both with Joey?"

"I did think so. It sure felt like it."

"Well, you think on it. But, anyway, this frees you up to do what we're supposed to be doing."

"Which is what, getting even with Letta?"

"No, spying on Annie and Mounty."

"Aw, Bren. It's the holidays. Are we really going to do this awful thing to our good friend around the holidays?"

"Okay, you're right. But right after Christmas, okay?"

Crap.

31.
Sally's Party

It wasn't the most imaginative prank but it was quick, simple, I could pull off by myself and it was mean. I was in no mood to be fucked with by Letta Steele. So I went to Wally World and got a roll of white duct tape, some waxed paper, a stack of poster boards and a package of heavy duty markers. Then I went to Lowe's and had a few small lengths of PVC pipe cut about eight inches long each. Then I went to work. It would be all ready for this Sunday night.

Miss Sally's Bluegrass Christmas Party, each Saturday before Christmas and Joey would be there with his famous lasagna. I was not going to let heartbreak stop me. I sucked up my pride and went with covered dish in hand because only a fool would miss out on Sally's Christmas party.

Everyone brings a covered dish. Bellamy calls them "weird food parties". It's not so much that the food is weird; it's more like you can't always tell what's in the dishes and I would like to know what I'm eating. It's always delicious so you know it's made any number of dangerous holiday ingredients. Butter plus sugar or bacon plus cheese equals' guilt, and I want to know just how conflicted I should feel about what I eat. So far this week, I have eaten a half of a large Amalfi pizza with sausage and onion with Bren, a large piece of egg custard pie with eggnog at Stella's and two of the five boxes of Belgian chocolate that I bought as gifts. I don't want to count the number of margaritas or chai tea lattes I purchased because I'm close to the breaking point of food-guilt saturation. And now I'm about to enter into the tempting world of Joey Vecchia's lasagna.

Goodfellas would kill for Joey's lasagna. I have personally smelled his lasagna baking and there is nothing homier than inhaling the aroma of a comfort food like lasagna. The mingling fragrances, the garlic and sweet basil in his red sauce, the union of the cheeses, soft varieties with the bouquet bubbling up between layers of pasta, spicy sweet sausage and the delectable salty scent of mozzarella and Parmesan melted and toasted to a thin golden crust.

Enough said.

Now let me say a few words about collards. These good people of Kernersville make collard greens that taste like angels prepared them in heaven before God. No one *ever* brings collards to a covered dish party. And heaven knows it is difficult enough to eat right during the butter and chocolate season, but someone should bring collards. I brought shrimp; Bellamy made a delicious salmon salad with spicy habanero sauce. Misty walked in with a fresh fruit tray from Whole Foods that must have cost a bundle, and Annie made a beautiful Waldorf salad. Bren's specialty is an Asian chicken dish that is almost as popular as Joey's lasagna.

A few years back, Sally added a large extension onto the back of her house. It's an ideal room for Linda's children to play in and a perfect place to have a music party. The high ceilings and great acoustics, I wondered if she'd built this just for musicians to play in.

Sitting amidst good music is much different than hearing it live in concert. You actually feel the music flow around you, through you and the feeling is captivating. It's real surround sound, fiddles and bass with guitars, a banjo, several mandolins and a dobro, it enfolds you. So with my eyes closed, I allow the music to take me, transport me to a place where there is no Joey, no Sophie, no Sally or Bren, maybe there isn't even space or time. I disappear into the cool-hot vibration of music as the waves of sound carry me where there is only rhythm and tone.

A solo fiddler began to play. His wife picked up her guitar and sat down next to him. She sang a love song, something ages old and regional. They were maybe Sally's age; a couple who I imagined may have been married for fifty or more years, united by their love of music. Tonight they seemed as much in love as the day they married. They were beautiful.

I turned toward the kitchen; and there was Joey, facing me with his hangdog expression. I sipped my wine. I was tempted to lick the edge of the glass suggestively, but I resisted. He already looked tortured so I left to refill my glass.

Linda was loading the dishwasher. As I poured more wine I wondered how I could ask her about Sally's overnights. "Hey Linda, you're a nurse. How old can woman remain," I lowered my

voice to a whisper, "sexually active?"
Smooth. I got an earful.

The five of us walked down the road toward the end of the cul-de-sac. It was as cold as I ever remembered and I drew my scarf tighter and wrapped the ends around my hands.

"It smells like snow," Misty said.

"Yes it does," I agreed, "I wish it would. I love the snow. It makes everything look so clean and perfect. Do you think we might have a white Christmas?"

"Wouldn't it be nice if we did?"

"Fuckin' New Englanders," Bren said and we nearly ran to my front door.

We sat on those comfy old stools at the breakfast bar and I opened a bottle of white. Bellamy mentioned how absolutely miserable Joey looked and that he watched me the whole night which, she figured, was close to impossible because Bren watched *him* with her harshest cop face; and that is not so easy to ignore.

"Well, didn't you see him?"

"Bell, I mostly kept my eyes closed. Could we talk about something else, please?" I think I sounded uninterested but I was truly miserable. Knowing that Joey was also hurting was no comfort to me.

"Why didn't Mounty come tonight? Isn't Saturday your night with him?" Misty asked.

"It's Tuesday. I thought Tuesday was your night." Bellamy seemed puzzled.

"And Mounty and I will be here on Tuesday celebrating Christmas with you fine people," she said sweetly.

"Wait a minute, Tuesday and Saturday? Is that why you always look so contented on Sunday nights at the bar?" Party-Cop-Bren was winding down. She glanced at me with her mischievous smile.

Annie caught that smile and knew what it meant. "Listen to me." She pointed at Bren and me. "I know you're up to something and it better not have anything to do with me and the Mounty."

"Whatever do you mean?" Bren asked innocently.

"I'm only going to say this once: respect my fucking privacy." And, of course, Annie stared directly at me.

I was taking a particularly long pull on my wine, hiding my face and trying really hard not to laugh. "What," I finally said.

"Bren, if you drag Sophie…" Bellamy started, but Bren cut her off mid-sentence.

"No, no, Sophie and I are planning, uh, a little something for Letta, aren't we, Sophie?"

"Mmhumph." I was half-noncommittal.

"What are you planning for Letta?" Bell asked.

"Oh, God help us," Misty sighed.

"It's a two-woman job." I was shaking my head like they wouldn't be interested.

"Ya, she only needs me."

"Ya, probably-definitely."

32.
Payback the Bitch

Misty asked me to meet her for brunch. I was late and she was on her second cup of coffee, which gave her the caffeine advantage.

"Just walk away from this. It's not worth it."

"Oh, but it *is* worth it. Didn't you tell me that anger is healthier than depression?" I nodded.

"It is slightly better, yes; but you are still acting on an unhealthy emotion. If you retaliate then Letta will look for a way to get back at you and so on. When will this ever end? Examine what you are creating in your life — anger begets anger and then more anger."

"I can't let this go."

"You can. Why do you think she singles you out? She never pulls this kind of crap with the rest of us."

"Then tell me how to make her stop. Give me a tactic."

"From the Law of Attraction point of view I would tell you to make a list of her positive aspects."

"Which means what exactly?"

"Think about her good points and list them."

"She doesn't have any good points."

"Can you see her as a person who cares?"

"She cares about getting laid."

"So do you and so do I. She hopes to find love and affection. Can you see her as a woman with hope?"

"Maybe."

"Can you see her as a person with faith?"

"I know she goes to church."

"So she must have faith."

"Do hope and faith make her a decent human being?"

"What about honesty? Can you see her as honest?"

"Letta? Honest? You must be kidding."

"She told you the truth about Joey, didn't she?"

"Yes, but that was to hurt me."

"Possibly, she's always been honest about how important

finding a man is to her."

"Yes and then cheating on him with Tommy Schull."

"Honey, we are trying to find positive aspects. You already know all the negatives. I want you to see there is good in her."

"Okay, she's cute and has a nice shape. She stays fit and takes pride in her appearance."

"She takes care of her mother. Have you ever met her mother? Take my word for it, her mother is a handful. It must require incredible patience to live with and care for that woman. She must have a strong sense of responsibility also, don't you think?"

"And you think that if I just make a list of all her good points, then she will quit being so nasty?"

"Yes I do. I would like for you to be able to see her as a spiritual being that resides in a physical body. She is just another human trying to get by the best she knows how to. And yes, try to see her good points. I know that once you allow yourself to see them, you will realize how much more alike you are than different."

"Alike? Are you kidding me? We are nothing alike. She's hideous!"

"*Allow* yourself to see it."

"See, that's what I don't understand. How do you just allow?"

"Well, take Joey, You used to be very opinionated about Joey, remember? Then you got to know him and allowed his good points to shine through."

"And he turned out to be a shit."

"I don't think so. I think he's being as honest as he possibly can in a completely impossible situation. I think he's sincere."

"You think so? I think he has a foot fetish. He sucked on my toes, you know."

"That's too much information." She raised her hands to stop me. "If you get too crazy, I'm going to have to start charging you. And *stop* trying to change the subject. If you knew more about Letta's story you might find more to like about her too or at least more to respect about her. Just let yourself see her as her true self, how you might imagine that Spirit sees her."

"How do you imagine Spirit sees her?"

"I think Letta would be like…" She paused to form a head graphic. "I think she'd be like a little ball of light with lots of little prickles, prickly like those stickers you see at the beach only made of light."

Prickly.

Ignoring Misty's advice and as soon as it was dark, I loaded up the car with bags, my supplies, everything I needed to punk Letta — and I was keeping it simple.

For some reason we used to call them ditty bags, bags full of anything one could possibly need for prank emergencies: tools, tape, glue, nail polish. I'd gone through mine meticulously and made sure I had Band Aids and a new pack of baby wipes and tie wraps. I laced up my running shoes and went to meet Bren at the Food Lion parking lot.

We went over the plan again. "This is your tool." I handed her an eight-inch piece of PVC. "Don't lose it. You put the pipe into the cardboard tube and pull away. Got it?"

"Got it." And she slipped the pipe into her purse.

"Shit, Bren, what the hell are you wearing, heels? Get in the Camry." I shook my head.

"What's wrong with these heels?"

"Would you have gone out on your beat in heels, Bren?"

"No."

"You don't wear heels in pranks either. You should friggin' know that. There are rules."

"Rules? What, you have your own punkin' rule book? And they aren't that high. Whoa! Damn it, Sophie, You cut that guy off. Will you be careful?"

"Didn't you have plan Z in your neighborhood?"

"I'm familiar with plan Z."

"Plan Z happens. You have to be ready to run. How you gonna run in those boots, Bren?"

"If I have to run I will run. Believe it, boots or no boots."

The entrance to El Mejor is on the street. The west side of the building is lined with windows overlooking a long, narrow parking lot. You know how people love to show off their cars? This parking lot is probably the reason everyone loves this place so much. It's the perfect place for people to show off or, at least watch their vehicles.

We usually sit by the window between the bar side and the bathrooms. From that vantage we can see most everything that goes on inside or out. Bellamy and Annie were already seated. Bren and I dropped off our stuff and went off to find Carlos. I had a prearranged agreement with him and had a nice hefty tip in an envelope ready to thank him for his help. I surveyed the bar but I didn't see him anywhere.

"Tito, have you seen Carlos?" I asked.

"Carlos got the flu. He's sick."

"Shit."

"What do we do now?"

"I don't know, Bren, but we can't be seen in the parking lot."

"Tito, can you lead us out the back way?"

"*Si, vamanos*. Let's go."

Carlos had agreed to flip off the breaker to the parking lot floodlights while we did the fun part. I didn't know Tito well enough to ask for his help but we followed him out through the kitchen while I scanned the walls searching for the breaker box. I wanted this to be done tonight.

The plan was so simple that I didn't think I needed a back-up plan. I needed one now, I thought as we walked out the kitchen door and around to the back of the building. The back lot was full of pebbles and dead weeds. Bren almost lost her balance and I caught her arm. The situation seemed impossible and I grasped for ideas on ways to kill the lights. "We can't unscrew the bulbs. We'd be seen." I was thinking out loud.

"I shouldn't have worn these damn heels."

"No shit." I reached down to pick up a good-sized rock, thinking out loud. "We can't break the bulbs. They're floods and I'm not that good of an aim. Even if I could hit them they wouldn't smash. We better postpone this for another night." Damn, I wanted Letta to have as miserable a holiday as I would. "Maybe I should go inside and just ask Tito if he'll show me the breakers."

"Well," Bren said. "Look at this wire. Where do you think this goes to?"

"I didn't see that. I bet that is the wire to those lights."

"What if I just pulled this wire?" She gave it a hard yank, the floods were off and the lot was pitch-black!

"Damn, Bren, you are brilliant. Let's hurry!" We made a dash to my unlocked car. "Have you got your tool?"

"What tool?"

"The PVC."

"Shit, I left it in my purse at the table."

I handed her a spare piece of PVC pipe because I was punk prepared. We plopped the stack of poster boards on the windshield of the car that was centered nearest the bar side and closest to the windows.

"Put the pipe into the tube on the bottom and pull the tape over the glass. You have to remove the waxed paper first, Bren."

Within seconds Bren became proficient. We did a few cars in front and a couple SUVs and trucks in the second row that stood up tall enough for our purpose. We did the entire prank in the dark and in only a few minutes then we ran back to the rear of the bar as Pedro and Tito exited the kitchen door.

"Tito. It's this wire, I think," Bren said.

"No problem, Amiga. I can fix that. Pedro, I need a screwdriver!"

"Phillips or flathead?" I had a cheap set of both so I handed them to Tito then we ran back in through the kitchen and occupied our seats before the repair was completed. I was pretty sure that nobody had seen us. The crowd was more interested in the commotion out in the lot. A few guys ran out to check their cars but most of them had their faces pressed to the windows, cupping their temples like horse blinders.

And then there was light.

White poster boards were taped on the windshields that were most visible; each presented a slogan suitable to describe our little Miss Loretta Steele. In very large, clearly-printed words, they read,

> *Letta whore*
>
> *Slut*
>
> *Had Letta?*
>
> *Booba Letta*
>
> *Steele your man*
>
> *Letta Blow Ya*   *Letta Delivers*

It took the crowd a few seconds while they read, rubbernecked and erupted into peals of laughter. They pointed at the signs, re-read them aloud, laughing at them, laughing at Letta. She sputtered and dithered and turned to study the face sitting next to her, the one we didn't expect to see that night, the face of Allen Predo. I felt a twinge of regret that he had to witness this. Allen didn't deserve to find out what the town of Kernersville thought of his woman, not in front of this hole of half-tanked, beer-drinking locals.

Her cellophane face asked *how can I recover?* His said, *Unrecoverable.* He whispered something in her ear, and she shook her head no. He verified her answer, mustered his dignity and walked out the door. Letta changed her mind and ran after him.

The Kernersville Police were soon in coming. They thundered into the lot with squad cars flashing. Patrons grabbed their jackets and stormed out to check their cars or just stand around dumbly with their hands in their pockets as strobing blue lights formed an erratic corona over the scene.

Tito was speaking with the police. He pointed his finger directly at Bren and me through the window.

"He's not going to get a very good tip from *me* tonight," I said.

"I've got this." Bren started and I followed her out, heads high, Butch and Sundance facing the law.

Bren strolled out, turned on that full-white smile and morphed into Cop-Flirt. "Why, Officer Roberts, you look so handsome in those blues, keeping fit, I see." She checked him out thoroughly. "And who is this fine young man? Are you new on the force?"

"Hey Bren, good to see you. This is Mullens. "Watch this one, Mullens. She's retired NYPD. Show him your shield, Bren. She proudly displayed the badge on the chain around her neck and spoke about old days on the force.

"No kidding, NYPD?"

"Thirty-two years." she beamed, tilting her head playfully. "Bren Sykes." She shook his hand and held it a second or so longer than needed.

Officer Roberts got more professional. "Ms. Sykes, were you behind the building when the lights went out?"

"Yes."

"What were you doing in the back of the restaurant?"

"I was trying to avoid seeing a certain someone so I asked Tito if he'd show me out the back way, isn't that right, Tito?"

"Si. Yes, that's right."

"The lights were on or off at the time."

"On, but it's very possible that I did it. I was trying to save my hat from the wind. I think I felt my bracelet catch on something. I can't be sure but I pointed the problem out immediately, isn't that right, Tito?"

"Yes," he agreed.

She faced Officer Roberts eye to eye. He asked, "And did you see anyone out here in the parking area that may have done this?"

"No sir." We both shook our heads.

Tito presented the two screwdrivers and indicated that he got them from me.

"And your name, please." He took them from Tito.

"Sophie Chase."

"And you just happened to have these tools in your purse?"

"No sir. These tools were behind the building and Bren almost tripped." And this was actually not a lie.

"And your hat?"

"What?"

"And where is your hat, Ms. Sykes?"

"I … ah … lost it. It just blew away…" I expected, even *waited* for her to say it was "gone with the wind", and I'd have wet my pants for sure.

"I see." It wasn't a particularly windy night, and I don't think we weren't fooling Officer Roberts one bit.

"There doesn't seem to be any real damage here. We'll take a few pictures, talk to the vehicle owners."

"Can I be of any further assistance to Kernersville's finest?" she asked from under those thick eyelashes.

He shook his head. "No, Bren, we got this."

"So you are done with us?"

"Not by a long shot." Officer Roberts said with a discrete wink at Bren.

"I'll be waiting inside where it's warm. Tito, put two coffees on my tab and bring them out for these fine officers?" We walked inside, trying not to appear too self-congratulatory and sat down at our widow table.

"Damn, that was a bitchin' good plan, Sophie," she said under her breath.

"I don't even know what you're talking about. We've been here the whole time. And you were brilliant, by the way." I kept my face as straight as I could.

"That certainly got your point across." Annie didn't seem to think it was funny.

"I thought it was hilarious, and so did most of the bar," Bellamy defended my efforts. "Tommy Schull went bananas. He laughed louder than anyone!"

"He laughs at anything."

"You annihilated her." Annie was kind of right. But this was my first prank with Bren, and she had performed well beyond my expectations. We completed a precision task in less than a few minutes. The police had been appropriately schmoozed. There was a lot here to feel proud of, even grateful for.

I tried to appear nonchalant. More than a few folks suspected me and it was essential that I play this role passably well.

"Did you do that, Sophie?"

"Sophie, that was so funny!"

"Way to go!" People were congratulating me.

"What?" I stupidly asked.

"She was right here the whole time," Bren confirmed.

"What are they talking about, Bren?" In the periphery of my vision I noticed that Letta had returned to the bar.

"She came back in. That's pretty brave of her, don't you think?" Annie quietly asked.

"Oh shit," Bren whispered, "she's coming toward us."

"Sophie," she asked, "could I speak to you in the little girls' room?"

"Well, Merry Christmas, Letta." I followed. I'd long been looking forward to a direct adult-like confrontation, and this just might be it. I made sad, crybaby faces behind her back. Then she turned and confronted me.

"You did this, didn't you?" The ladies' room door swung shut.

"Why would you think that?"

"I know it was you, and I saw the cops talking to you."

"They're friends of Bren."

"Only you would do something like that."

"Why, because you think I'm the only one who knows you're a dirty, husband-stealing slut?"

"Are you blaming me for your failed marriage, Sophie?" She seemed self-satisfied with the question and she sounded a little bit on the arrogant side.

"I think I can muster up some blame for you."

"Well, who is dating a married man now?"

"He's been separated for fifty-something years and I didn't know about the wife."

"Well, how does it feel to have done the same thing you've been blaming me for all these years?"

"You knew Jim was married with a young family."

"You can't blame me for Jim leaving because you weren't takin' care of him like he needed."

"And how would you know what I was or wasn't doing with Jim?"

"He told me."

"Well, that seems to be your main problem, Letta. You believe everything a man tells you."

"Jim told me all about you and if you want to hear about yourself, I can tell you a heap. He trusted me."

"Right, and he loved you, heard all about it."

"He did love me."

"Which is why he ran off with Edith Marsh, Letta, he screwed you just like half the women in the county till he found the highest income on the longest legs. Jim always liked to get the most buck for his bang. Jim was out for Jim."

"Jim was everything. He was handsome, smart, and funny; and you can't blame me for that. Nobody can help who they fall in love with or when it happens so don't blame me."

"Is that how you justify all your affairs, Letta? Well, don't take it personally but Jim was too much of a mercenary for your secretary's salary. It just wasn't big enough."

"You think you're so much better than me because you got college. You ain't no better than me, you fat pig. That's twice you ruined my life, you fat, ugly Yankee ... pig. "

I could feel the anger rising. I took a step closer to her thinking how easy it would be to grab her windpipe and snarled. "So what are you gonna do about it, call for your mammy?"

"This used to be a nice town before all your kind of people moved in."

"You have despised me since the day you met me. Why is that?"

"Because you're a Yankee heathen, and you don't even believe in Jesus."

"Leave Jesus out of this. You hate me because I'm a Northerner and because I was married to a man you wanted."

"Well, your taste in men has certainly changed. Old fat Joey? He's so old and ugly and disgusting. You make a good pair, another fat pig … just like you."

"Love to have Allen hear you talk about his family like that. Oh, but I think he broke up with you tonight, didn't he?"

"Don't worry about me and Allen. I'll get him back."

"He knows what you are now. He saw it in writing with the whole bar laughing."

"You shamed me in front of Allen, and in front of this whole town." She grabbed her sweater just over her heart. "How can I even live here after this?"

What a whiny little pea brain. "Why don't you buy a boat and go oil rig hopping? I know of a lumber camp in Maine that would pitch a tent for you. I think you'd feel right at home there."

"That's why Jim left you because you say mean, ugly things. You have a real nasty streak and the language to match. You were like poison to Jim. Living with you was making him sick! His back was sore all the time and he had all those headaches."

"Bet you were there to rub his temples and massage his back. Well, guess what, Letta? There's nothing wrong with Jim's back; he just liked to be worshiped. And Jim doesn't get headaches. He *gives* them."

"You Yankee women are pitiful, and you know you can't compete with us Southern women. We know how to treat a man. That's something you never learned how to do."

"Ya, we expect our men to act like grown-ups. We want the kind of man who doesn't need an idiot to iron his socks and hold his dick when he pees."

"You're just jealous because I know what a man wants and plenty of men want me. How many dates have you had since Jim left you?"

"That's none of your business."

"None, that's how many."

"How would you know?"

"I know."

"I just don't make it a spectator sport like you do."

"You gypsy witch, no man wants you, you ugly old Greek." She walked up close to within six or eight inches of me, which was, again, pretty brave of her. "You ain't but two shades lighter than that nigger bitch that helped you do this."

My eyes narrowed, and my heart pounded wildly in my chest. She just called Bren the *N* word. That windpipe was pretty near to my hand, but what would it serve to grab for it? Her back wasn't near enough to a wall to make it count. I considered grabbing her hair and smashing her face into the sink, but a palm thrust to the nose would be the move. Ya, palm thrust to the nose. But any of those moves could potentially kill her. I was actually thinking I could kill her, wring her skinny little neck, right here, right now.

Jail, Sophie, she's not worth jail ... I took a deep breath and stepped back.

Every living person on this earth came from Africa. It is where Homo sapiens evolved from. I wanted her to know that but with my frighteningly unparalleled anger, what would it serve to tell her? I needed to remove myself before this escalated any further and I was not about to explain the theory of evolution to this bigoted bitch in the bathroom of a bar. I took another breath and let it out.

"You know, you are absolutely right." I spoke particularly slowly, brown eyes to blue. "And I am extremely proud of that." I turned and left the room.

A fresh margarita was waiting for me back at the table. I took a sip and considered the chips and salsa.

"So are you going to tell us what happened?" Bellamy wanted to know.

"Oh, I ruined her life and Jim really loved her. It was like debating with the argumentatively impaired." I was putting on a brave front, and I didn't want anyone to know how close I was to berserk.

"I think you wrecked her chances with Allen. He looked pissed," Bell pointed out.

"He was pulling away from her anyway. Who wants someone

that clingy, that needy? It's a blessing for him to know that she's not quite the sticky sweetness she pretends to be." I munched on a chip.

Bren held up her drink up for me to clink glasses. "That was great! We make such a good team. We pulled it off perfectly. What's wrong? What did she say to you in there to make you so …?"

"Uncelebratory?"

"Ya, uncelebratory."

I clinked her glass none the less. "It was a nasty prank. I knew it was mean; but I was angry and I didn't care. I don't care." I took a long pull on my margarita and a hint of revulsion bittered my drink. I crossed my arms, mostly to warm my hands. I remembered Allen's face. I really felt bad for him.

"Seeing those posters all lit up like that, I'm sure glad you like me," Annie added. "I feel kind of sorry for her."

"Sorry for Letta?"

"A little, yes."

"I think all this Christmas music has damaged your brain." Bren patted Annie's arm in mock comfort. "I feel your pain, but there are only a few more days of it and you'll be back to your normal self. I'm hungry, Sophie, you going to order?"

"No, these chips are fine. I'm going home early, kind of tired. Will one of you take Bren back to her car? It's at Food Lion."

"No way are you leaving now."

"G'night, Bren." I finished my drink, threw cash on the table and I waved at the gals who I knew loved me in spite of myself.

I was shaken and truly frightened to know how close I had come to violence. I could have killed her. With my bare hands I could have actually killed her dead! Okay, Letta is repugnant, what she said was revolting; but she is basically so… pitiful. Why does she make me seethe and fume with such hatred?

And she was right about one thing: I couldn't compete. I would never be able to indulge an able-bodied man and that is what most Southern men have come to expect in a relationship, I thought.

I should feel sorry for her. She was ignorant and so utterly desperate for a man; almost any man would do and she'd do anything to get him. Finding someone with a decent income was probably the only way she would be able to manage a retirement that didn't include dog food.

And she'd been in love with Jim. She had probably trusted and counted on him to marry her, to provide for her future.

Both of us had been manipulated, used and abandoned by Jim. I remembered what it felt like to worry about how I would make ends meet. Letta had that same kind of fear in her eyes. And she had been abandoned again this night by another man, Allen Predo. I was mostly to blame.

I liked Allen. A nice guy like him did not deserve to be mixed up with a ninny like her; but, like Joey said, what happens between a man and a woman was not my business. I had inadvertently contributed to that break-up. I had humiliated her and ruined her chances, for what? Revenge? My ego?

I tried to relax but couldn't. I kept reliving the night, rewind, playback, rewind, playback.

I'll go see Misty in the morning. I need help with this. Deep breath, relax, deep breath, relax. Again, I took a Benadryl which carried me to an unrestful slumber until...

I was in a large house, but it was packed full of junk. Two dolls—two old ugly baby dolls with hollow eyes like they were dead — dead dolls were standing on a shelf at about eye level. I had to squeeze by them, and they were scary. A Native woman took my hand and led me away. She pointed at them: "Old fear," she said. I followed her through a maze of effort. Every space was crammed full of stuff. Junk. We climbed over piles of it to get through to a narrow decrepit stairway. I felt compelled to follow her up. The room above appeared more open, but I couldn't get past all the stuff blocking the top of the stairs. The woman beckoned, pointed at an eagle perched above her. I felt lost in the room but I could hear a baby bird chirping. I knew it was hungry. I walked toward a big bowl-shaped container in the center of the room. The bird was at the bottom of it. I picked it up and held it, but I had nothing to feed it. I frantically searched for bread or seed, something to feed it; but then when I looked back at it, the bird's head had changed into Letta's... I was holding a Letta-bird, and it scared the piss out of me.

I woke up startled and couldn't get back to sleep.

33.
Misty Morning

"Feeling remorseful?" she asked as she answered the door, dogs barking from every corner. "Come with me' I have to get a rescue. We got into her beat-up wagon. It smelled strongly of the animal of the week. "This has to be important for you to come over cuz I know the cats bother your nose."

"Misty, it was bad. I'm glad you weren't there to see it."

"It wasn't going to make me smarter, happier or better-looking, was it? You want to tell me about it?"

"Not really. You'll hear about it soon enough. I want to talk to you as a psychotherapist and a friend. I'll pay you this time."

She smiled. "Sophie, I can't take money from you. What is it you want to talk about?"

"I came close to violence, Misty. I think I came very close to seriously hurting her."

"What in the world made you so angry?"

"Please don't tell anyone; she called Bren the N word."

"Oh no."

"Honest, I was tempted to kill her. Then I had this weird dream last night." I described it.

"So you want to know how I would interpret it. Usually in session, we could take hours, weeks even but I can give you my quick version. The house is you, your inner being; and if it was cluttered and decrepit then maybe you have some inner housecleaning to do. Climbing the stairway may mean that you are willing to reach a higher level of consciousness. The eagle is a powerful symbol, and we'll get back to that. The little bird is, of course, Letta. Perhaps the bowl-thing is showing you how fragile we all are in a world too big for us. Did you wake as soon as you saw her face, or did you try to comfort her too?"

"I woke right away. It was too weird. I maybe even dropped her. Are you sure there is no retribution? I feel guilty."

"Retribution? You weren't even brought up to believe in retribution." Misty has a certain wise woman look. I can try her patience and drone on for hours about stupid shit, and she will listen patiently to whatever spew-able drivel I can muster and then, wordlessly, she shoots that look of hers at me and it all comes instantly clear. And I say to myself, *that's so obvious! Anybody could see that. I must be a pinhead to have missed that.* It's her 'wise woman' look. It's silent, and yet the message is thunderous.

"You get what you believe. Do you feel like you need guilt and punishment in order to grow?"

"No, I think… " I twirled the end of my sweater. "Letta was in love with Jim, and he led her on, right? He made her believe he loved her."

"And that bothers you?"

"Not the way you might think. Jim took advantage of her. I feel like we were both his victims."

"Victims, smicktims. Get that victim mentality out of your head. You decide how to feel. You and she have something in common — namely you both chose to have a relationship with Jim. What you two do with that is entirely up to you."

"The dream, Misty, can we get back to my dream?"

I don't think you realize how much symbolism and mythology is involved here, the eagle, the Native Mother."

"What do they mean?"

"In animal lore? That's way too complicated to explain. Every group of people that has ever been in contact with the eagle has a mythology about them."

"Well, what would your best guess tell you?"

"Well, the meaning can be anything from creativity…"

"To?"

"To flying too close to the sun. Eagles are birds of prey. They are killers. They are important symbols of power."

"And the eagle was perched over the little bird, easy prey."

"Remember when Annie said that passions could burn down the house?"

"I do."

"This is passion. Do you want to immerse yourself, waste your time in this ridiculous and unnecessary imbroglio with Loretta Steele?"

"Yes."

"Why?"

"I don't claim to know why."

"Do you want me to tell you why?"

Now, as I think back on this, I feel kind of stupid that I missed this. I could have easily explained to you in scientific detail how receptor sites on the exterior of each of my cell's walls were practically yelling, *feed me, feed me anger* and I willingly fed that hunger with anger neurochemicals that were, of course, manufactured personally by my own body. Somehow I didn't put that together with like attracting like.

"Yes, spell it out for me like I'm a two-year-old."

"A two-year-old would get it right away. It's too easy for your left brain thinking to grasp. Are you choosing to feel like a victim now? Is that what I'm hearing?"

"No, I felt that way for a long time and I think Letta still feels that way still."

"So you are recognizing some of the Letta in you. You are so alike."

"How can you say that? She's awful."

"Like attracts like, period, done. The universe is holding up a mirror to you right now and asking you what you are going to do with it. What feels right to you this minute?"

"I feel sorry that I did this, and I think I should start by apologizing."

"You realize that could create more drama and escalate the situation?"

"I did something wrong and I think I should apologize."

"If that is what makes you feel better, then that is what you should do. You have to accept responsibility for your own actions. Guilt and apology are certainly a step-up from violence. So go and apologize then release it; get rid of it. Forget it and try to find happier thoughts."

"About Letta."

"About everything. Sophie, about *everything*." She brushed her hair back with both hands. For a second I thought she might pull it; then patiently she explained it all again.

I had to start shopping; I was making Christmas dinner for seven people, and that was tomorrow. I picked up a leg of lamb, packages of both ground lamb and bison for my healthier Greek meatballs, potatoes and green beans for the garnish, cheese and olives. Annie and Mounty were bringing bread and wine, Bell and Sam the desert. Misty said she was bringing something; what was it?

On the drive back home I was thinking about that apology and wondered if I really could do it. Could I look into her eyes, a woman who I despised, and sincerely, with my heart hanging all out and exposed say the words 'I'm sorry' and mean them? I imagined myself doing it and felt nauseous.

Crap

When I emptied the shopping bags and realized I had no filo for the pita. I had tons of spinach and feta cheese but no filo dough. I considered getting it in the morning or having one of the girls pick one up but pita is labor-intensive and I wanted it oven-ready in the morning to bake fresh. I got back in the car and drove to Food Lion. *Just in and out,* I told myself as I strode up the freezer aisle searching for the filo dough and making a mental checklist. *Christmas is tomorrow. Is there anything I have forgotten? What a crowd. I bet the line will be long. How could I have forgotten the filo?* Too pre-occupied to pay attention to my surroundings, I almost ran into an old woman in a tired grey coat. She had limp white hair and weird eyes. She pointed a strong-looking finger tipped with a thick discolored nail and asked in a raspy voice, as if she had been smoking Salems for a hundred years, "Have you found Jesus?"

Now this was Christmas Eve day and I saw no reason to upset a creepy old woman with my fake grandmother story so I replied, "Yes ma'am, we are very close. Have a Merry Christmas." Then I turned toward the piecrust section and was face-to-face with Loretta Steele.

"Letta, I am... so sorry for what I did to you last night. It was mean and wrong of me, and I will do *anything* I can to make it up to you. I'll talk to Allen. Please forgive me. I have said and done some awful things to you, and I have been a complete jerk."

"I ain't never going to forgive you as long as I live. C'mon, Momma." And they walked away towards the rear of the store.

Maybe that was too soon.

Christmas morning I was chopper-ing the parsley, mint, onion and peppers for the meatballs when Joey knocked at my door. I opened it a crack. He held a vase, a vase full of white hydrangeas, one of the prettiest Christmas bouquets I had ever seen with red roses and Christmas greens as the filler. It was gorgeous. "Merry Christmas, Sophie, could-I please come-in?" I let him.

"I'm cooking." I gave a bit of raw bison to Chica.

"You let me-in and that's-a good sign." He followed me to the kitchen. "Sophie, please forgive-me. I didn't know how-to tell-you."

"I forgive you."

He gazed down at the vase. "They say flowers-work, but I didn't-know they worked this-good." He handed them to me.

"It's not the flowers, Joey. I mean, they're beautiful but I thought about it and I think you didn't mean to lie. You still lied, but I think you didn't know how to tell me the truth."

"I should-of, I'm sorry. This smells-wonderful."

"It's all the garlic in the lamb."

"Maybe-I should-a accepted your-invitation."

"It's still open. Bren won't be here to scare you with her cop face." I smiled.

"Naw, I can't. Allen broke-it-off with-Loretta, did-you know?"

"I was there."

"He's pretty-upset."

"So he really liked Letta?"

"Naw, he didn't like-her that-much but nobody likes breaking up-on Christmas. Besides, she has-a sick mother. That's a-lot to take responsibility for. He's-going to Sally's wit-me for dinner. I got-her one like this, only smaller," he said as he gestured at the vase. "She's mad at-me for not telling-you."

"You should have."

"But you forgive me. So can-we be together? We were great-together. I-miss waking up to-you, Sophie; you are so-beautiful." He took my face in his hands, and I turned away before he could kiss me.

My mouth quivered. "Maybe when Viviane comes down, if she wants to give you permission. I don't promise anything, but I'll try to keep an open mind."

"Thank you, Sophie, for giving me hope. I got hope for

Christmas." And he gave me a one armed hug. "Merry Christmas, Sophie."

The first dinner party in my newly-renovated kitchen was our Christmas dinner together. The food was delicious. The wine glasses were full. Everyone was charming and we all looked good.

There was a big stack of paper towels which had been individually torn and separated on my counter. I had patiently unfurled and detached every single sheet of several rolls in order to get at the cardboard centers. I had cut them. I'd wound duct tape *inside out* onto those cardboard cylinders and covered the sticky side with waxed paper. I did all this to humiliate another woman and to make sure her Christmas was ruined.

That may be the definition of insanity.

34.
The Burning Bowl

Misty and her spiritual outings, I cannot believe that I let her talk me into another one. The last one was about how we as humans will grow to be seventeen-foot crystal beings, and the lecturer said that there is a sun in the center of our galaxy.

"I can't believe I'm doing this, Misty."

"You'll be very happy you came."

"Church? I'll be happy I'm in church on New Year's Eve? I'm missing the party at the Roof Top Club for this." I parked the Camry on the street in front. The lot was already crowded and we were early.

"I know you are missing the party but this ceremony will be good for you. It will be worth it."

"Now help me to understand why this is so important. They aren't going to talk about a sun in the center of the galaxy, are they? Because I'm pretty sure there is a black hole at the center of our galaxy. You didn't believe that stuff, did you?"

"That was not the point of the message. The point was the feeling, the energy in the room. Didn't it feel wonderful to be amidst all that love and super-high energy?"

"Yes, actually, it did, but the information was incorrect. I have a problem with information that is so far from reality. I mean this is reality I'm talking about."

"I think you're taking reality a little too seriously."

"Seriously? How can you not take reality seriously? This is science we're talking about."

"And isn't science constantly changing, evolving?"

"Yes, but… "

"Is a black hole a powerful source of energy like a sun?"

"Different, but yes."

"So how do you know reality isn't subjective?"

"Okay, I get your point. I don't believe it but I can't argue against it. So what is important about this ceremony?" I rolled my eyes.

"It's about closure. You write all your problems on a piece of paper and burn it ceremonially. All the people you need to forgive, all the bad habits you want to transform, all the old emotional junk that isn't serving you; you write all that down, say good-bye to it, and you drop it into the bowl and ya burn it."

"So it's about forgiveness and closure. I need to forgive myself for almost killing Letta after I completely embarrassed her and maybe ruined her life?"

"Don't stop there. Forgive Joey and Chuck and Jim and your mother and father, your siblings. Cut all the etheric and emotional cords that are holding you back. See this as setting yourself free from anything that binds you on any level."

So I did. I wrote a list of all the nagging issues that play over in my mind as I lie awake at night, Joey and Letta, for sure. I listed all the people I'd had difficulties with or that in any way I had blamed for my predicaments. Both of my parents' names were listed. I'd blamed them for what they'd done or what they failed to do. I'd blamed my brother Nick for having taken our family's fortune and not offering to share. And then I listed myself for being my own worst enemy. I continued on to Jim and both of my children for leading me to, and eventually trapping me, here. Lastly I listed the entire state of North Carolina and especially the town of Kernersville.

I was forgiving a town.

We lined up by pew to approach the fire pit in silence. I finished my paper while still in line. Misty suggested that I include the words "I cut and release all etheric cords that bind me on any level, all for my highest good." Quietly and meditatively we cued to the flame.

When it was my turn, I dropped the paper into the fire picturing myself letting go and being free of all the old grudges and regrets, the anger and the need for revenge. It wasn't pivotal. It was a moment just like any other moment. I may have felt a little freer. It's hard to say. We returned to our seats and were asked to write what we want for ourselves in the coming year. I wasn't prepared to do this. I don't really know what I want. I don't even know what I want in a man.

"Misty," I asked. "How do I know what to ask for?"

"Well, what do you want?"

"Besides plastic surgery?"

She gave me the homey accepting smile that I love. "Maybe you should just set an intention for health and guidance on your path for 2013."

I wondered why such a wise loving woman is a friend to me. I'm so crazy and flawed. How incredibly lucky am I to have this person who favors me with her love? I had been to other spiritual adventures with her, some helpful and interesting, others highly questionable. Why had I agreed to come here tonight? But the answer didn't matter. I was, as she predicted, just happy that I came.

I gazed around the sanctuary. Ornate lanterns hung from a cracked ceiling. Light fixtures were old but still beautiful, and now dimmed as if out of reverence for the flame. This was a Phoenix night for fire and rebirth, intensities calmed by peace, shadows and doubt replaced with illumination. This was a night for small flames, for the myriad of flickers that together form One Great Light of benevolence and love.

I felt soothed, peaceful as I regarded other smiling faces like mine who also seemed calmed, comforted and, if not entirely relieved of their burdens, at least they were filled with hope.

And then …. I felt a rush, the rush entered and swelled within me, a warm loving stream flowing through my body, calming and exciting, centering yet scattering, bringing peace and an emotive love to my heart. Sweet tears burst from my eyes, tears of joy and … gratitude; I was filled with love and joy and bliss as if my little spark contained the entire sun, like an ocean had filled my cup, like every single one of my cells contained the entire universe.

That is why I came here tonight, so that I could receive this experience of Grace. It was both miraculous and ordinary, this most beautiful gift of ecstasy and tears traced down my face.

Misty recognized the experience. She held my hand tightly as we left the church that night loving the whole world and everybody in it.

"I'm so lucky to have you."

"We're lucky to have each other. I don't know how I'd have made it through my divorce without you, Sophie."

"You're kidding. You are always there to save me."

"Seems like," she chuckled. "Learn anything new about yourself tonight?"

"Yes."

"You want to share?"

"Feels kind of stupid; I listed the town of Kernersville as one of the things I needed to forgive."

"That's so funny. I did too."

"Did you really?"

"Well, let's face it Sophie, Kernersville hasn't exactly been kind to either of us."

"I'm surprised to hear you say that."

"Well, we create our experiences. I still hold to that. I expected that I'd see a ton of subjugated women and spousal abuse in my practice and what did I get? Jet increased his drinking and started smacking me around. What did you expect to find here?"

"I expected happily ever after."

"Right, you're going to tell me you didn't have any preconceived ideas of the kind of people you would meet here. You came here with a completely open mind."

"No, I had the regular stereotypical regional expectations: Andy Griffith, Dukes of Hazard and Petticoat Junction. It wasn't as funny when Daisy Duke and the Hooterville girls were after my husband. I didn't like most of the people I met when I first moved here. I expected to find closed minds and ignorance but I eventually found kind people and intelligent people like Stella and Sally."

"That's the thing; you see exactly what you choose to look at." She was quiet a minute as I parked in her driveway. "You know, Soph? There's no doubt about it. Jim and Jet sucked, but did you ever think of this? If it weren't for them we would never have met."

"And in the town of Kernersville, go figure."

It had been an eventful holiday season. Hell, the whole year had been wildly momentous. I thought about Letta some. What was it that she had done to me to make me so angry? She'd made a few crass remarks, had given me some dirty looks and had fallen for Jim-shit. She hadn't mass murdered or invaded defenseless principalities in Eastern Europe. She was just easy to hate.

Hate was the only four-letter word that I didn't allow to be said in our home. I didn't exactly encourage my children to swear, but I did explain that there was a time and a place for the bad language which they occasionally heard in our home. We saw the movie

Titanic together, and I used it as an example. "When you are chained to a drain pipe and the ship is sinking, it is perfectly appropriate to say the word "shit"," I told them. "Oh, *poopie* just won't do. But hate," I told them, "was the worst word of all. It was never appropriate to use it." Yet our home was rife with it. I'd hated their father, hated him till it made me sick.

When we moved here from South Florida it felt like a breath of heaven for my family. The air was clean and crisp in the late fall and the land reminded me of the rolling hills and farmlands of Massachusetts. Here we could provide the kids with a large yard and a gentle change of seasons. There was ahead the promise of snowmen and family evenings by a warm fire with a warm mug of cider. When I saw Kernersville, I loved it and I wanted this life for my family. But I didn't get that happily ever after and it was too late to claim my old life back. I felt chained to a picket fence in a stinking marriage. After my first year here, I was so culture shocked, so spurned and unaccepted, so completely traumatized by Jim's behavior that I could have easily lobotomized myself with a fire ax. "Shit" wasn't a word strong enough for the peril I had faced.

And to admit that I felt resentment towards my children, that was excruciating. They weren't to blame for the choices I'd made. Misty explained that it's fairly common for mothers to resent their kids but that hardly any mother admits it. "We give up so much of ourselves and it all seems worthwhile because you want the perfect life for them," she said. "They mistreat you in their teens, cost you a fortune in college, then leave home and hardly ever call." In my case I'd stayed with a man who I hated in order for them to have two parents that might possibly drink cider.

Willingly I'd left the dynamic mix of people from everywhere and the five-star restaurants of Florida. Readily gave up my career and the security of my own paycheck. I left what was a bigger life to follow Jim, trying to do what was best for the family. That choice led me to this small life and a huge chunk of savings recently exited my account in order to save the family home which those children, now grown, might only visit once a year.

And it all came down to one huge-small point. I didn't have the amount of love that I wanted in my life; according to the *Book of Misty*, I had to take responsibility for creating this.

35.
Get Back, Loretta

The screeching train streamed past her window. She'd slept in this room for most of her life. This was where she'd hid from angry parents, the bickering of older siblings and the relentless crying of the newborn who replaced her as youngest. They'd sat on this bed when he told her he was leaving. She begged him to take her with him but even the visits he promised never followed. She prayed long and hard that Daddy would return someday. He didn't.

Each night, as a child, when she heard that train she thought it would skip the track, plow into the house and smash it with everyone and everything in it crushed dead.

Maybe that would have been a blessing, she thought. It would have saved her from the many disappointments of her miserable life. Death would have prevented her from the shame of having to marry Orvis Steele because of a swelling belly. People had talked and her new husband had listened. A train wreck would have saved her from the mortification she felt when he asked her if the child was really his. Orvis brought her back to this house then reenlisted in the Army; he'd chosen another tour in Viet Nam over a life with her. This was where she'd miscarried and cried… here alone in the dark.

Damn that Sophie Chase, that evil witch. I bet she's laughing about it, laughing at me with her damned Yankee friends right now. I hate her. I hate her so much. She wrung the coverlet. *I'd like to do something to embarrass her, wreck her life for a change. What if I snuck up behind her with a pair of scissors and cut a big thick chunk out of her hair? She wouldn't be laughing then. Or dumped a pitcher of margaritas over her head; I might could do that. People would be laughing at her for a change.* She twisted the coverlet and held it against her knotted stomach.

"Letta?"

"Yes, Momma, I'm coming."

"I spilled."

"Oh, Momma." She hurried to her side. "You wet again." She filled up the basin, undressed her and cleaned the woman with soap and warm water.

"I'm cold, Loretta."

"I know, Momma. Wrap yourself with the throw — no, that's wet too. She ran to the linen chest, got dry sheets and another blanket. "Now let's get you in a clean nightie." She placed an adult diaper and dressed her in a warm flannel gown and socks. She eased her mother into the recliner and covered the frail body with a heavy quilt. Then she wiped the mattress cover and changed the bed ... again.

The soiled laundry she brought to the washing machine on the back porch and started another load. The air was cold and damp so she quickly returned to the warmth inside. *Is this the only life I will ever know?* She wondered as the wind howled pitilessly outside the door.

Her mother dozed comfortably. Letta grabbed her jacket and walked out the front door to the night and this neighborhood of small houses. An old bare myrtle tree lashed in the wind as the hopelessness of her predicament set in yet again. *Allen was my last hope of happiness.* She checked her pocket for a tissue and wiped her eye. *Maybe I could move to another place where nobody knows me, a place where I could have a fresh start.* But she knew that she could never leave until her mother passed. A twinge of guilt — *had she just wished her own mother dead?*

Born, raised and trapped in Kernersville for the rest of her life. She shrank at the sound of snarling cats and quickened her gait, holding her hood with reddened knuckles against freezing rain that pelted her face. It was cold and miserable but she was accustomed to that feeling so she walked on.

The whistle blew, another train was coming. She waited on the side of the tracks. *I could do it, just walk in front of it.* To end it all would be so tempting but Letta had been sitting in the same church every Sunday listening to the same message for the last fifty-seven years, knowing that the glory and kingdom of heaven was before her and to beat Sophie Chase to hell would be the final disgrace. Despondent and alone, she watched the train pass by as she had done hundreds of time before.

She found herself in front of Tommy Schull's and knocked on his door. "Hey, Tommy," she said when he answered, "it's really cold out here. You want to warm me up?"

36.
Wired

Bren and I met for lunch at that coffee and internet place, *Wired*. I expected her to pressure me to spy on Annie and the Mount. I had a tactic readily in place. It was to stall her. I don't know how Bren manages to talk me into these things. Maybe I have an excitement addiction problem too.

She arrived a few minutes late wearing total black leather head to toe. It was fabulous. "Where did you get those pants? They are great!"

"I know. I bought them for myself for Christmas. They were hugely expensive but I had to have them. Maybe I need to buy a Harley."

"Well, a gal does need to accessorize. I think a blue one would look excellent."

"Wouldn't it? Hey, let's get our coffees to go and drink them in the park."

"Well, it's a beautiful day. I think that would be lovely."

"We may as well take advantage of this nice weather. There's an ice storm coming." And we talked about the weather with the barista until our order was ready.

We should have walked to Harmon Park but lazily we chose to sit in the courtyard. It was sunny and easy.

Bren carefully wiped the chair before she sat. "So how are you doing there on your street with all those neighbors of yours?"

"You mean, have I seen Joey?"

"No, I want to know about Linda and Betty Lou. Of course, I want to know — have you seen Joey?"

"He brought me flowers on Christmas morning."

"And?"

"I forgave him."

"You what? Sophie… "

"Hang on. I'm doing exactly like you said: waiting for the wife — Viviane is her name — and I am not sleeping with him."

"Okay, if you're sure."

"He's hard to miss. I'd notice if I were."

"So you're sort of free now, got some extra time on your hands?"

"And you want me to help you spy on them."

"Well, you said after the holidays."

"No, *you* said after the holidays."

"The holidays are over."

"Not officially."

"What do you mean *not officially*?"

"The holidays aren't officially over until after Epiphany."

"When is Epiphany?"

"I'm not sure. I'll ask Misty."

"You are stalling. I know when I'm being stalled."

"Aw, Bren, my heart's not in this."

"You said you would."

"I know, I know." I had promised at a weak point. "Listen, there is something I want you to be aware of before we jump into this."

"What?"

"You know why they call him Mounty?"

"Isn't it obvious?"

"That is not the reason."

"Then why do they call him Mounty?"

"Because he really was a Mounty, he was one of the Royal Canadian Mounted Police. Misty told me."

"I didn't know that, just like Dudley Do-Right?"

"Yes, exactly like Dudley Do-Right. He's probably rescuing damsels tied to the railroad tracks right now, Bren. I'm serious. I'm telling you that this is serious business."

"All this time I've known him, and I never knew he was a cop too."

"Apparently he doesn't advertise it, but he calls himself Mounty. It's weird. But do you see that this is another problem? Mounty is an ex-police officer. You are an ex-police officer. How easy would it be to trail you or spy on your home without being spotted?"

"Not too easy."

"That's what I'm saying."

"Well, it won't hurt to just case the place."

"Okay, but if this feels dangerous in any way, I am bailing."

"You promised."

"Promises only go so far. He could be armed, and I'm not getting shot at."

"He's Canadian. He probably just has a yard full of bear traps."

"Bren! Quit it or I'm leaving."

"Okay, I agree, if it looks dangerous."

"Or feels dangerous."

"That's subjective, but okay."

"There is something else. Annie and the Mount meet on Tuesdays and Saturdays, right?"

"Right."

"What if I know someone else who has regular sleepovers on the same nights?"

"Who?"

"You got to promise not to say anything to anyone. I have no proof, no evidence that they are connected in any way."

"Who is it?"

"Miss Sally."

"Holy shit! Do you think Miss Sally is into some kink?"

"God, I hope not." My hand held my head.

"Holy shit! She and Annie are in the garden club together."

"So what are you doing? How far are you planning to go with this? Are you going to bust in on them and find, say, Annie dressed up as Elvira with Miss Sally wearing a ball gag and Mounty half-asphyxiated in a closet?"

"Wow, that's an image."

"Oh crap, don't make me laugh; the restroom is way over there. But I'm serious. Think about this."

"I'm thinking that I'm gonna bring my camera. That is a Kodak moment."

"Bren! Stop! Damn it I need to wear Depends when I'm with you." I ran across the courtyard back to the cafe.

When I returned, Bren finished her coffee contemplatively and asked. "Hey, Soph?"

"Ya?"

"What was it about Joey's technique that made him so good?"

"You promise not to say to anyone?" She nodded. "He would work my clitoris with his tongue and thumb interchangeably while he had two or three fingers in my vagina. That left his very large baby finger to… "

I paused, thinking about that flying pee orgasm. I had no idea how to describe that.

"To?"

"He would stimulate my anus with his finger, even penetrate it. My butt hole!!! Where no man has gone before!!! Honest to God, Bren, I craved his touch." I sniffed and frowned. "Bren," I mewled, "I want my orgasms back."

"Ya, ya, there, there. Sophie, you realize that you just described jail sex?"

"What do you mean 'jail sex'?"

"What he did to you was woman-on-woman sex."

"You're kidding."

"It makes sense. Joey has a gay wife. What if he specifically tried to learn and stupidly thought that he could satisfy her? I bet he has a porn collection which he has studied and memorized the techniques. Do you think you can get into his house without him knowing it and check?"

"That's breaking and entering. Are you sure you were ever a cop?"

"And you never had anal sex. Are you sure you're Greek?"

The more I thought about it the more curious I became. I knew how to get into his house, if the key was still under the stone. I knew enough about his habits to guess where he was and how long he would be away. There was no guarantee I'd find it. It might be on his computer but probably it was on DVD or VHS. Hell, it could even be on nine millimeter film for all I knew. I couldn't give a rat's ass that he *had* porn. It was which *format* the porn was on that would be the most telling, the most intriguing and most significant piece of the evidence.

It was a cold drizzling morning, and I was feeling the weather in my hip. I would have loved to linger in a hot bath but I forced myself to get up and dressed before dawn. A strong pot of coffee had just finished brewing, and the aroma filed the house. I poured myself a large earthen mug. With heat-seeking fingers I clasped it and walked into the still dark comfort of the front room. I turned the baby rocking chair around to face the window and sat furtively watching, watching the morning lighten to a barely-invisible grey.

Because the traffic annoyed him so Joey was in the habit of doing all his errands as early as possible so it wasn't very long before I viewed the tail lights of his minivan disappearing into the mist. I slipped on my parka and sneaked up to his house in a pall of hovering fog. I made a mental note to find this exact shade of invisible in an umbrella and maybe one for Bren too. No gloves, as usual, but I was fairly sure that I had been unobserved as I disappeared into Joey's backyard. The key was still under the rock and I let myself in.

Joey had a nice collection of old movies, so I went right to the video cabinet and searched the bottom shelf first. There I found a row of unlabeled DVDs in their milky, generic, plastic covers. I popped one into the player. No trailer, not even a title page, it went right into raw-wild sex scenes. The video was riddled with the glitches of unprofessional edits. I made a quick assessment of the collection. Bren was right. There was lots of porn and most of it was woman-on-woman. Some of it was old; I could easily tell that from the hairstyles. But the video tech in me saw the grainy, scratched quality of film transferred to video, probably VHS and then again to DVD. I cringed at another glitch leading to more sex on bad video. He had edited out all the old ridiculous story lines and just kept the steamy parts.

I flipped through the stack of unmarked cases. Most of them, I guessed, were transfers. But more than a few of the disks were newer and had labels; the cover packaging had been discarded, but they were fairly recent disks. I ejected the old one and replaced it with a labeled one and I was not surprised to see clean digital video as one beautiful women was doing another the same way Joey had been doing me. I had to admit that some of it seemed pretty interesting but I had no time to sit here leisurely watching girl-on-girl porn.

I was holding a handful of DVDs when the front door opened. Joey scanned the room, the opened movie cabinet, the stack of unmarked cases and me with a handful of disks. I was caught red-handed in the act of snooping but Joey appeared mortified. He shuffled his feet and started to sputter.

I took the offense. "Why didn't you tell me?"

"Tell you-what, that I-own some blue-movies?"

"I asked you how you knew my body so well. The correct answer to that question would have been, 'I've seen a little porn.' You said that you just paid attention."

"Yes, to a little-porn."

"That's another lie, Joey."

"I didn't-lie. I just didn't tell-you."

"How is that different from lying?"

"What do-you expect me to-do, wear a tee-shirt that says 'Hello, my name is Joe and I like to watch porn'? Be reasonable, Sophie. Am I-allowed to-have a secret?"

"You should have been honest about it when I asked you."

"Do you tell-me everything you-do?"

"Pretty much."

"Did-you tell me that it was-you that pasted 'Slut' and 'Whore' signs all-over the-cars at El Mejor on Sunday before Christmas? You could-a told-me that on Christmas morning when we talked about-it, but did you? You're no-angel either, Sophie."

I mentally searched for the distinction between a lie of omission and a secret? "*That* had nothing to do with us," I said. "*This* does."

"How?"

"You were doing woman-on-woman sex to me. I think I would have liked to have known that."

"Why, what-difference would that-have made?"

"You don't understand. I thought… " *Damn, did I really want to admit this to him? Shit.* "Joey, I thought… I thought that you had ruined me for all other men and that I would never find somebody else as good a lover as you."

"Oh, Sophie." His face softened, and his eyes got all velvety chocolate.

"And, now, here I find out that all I needed… was a woman."

"Sophie." He made a step towards me and opened his arms to hold me. It would have been so easy to fall into those big strong arms but I had found newer DVDs and that was the sticking point.

"Please don't. Right now I feel a little, I don't know, violated and deceived maybe. I'm not sure how I feel… confused." I did not want to ask the next question but I had to. With tears flooding my eyes, I took a few seconds and a deep breath and then I asked him, "Tell me the truth, Joey. Were you practicing on me to get ready for Viviane?"

"Sophie, no. I really care about-chou."

"I wish I could believe you, Joey; but if you lie about the small dumb things, how can I believe you about the big important things?"

"This doesn't make me-a liar."

"Maybe not, but it doesn't make you overly honest either."

"Then what does-it make me?"

I looked down at the DVDs and placed them on the end table. "I guess this makes you my prison bitch." And I walked out the door.

37.
The Ice Storm Cometh

As I have said, the winters in Kernersville are mild. We may get a few inches of snow a couple times a year. As far as I can tell, the snow plan here is "wait until it melts". The whole town shuts down until the roads are clear and that is a good thing because nobody has snow tires or much experience driving on slippery streets. Ice storms are fairly common here and everyone panics like it means imminent destruction and woe. As soon as an ice storm is in the forecast, the grocery stores are inundated with desperate shoppers in search of bread and milk.

Bread and milk, for chrissakes, bread and milk?

I needed batteries and a butane lighter because the brittle trees like black pines are prone to falling on power lines, but I also purchased an extra bottle of wine and some good hard cheese. A woman in the checkout line had a cart full of beer and nacho chips. "So you're a Northerner? Where are you from?" I asked.

"We're from Rhode Island, Providence. How did you know?"

I pointed to her cart. "Not bread and milk." I held up the bottle of wine and chunk of cheese. "We have different priorities." And we smiled and nodded.

Ice crystals whipped at the glass but we still had power. I curled up on the sofa with Chica and covered us with a soft thick comforter. I tried to read, but the book was an ineffectual diversion. My mind tossed like the branches outside in the wind.

I sipped a second cup of chamomile tea and reflected on what a year this had been. It went by so fast, like time was speeding up on us and we had only equally sped-up clocks to measure it by.

I thought about the past year, reviewed the events but I needed more than just a mental review. So I got up and found a piece of paper and a pencil and I wrote.

First I met Albert, who was possibly psychotic, and Kenny, GQ with a listening problem. Will was overly married, and then there was that footwear-impaired guy. I got torpedo-tongued and almost went out with an ex-convict. I said "yes" to Chuck, a practical fucking joker of all the freaky things.

My mother died. My house was half-destroyed, and I found a very lonely man who dressed up in an expensive suit to convince his lesbian wife to come to Kernersville to retire and grow old with him. He also has every fucking blue movie made in the last half-century edited down to just the sex acts.

And poor Letta should probably be on suicide watch because I displaced the anger I felt for Joey into hurting her.

I stopped and reread what I wrote and said out loud to Chica, "I don't think I like what I'm creating in my life. What do you think Misty would say to that?"

I started to reach for my phone but stopped. *Let me try to reason this out for myself.*

I turned the page over and wrote.

I met some interesting men, way more than I would have expected. They took me out to some lovely places and we had good conversation and I even snuck a few cuddles. Mom died. That's life and it was probably a blessing.

Not only did I pop the 'old cherry', but I also had a great passion with a super affectionate, romantic man who gave me the most pleasurable sex and best friggin' orgasms of my life.

I catapulted a contra dancer into the start of a comedic career. And ya, sure, the kitchen happened but it all got fixed up better than it was before and for the best possible price... and all just in time for Christmas dinner with all my adopted family. I'm so lucky to have such smart, wise, fun, cool friends. They have enriched my life in so many ways.

I even was able to help a passive-aggressive, patriarchal-ly indoctrinated and culturally deprived to woman channel her anger in an honest and direct way. Everything will work out for Joey. He'll go back to plan A knowing that he had a lovely romance; and I know, deep inside that there is someone out there for me. I'm healthy, educated, fit and I have reasonably good brain cells. I have a good sense of humor and... I have no electricity.

I lit the candle on the end table and used it to light the paper and kindling under the wood pile, already prepped in the fireplace. I made sure the screen was safely positioned. Then I snuggled back under the spread with Chica and I privately murmured infantile language, "Now isn't this cozy and aren't I such a good little Girl Scout? Your mama is always prepared for emergencies and your Auntie Misty would be so proud of me, yes, she would." I kissed her good night on the top of her head, curled up near a toasty warm fire; I listened to its soft crackling and enjoyed its warmth enormously.

The morning sunshine back-lit branches sheathed in a thick coat of ice, it is indeed one of the most magically stunning of all winter scenes. Smaller trees and bushes whitened and weighted, bowing to the powers of nature. I enjoyed this visual from my baby rocking chair which was again turned toward the window. I sipped my second cup of coffee. Duke Power already had us up and warming. Look at that sparkle. Look at that sky.

A tall pine had fallen into the creek overnight. It was mostly in the neighbor's yard and not my responsibility to remove. But the direction of the havocked stream flowed over the lower section of my yard. By nightfall it would be a solid sheet of ice.

I spotted the paper on which I had written the year's review. I quickly read over one version and then the other. Wow, I think I did something like that positive aspect thing Misty told me about. That's incredible. Both sides tell the true story. They are just different sides to the same page.

January temperatures plummeted. Since Bren is not particularly fond of the cold, I was able to easily put her off Annie's trail for a few more weeks.

When I could delay her no longer, we set out in the Camry (because it was much less obvious than Big Red), and we headed down Route 66. Mounty's address was not so easy to find. By the street numbers the place didn't seem to exist until we caught the dirt road on the left covered with bare winter vine, something like the secret entrance to the Bat Cave.

"Go up this road, ya think?"

"We don't even know if they meet here." I turned onto the road but didn't get far. There was a gate with a "no trespassing" sign. "Well, if we continue we could get into some trouble, never mind if Mounty catches us snooping here in broad daylight," I added.

"We might have to traipse through all this brush."

"Nope."

"Why not?"

"*You* walk through all this brush. These woods are probably full of poison ivy. I'm not doing it. That is clearly dangerous. Imagine these woods at night. Bren, be serious."

"We could wait up there at the bend on Tuesday night and see, at least, if the people are coming in or going out. That would be easy. "

"Tuesday is contra night."

"Both of their nights are contra nights. You can't play the contra card. It gets dark early and you can bring your dance clothes with you. We'll just sit here and watch for a while." She pulled a map up on her tablet to find out what was behind the property. The map guided us to an old tobacco field on high ground, high enough to see into Mounty's back yard.

A scrim of bare trees could hardly obscure the play area, but his pergola and privacy fencing partially succeeded. From what we could see this place looked like a party waiting for spring. Even at this distance we could see how cool it was. I popped the trunk to get my binoculars. Bren brought a pair also and we peered at a multi-leveled deck descending toward an oval-shaped pool. We guessed there was a hot tub behind the privacy fence and we spied a full outdoor kitchen under the covered porch and a tiki bar. Even in the cold of winter you could imagine entertaining in that backyard.

"That will be where they meet," Bren stated.

"How can you be sure?"

"Look at the place; it's built for a party. Shit, even I want to party there. This Tuesday night we are gonna sit here and see what we can see."

"And that's because … you think they will be having an orgy in that backyard in the middle of winter?"

"Hot tub! Warm in the winter and see those big windows. We'll be able to see into them when the lights are on." *You keep thinking, Butch. It's what you're good at.*

Tuesday I brought a skirt, and we drove to the top of that hill to watch the rear of Mounty's party palace. There was one light from a shaded window in the back of the house. We spent hours just watching that dim light and then it went out. We didn't see an orgy. We didn't see a party, not a person. We didn't even see a car drive to or from the property. No one was there and the light was probably on a timer.

"Could we go? I'm going to be late for the dance." She started the car.

"So we go again on Saturday night?"

"Saturday I have to travel for contra. It will have to be next Tuesday."

"That will take us into February."

"Ya, February. I don't want to do this in February."

"We may have to. Jaysus, it seems like February was just last week. How can it be February again?"

"Bellamy will need us."

"She has Sammy."

"We'll play it by ear." And we shook hands on that. Ha, I had negotiated skillfully. I could play the 'Bellamy's grief card' for the next four weeks. Hit the easy button.

38.
Belle Amie

"I don't know, Misty. I can't get past this. It's too much, too much hurt and too much pain. I'm not even living my life, like you said. It's like I don't know how to live it anymore."

"I don't think I said that. You *are* living life, but you could be getting so much more out of it if you let go of the past."

"So how do I do that, let go of the past?"

"By living in the present, Bell," she repeated. "I think that when you get off all this medication, you might be able to see it all more clearly."

"I don't want to think about how awful the withdrawal will be."

"Honey, on drugs you live in a cave. It's maybe warm and comfortable in there, but it's dark and there is no chance for you to grow. By detoxing you are choosing a life under the sky where there is sunshine and light and you can see the stars above you. It will rain some of the time but it's the rain that helps you grow. Rain is what colors the earth."

"I'm so afraid." She bit her thumb, and Misty handed her the box of tissues.

"Let's set a plan and a target date."

"No, not now, I'm not ready. Can we wait for spring?"

"We can, but I want you to start cutting down now. We will save a half a pill here and a full one there so that when you are ready, you don't have to go cold turkey. I will help you and the more pills you save now the easier it will be on you later."

"And you will keep the ones that I save?"

"Oh yes. And when you are drug-free, you can quit the pain clinic for good."

"Misty, do you honestly think that I would be over Eddie's death by now if I had never taken the pills?"

"I do, but it won't be easy. Can we try for April when it's warmer, when the flowers come up and you can spend some time outside in the sunshine?"

"Okay." She wiped her eyes.

"Now do you want to talk about Sophie?"

"It's always about Sophie. Did you ever notice that? It's always the Sophie-Show, Sophie's anger, Sophie's reluctance, Sophie's dates, Sophie's orgasms. Aren't you sick of it?"

"Like you said, Sophie lives out loud."

"Well, why does she have to be so loud about it?"

"Because she is honest about who she is. Bellamy, you have been hiding all your secrets. Nobody knows about your abortion, the hysterectomy; nobody knows about the pain clinic and nobody knows about how much you resent Sammy. Honey, everyone thinks you lead a charmed life. We have known you for years, and none of us know who you really are."

"So what, do I have to divulge every little secret flaw that I have?"

"Of course not, but you are the one who said you wish you were more like Sophie. Is it that you wish that you could be more honest about who you are?"

"I don't know. Maybe I don't even know who the real me is anymore."

"You are a beautiful soul who has friends that love you, and right now they all think you haven't got a care in the world."

"Maybe they won't like me so much when they find out how broken I am."

"Maybe, Bell, just maybe, they will love you even more."

39.
February Again

Candy had a new man in her life but we talked often. She said that she saw Chuck at a dance in Concord. She heard that he was going to be home in mid-February so I should not be surprised to see him at a few of the dances. There was one in Carrboro on the Friday before Valentine's Day. It was going to be a great dance with a fabulous band. Life wasn't too complicated at the moment and it's a big enough dance that I don't even have to see him. I could skip lines all night and he might not even notice me. Contra is a good stress reliever and exercise. And besides, going dancing will keep me from cavorting with Bren.

I drove to Carrboro with Barbara and her daughter, Allie, who sat in the back texting and playing games on her smart phone during the ride.

"You heard that Chuck Loughlin is going to be here tonight?"

"Is he?" I hoped I sounded uninterested.

"It was on his Facebook page. Aren't you two Facebook friends?"

"No."

"You'd have to be pretty good friends to punk him like that. So what was that male stripper joke about, anyway?"

"Oh that? That was Sam and Candy's joke. I just helped a little."

"You know, you and Chuck would make a nice couple. Would you ever consider dating him?"

"We went out for drinks once or twice. He's okay. I don't know. He's probably busy traveling around now. I bet he has a ton of ladies after him."

"I don't think so. As long as I have known Chuck, he has always been very particular about whom he dates. He's cute and a lot of women try, even younger ones, but he's definitely not a man whore." If she only knew how right she was. "What if I asked him discretely, you know, if he'd be interested?"

"No, Barb, don't do that."

"But he's the best guy. He's so talented and full of life. Both of you are funny, both artistic and I think you would be good match. Sophie, he is a really nice man and he deserves to have someone like you in his life, someone to come home to. He's cute. Don't you think he's cute?"

"Ya, he's cute, alright."

"I'm going to tell him. Can I tell him you think he's cute?"

"Are we in high school, Barbara? Stop it."

"Mom, stop it. Leave her alone." Allie showed her annoyance. "Old people are gross."

I managed to avoid Chuck for most of the first set but he waited for me outside of the ladies' room during the break.

"Dance with me?" He offered his hand.

"Sure." *Asshole.*

"I talked to Barbara."

"Ya, so?"

"Barbara says you think I'm cute. Do you think I'm cute, Sophie?"

"You're fuckin' adorable, Chuck." *I'll kill Barbara.*

The dance started and Chuck turned into the charming dancer that I had originally been attracted to. He was, actually, fuckin' adorable. I was trying hard *not* to enjoy dancing with him.

"We got off on the wrong foot, Sophie. Do you think we can be friends?" he asked as we balanced and swung, and I went off to allemande my neighbor.

"Sure, Chuck, BFFs." I maintained a serious demeanor.

"You know you like me." We gypsied and swung.

"I'd like you… in the dumpster behind Arby's."

"Let me make it up to you," he said when the dance was over. "Let me take you out to the Birchwood for Valentine's dinner. We'll sit by the fire and drink good whiskey."

"Ya, sure, I'll meet you there at seven."

"Let me pick you up."

"No, I'll meet you there."

"Okay, at seven."

"Seven." But I expected that he would stand me up. I was certainly planning to stand *him* up, and I knew that he knew that neither of us would be at the Birchwood. Valentine's Day was on a Tuesday and Tuesday was a contra night. We'd both be dancing.

Bren's family had a Valentine's gathering to make a point of loving one another. I thought it was a wonderful idea, a great way to celebrate this holiday, and it also freed me from having to spend hours in a parked car on an old curvy road in the woods.

I pulled into the dance hall parking lot and Chuck's Jeep pulled in right next to the Camry. What were the chances of that happening? I gathered my dance shoes and water bottle and pretended that I didn't see him.

"You stood me up," he said as he opened my car door.

"You stood me up."

"I waited for you."

"You did not."

"I did."

"At the Birchwood?"

"No, at the bottom of your street."

"Did not."

"You passed me at 7:38, and you stopped for gas at the BP on the corner where Route 66 turns right."

"You followed me as in, like, *stalking*?"

"It was that easy." He snapped his fingers. His mouth curved into his impish grin.

I walked away and he followed. "Sophie, listen to me. My pride was hurt and it was a bad joke and I'm sorry. I like you and I want to see you."

"It was an insult. Why would I want to see you after you insulted me like that?"

"Because I'm such a good kisser." That stopped me in my tracks. He smiled and took a step closer to me like I was going to make out with him right in front of the contra hall.

"That's not how I remember it." I backed him up with a finger to the chest.

"Well, you looked so beautiful on that first date with your hair blowing in the wind like that."

"Huh?"

"I was drooling, Sophie." He couldn't even say that without laughing. "I was drooling. Let me just refresh your memory a little."

Grey eyes glinted with suggestion.

"Nothing wrong with my memory, old man." Damn, he was cute.

"What would it take for you to date me again?"

"Bag of tie wraps and a ball peen hammer."

He half-grinned. "Funny. First dance?"

"Ya, sure." And get it over with. We walked into the hall together which made Barbara especially happy.

We waltzed at the break. He told me that his comedy troupe would leave for Florida on Sunday and how happy he felt to be headed towards warmer weather. They had been on an East Coast tour. He said he played at an open mic in Boston, describing my city as "cold as shit".

"So, Friday night I would like to really take you out for dinner. You pick the place, and I will pick you up in the Jeep; we could maybe start again from the beginning, a clean slate?"

It was too tempting. "Fine, Friday night, just dinner. "

"What time?"

He came to my door looking all … Irish, wearing a tweed jacket and he carried a small bouquet tied with a cloth ribbon. I think they were leftovers from old Valentine bouquets. Maybe he had purchased one for me last Tuesday. I imagined him picking through the flowers, saving the best, trimming and cutting the stems to make them look fresher, then wrapping them as a creation of his own. It was romantic and all the more endearing to me. Bell would have called him cheap.

I ordered pecan-encrusted scallops on his suggestion, and we split a bottle of white. He said that he grew up in New Hampshire up in the White Mountains. I knew the area well. When the city got too hot we'd travel north in caravans, carloads of freaks invading the Indian Head, taking acid and running around the trails at the Flume and the Basin. We took pretty frequent ski weekends at Loon Mountain in the winter too. Chuck had worked at Loon. He'd manned the gondola. Maybe he had helped me into the lift at one time or held my skis. We were around the same age so while he cut firewood for extra cash in the summer, I ran around the streets of Boston, listened to unbelievably good band-bands at The Tea Party, at Boston Garden or at the Orpheum. In those days you could smoke a joint almost anywhere in the City but we'd had to hide it up there in the woods of the White Mountains. We were from very different childhoods but both of us were New Englanders and both artisans. That's a fair amount to have in common.

Chuck had dreams. His life was full of opportunity and possibility. At our age, dreams like his are a luxury. He dared to believe he had a future in show business and what kind of fame and success it could hold for him. Life on the road was tough but he was having more fun than at any other time in his life. That was nice to hear, a man my age who looked forward to what was to come. He was what I wanted to be, the outlier.

"I have a present for you, Chuck."

"A Valentine's present for me?" He smiled like a little kid.

I gave him a package, plainly wrapped. "You should have this. It's the video from the night you sang with *Contra Crossing.*"

"It was you who did that?"

"You didn't know?"

"Lenny said he was hired by some pharmaceutical guy. I assumed it was Jeremy Sanders. He's the only one I know in pharmaceuticals."

"Sammy is in pharm. He is a friend of a friend."

"Sophie, that must have cost a bundle." He studied my face and nodded. "You must like me a lot."

"Sammy put it on his expense account. You know how strippers and big pharm go together. It didn't cost me one nickel."

"You want me bad."

"I want you … headfirst in a Boston snowbank."

"Hello, Sophie, fancy meeting you here." She extended her hand to Chuck. "Hi, I'm Bren Sykes and this here is Bellamy Hays."

"Bren, Bellamy, pull up a chair." There was no use in fighting it. If they wanted to meet Chuck it was going to happen. Hell, I'd invite their commentary.

"What a coincidence," I said sarcastically. "Chuck, these are two of my closest friends. I'm guessing that they made a special trip just to meet you." I narrowed my eyes at them.

"Ladies, can I buy you a drink?" he asked.

"Thank you, Chuck." Bren-Flirt Smile. "I'd love a martini."

"Vodka cranberry," Bell said. "It's so nice to meet you."

40.

More Mejor

"Don't you dare steal my guy, either of you. Keep your hands off him!" I pointed fiercely.

"Oh, for chrissakes, nobody is stealing Chuck." Bren's fist was on her hip. "So let me get this straight. Last February you had zero prospects, and now you have this very cute Irish guy and an old horny Italian both wanting to date you." She was nodding.

"So what did you think of him?"

"I thought he was very nice, nice-looking, and good conversationalist," Bell began.

"I think he's a dragonfly."

"A dragonfly? Why do you think he's a dragonfly?"

"They transform from one life to another, change their path of flight easily. They have two pairs of wings and everywhere they go they bring sparkle."

"He's a dragonfly." I pondered.

"So what do you want to do with these choices?" Misty asked.

"Chuck would be away a lot, spreading his double wings, I guess. I doubt that I could expect that a relationship with him would be exclusive."

"So neither do you have to be monogamous. You could be having dolphin sex when he's traveling," Bren stated.

"Dolphin sex?" Bellamy asked.

"Yes, dolphins have multiple partners and the sex act is more of a social affair to them, more like play," I explained.

"And you are going to get very social with whom?" Annie asked.

"I'm still deciding. I'll see Chuck when he is home from touring. Joey is still an option."

"You are becoming such a slut!" Bren nudged me with her knee.

"Feels weird, it was weird enough just with Joey."

"So what? It's your life, Sophie. You're not hurting anyone," said Little Annie. "So will this satisfy your kink quota, and you can leave me and Mounty alone?" she asked.

"I have no idea what she is talking about, do you?" Bren turned to me.

"You both know what I'm talking about. Don't waste your time because you'll never find us," A corner of Annie's mouth turned up.

"Don't goad them, Annie. It will only make them more determined," Misty said.

Bren ignored the comments. "So Chuck left this morning for points south with his troupe?"

"Yup."

"What are they calling themselves?" Misty asked.

"Rude Remedy."

"Cute name, how did they come up with that?"

"It has to do with something Lenny Bruce said, that if people weren't sick, there would be no need for him. He'll be back for a week in the spring. It would definitely be a part-time love. But that sounds appealing and free, something fun to look forward to."

I dropped Bren at her front door. We hadn't exactly been arguing, but I had a different perspective on Annie's situation now. I pushed the case for letting her and Mounty alone. She countered using the P word on me.

"You *promised*," she narrowed her eyes and pointed a weighty finger.

"You," I pointed back, "have voyeuristic tendencies. Maybe you need to see Misty professionally."

But since I *had* promised, the following Tuesday evening, I dressed in a contra skirt and assumed we would be warm enough in the car. "I'm freezing, Bren! Don't you have any heat in this car?"

"It doesn't seem to be working. I may have to take it in to the shop."

"Do you have a blanket or anything?"

"No, why would I have a blanket?"

"In case your heater stops working. I can't believe you are taking us on a stakeout in this big red vehicle."

"What's wrong with taking Big Red?"

"It's fuckin' big and … *red*."

"Oh, quit whining."

"Pull over into that discount store. Maybe I can get some heavy socks and an inexpensive throw or something."

"Well, why are you wearing a skirt on a stakeout? Haven't you heard of plan Z?" But she pulled into the parking lot anyway.

"Oh, shut up."

"It isn't usually this crowded. There are no parking spaces."

"Check to see if there is a parking spot on the side," I suggested, and she pulled around to the side lot and parked.

"You coming in with me or do you want to wait in the car?"

"Well, I shouldn't." But she got out anyway and walked towards the store front. She stopped for a minute to straighten her jacket and began to feel for something in her pocket. She turned towards me and said, "I want to know what the… "

I felt it immediately, it was the vibe. Bren backed up a step. She felt it too. From the night's shadows a man appeared with a long and menacing knife. I tried to appear frightened and vulnerable (I *was* frightened and vulnerable). I began to assess the situation. His lower body was slender but it was difficult to gauge his upper body size. I guessed he was slight and that he used his oversized hoodie to disguise that. *Look stupid, Sophie, look really stupid and scared.* His face was shaded by his hood but his body language communicated a combination of confidence, desperation and a touch of lunacy.

I knew Bren would have already checked the periphery. It had become clear to both of us that he had us backed against the row of cars parked too close to the building. If we retreated we'd most likely be cornered, probably trapped and stabbed. He had picked this spot carefully to his advantage and we were well out of plain view. *There is always a way out, find it.* The knife's reflection glinted from the streetlight behind him and we both guessed that he had some skill with a blade. "Give me your wallets, both of you."

"Come on, son. You don't want to do this," Bren started.

"I'm not your son. I'll take those earrings and that ring too." He pointed at Bren's hand.

"This ring?" She scrutinized her hand. "This ring right here?" Deliberately, she filled her right fist with her car keys and she made damn sure that he saw her do it. *That's the only way out. We have to fight our way out.* "Oh you ain't getting *this* ring." Bren took a step

223

forward making a show of the overstuffed fist, bulging with metal and expanded by that large boulder of a gold ring. Bren showed not one drop of fear or hesitation. She had his full attention ... but I was the one who had the clear shot.

Only *one* chance, that's all I'd get... one. I said a prayer and went for it; I shuffled in and snapped a right hammer fist to the center of his face, bam. I heard a sickening crunch. His shocked head tilted back and his hands instinctively went to his face. I stepped low and to the left to land a right forward kick. Bam, I got him cleanly in the beets. He bent over cupping his junk with one hand and twisted his body in unexpected pain. He shouldn't have done that. It exposed his back. I cupped my right fist with my left hand and used both arms like a battering ram. With all my body weight behind me I jammed my right elbow to that kid's kidney. He fell forward onto the pavement with a groan.

Bren stepped on his wrist, disarmed him and then she tied his hands behind his back with the strap from her purse. She pressed her knee between his shoulder blades while I dug my cell phone out and called 911.

Whoa, that felt good. A right hammer, a right kick and an elbow to the kidney. I just beat the piss out of a robber and I wasn't even out of breath. I was filled with adrenaline. Six seconds and it was over. He was toasted, tethered and down, *damn*. Super-Sophie! *Feeling good now, yeah, feeling good, and feeling strong.* I even looked around to see if there was anyone else I could punch. But the adrenaline rush soon faded and I was wasted, felt woozy and limp. *Feeling old now, feeling old, shaken and boneless.*

"I need to sit." I held onto the back end of a nearby car. Bren tossed me her keys but I missed catching them. I squatted and tried to find them so I could open the door to Big Red. The 911 operator was speaking to me, asking questions but I could barely get my words out, "South Main, we're behind the store," I managed to say, "beside the dollar place, left, left of the dollar place" I could see a sign in the distance that gave a name to our location. "Behind Hardy's."

"I bet that warmed you up," Bren chuckled. I sat cross-legged on the cold asphalt in a raspberry pink twirling skirt and no socks, while we waited for the police to arrive.

Bren described the whole scene using words like "suspect advanced" and "perp". My mind seemed to fade then sharpen and fade again. I was clearly sitting in the front seat of Big Red with a blanket around me but couldn't remember how I got there.

Bren dropped the names of a few friends she already had in the Kernersville Police. She flirted with and entertained these officers. Then, of course, she showed off the gold shield, making lifelong friends with these men.

I heard her say, "No, not me. Sophie … ah … Ms. Chase did that damage." She pointed at the boy who was now properly cuffed and faced down on the ground. "All by her-bad-assed-self, you should have seen it!"

A news photographer was on the scene snapping pictures. An officer helped me to stand and he began to ask questions like my name, address and more inquiries pertaining to the attempted robbery. My brain scrambled and it was an effort to form simple words. Then he asked me where I learned to fight and my mind sharply cleared. "I do the senior's kick box class with Rita Jones at the Kernersville YMCA," I said.

They helped the young man into the back seat of the cruiser as Bren yelled, "You be sure to tell all your friends that you were beat up by an old white woman!" And they drove the suspect away.

"I need whiskey." Instead they made me go to the police station to fill out paperwork. It took a very long time and all I got was a Diet Coke.

"Have you seen the morning paper?" Bren asked. She, Bell and Annie walked in through my kitchen door and slapped it on the granite. Front page of the Kernersville News said, "Senior Thwarts Robbery." Below that was a picture of me, an ugly *newspaper* picture of me and I looked fat.

"Oh no," I sank onto the stool.

"Sophie, you're a hero!" Annie beamed.

"And here's the *Winston-Salem Journal,* and Greensboro has the story on page two."

"How embarrassing." Tears clouded my eyes.

"What's wrong with you? I expected that you would be elated," Bellamy said.

"Bren and I could have been killed. We could have been killed, Bren."

"No problem, Baby, we're a team." She came forward and hugged me. Bellamy surrounded us both with her long lovely arms, and then we tucked Little Annie into the fold.

"I'm getting to be such a cry baby."

"Don't cry, Baby. We're all safe."

What kind of desperation sent that boy to that parking lot armed with a knife? What about his mother? For God's sake, *what about his mother*? I could see his face in my mind and I imagined what it would be like for him in jail if the other inmates ... I mean *when* the other inmates found out that I beat him up. This story was in three newspapers. What was going to happen to him now?

I took a few moments to live in gratitude. I thought about my grown children who were safe and fed and warm and employed. Misty texted me. "Drink lots of water today and take your vitamins." I did.

She came to my house after work with ashes on her forehead.

"Misty, you get religion at the strangest times."

"You think Ash Wednesday is a strange time for church? You're from Boston; wasn't it compulsory? I was near Holy Cross, and I lit a candle and said a prayer for the young man."

"Thank you for doing that. Bren thinks I'm nuts for worrying about him but he was so desperate. Misty, I beat the crap out of him."

"You acted on instinct. You have nothing to feel remorseful about."

"I could have just as easily given him my wallet. I keep remembering words that I heard long ago, that it's worse to have to steal than to be stolen from. I think there is some truth to that."

"Maybe, you never know. It could also turn out to be the best thing for that boy. Maybe what you did last night saved his life or redirected it toward a better destination. It certainly lent him some humility. Maybe it could lead to something completely different. Maybe he could make it work for him. 'Yes, I'm the man who was beat up by an old lady,' and he could go on Oprah then on to fame and success and have his own talk show. It's all up to him."

"Yes, Misty, you could spin it that way. But what is the reality for that young man?"

"You don't know. It's not your job to know."

"So how did I attract that into my life? Why did I attract it?"

"The question is only this: what do you choose to think about right now?"

"Right now I want to understand why and *how* I attracted this to me."

"Okay, let's brainstorm it. What were you thinking when it happened?"

"I was kind of pissed at Bren. I never really wanted to do this."

"Do what?"

"You know, spy on Annie and Mounty. Well, I did promise that I would help her but I didn't think it was right, and she was holding me to my promise. You'd think that at our age we'd be more grown up."

"Well, can you think of a more brilliant plan to prevent that from happening than what you did? You thwarted Bren's spy mission by thwarting a robbery."

"No sah."

"And I vaguely recall a period of your life that was somewhat dominated by anger towards men. Remember that? And you were ready to kill Letta Steele! Did you get to release some of that residual anger on an actual person? And right now you have some interesting romantic possibilities in your life. Could there be a little fear mixed in of the … unknown?"

"Hmmph. You are such a know-it-all."

"I know." She got up and stretched. "Nobody sets out on a Tuesday night and wants to get robbed. It is what you are doing and thinking and feeling leading up to the event that affects the event. You were feeling anger and fear, resentment toward Bren. What do you expect to manifest from anger and fear, Tootsie Pops?"

"Hmmm. So what do I do now?"

"Go forth and sin no more."

"Huh?"

"Only kidding. Forgive yourself and think about happy things. Hey, maybe that's the same thing!"

"Really?"

"Really. I have an idea. Do you have any sticky notes?"

"Ya, sure." I pulled open a drawer. "Yellow or pink?"

"Both. Put them everywhere. All over the house, in your car, put them in your wallet, your pockets. Every time you see a pink one think of a loving thought and keep it going for as long as you can. When you see a yellow one, think a happy thought and then keep that one going. It can be a memory, a fantasy, anything. Now do this for one week and see what you manifest. I bet it won't be a robbery."

"I have these silly blue star-shaped ones too. Can I think of something funny when I see those?"

"Whatever you choose, Sophie. You want to go out to eat?"

"You gonna wash your forehead?" She tittered a little. "I have soup. Let me warm up some soup."

Everywhere I went someone asked me to describe the fight. It was a lucky punch, *a very lucky punch*, and it could just as easily gone very wrong but people were calling me Rocky, for chrissake. The sticky notes saved me. I'd feel a sticky in my pocket. If it was pink one I would remember the feeling of holding my babies or imagine what it will be like to hold my first grandchild. I'd spot a yellow sticky and I'd remember shushing down the ski slopes at Loon or I'd think up a perfect fairy tale life for the next child I'd see. The blue stars were fun. I'd think of old Buddy Hackett routines or Monty Python silly walks. All in all, this was very pleasant experiment, thinking just about stuff that makes me happy.

I walked into McDonalds to get a senior coffee and who did I see inside? It was Hook. He was having a senior coffee. I sat across from him.

"Hi Sophie."

"Hey, the last time I saw you my friend was kind of rude. I want to apologize for her."

"No big deal, I'm used to it."

"How do you ever get used to everyone being nasty to you?"

"You're right. It's not that easy," he searched into his cup. "I don't want to sound like I'm bitter or anything ... but I am a little bitter. I got a rotten deal handed to me and I gotta live with it."

"So, ah ... I don't know how to ask you this but... "

"You want to know what I did."

"I was going to ask you why you picked Kernersville to live in but ya, I really want to know what you did."

"Well, it's a matter of public record. I guess I should thank you for having the balls to just plain out ask me. The public only tells you what I was convicted of."

"What… were you convicted of?"

"Rape."

"Rape?" I had been hoping that it was something less serious than rape.

"I told you the truth. Now if I ask you some questions will you tell me the truth?"

"I will."

"How old were you when you first had sex?"

"I was fifteen."

"Was it your choice?"

"Yes."

"Nobody forced you or talked you into doing something you didn't want to do?"

"No. I was curious and wanted to know what it was like."

"Did you feel competent to make that choice at fifteen?"

"I suppose I did."

Hook nodded. Again he searched for answers in his coffee cup. "Tell me."

"My family owned a parking garage in Philly. It was next to a private girl's school. We had a contract with the school so most of them parked their cars there. I saw these girls every day. Wishes, that's what they used to call me, short for Aloysius." He took a sip, remembering better days before the incident. "They are all beautiful at that age and in the afternoon, on their way out of school I would see them roll up the waist bands of their skirts. You probably did that too after high school got out for the day."

"I did. Most of us did. It was the sixties and miniskirts were in style but the school didn't allow them."

"Well there was this one girl, Sarah Adelheid. I would see her roll her skirt up and she'd smile at me. Sometime she would stop and talk. She was funny and smart and very flirty. Sometimes it was just a smile as she walked by to get her car, a powder blue Fiat

229

Spider convertible, the exact color of her eyes. By the time she would get to the booth she would have unbuttoned her blouse and tied her shirt tail around her midriff. My God, she was so beautiful. On warm sunny days she'd stop and ask me to help her put the roof down. She would drive off with the wind in her sandy hair. I was so in love with that girl. She was all I could think about. Those eyes, those legs, those beautiful breasts, I would have done anything for her.

"So one day, after school she walked up to her car then came back to the booth and told me that the Spider wouldn't start. I didn't know much about cars but I was sure willing to try. I followed her up the ramp watching her cute little ass in that skirt swinging back and forth. When we got to the car... well I just couldn't help myself."

"So you raped her?"

"Believe me; this girl knew what she was doing. There was no forcing. She was eager. So we were fucking in this tiny Fiat, I don't even know how I fit in it. Anyway, I forgot about the booth. The girls were lined up to leave and there was nobody there to punch their ticket and before you knew it we were caught."

"She was underage?"

"Seventeen, and there were eight witnesses."

"Holy crap!"

"She swore that it was consensual but I served seven years in jail for statutory rape."

"I'm so sorry."

"After I got out I tried to get my life together. I moved around a lot but being in jail does nothing to really encourage sanity. When I was released I was a pretty fucked up guy and I couldn't get any good jobs. If I got one I had trouble keeping it."

"So what did you do?"

"I settled in Tampa for a while, worked in a strip club and then I moved here."

"Why here, of all places, why here?"

"Because of the kink scene in Kernersville now I work at the dungeon."

"You work in a... dungeon?" He could see my face was puzzled.

"An adult play space for kinky people, you know? Whips and

floggers, fantasy scenes, bondage, I assume you have heard of this stuff. Since that stupid fifty shades book most everyone has heard of it.

"Are you telling me that there is an actual dungeon in Kernersville?"

41.
March 5th, 2013

I unfolded it and read aloud.

Dear Sophie,

Joe asked me to write to you. Because he is the best friend I ever had and the finest man I have ever known, so I'm doing what he wants.

Joe and I met in high school when we didn't know anything about sex. After we married I figured out right away that I didn't like sex with him at all. He gave me permission to explore my own sexuality. Back then that was a big deal so I want to return the favor to him now.

I give you and him my total permission to have sex as often as you want.

I look forward to meeting you and having you as a friend and neighbor.

Sincerely,
Viviane Vecchia

"Wow," Bren exclaimed as I poured another cup of decaf.

"Seriously, that's a bona fide offer."

"So you think I should do it?"

"Only you can make that decision," Misty said. "Do you think you should do it?"

"It's a free ticket to enjoy wild sex with somebody who really knows how to do it. Who wouldn't want that? And I can still see Chuck when he's home."

"Listen, I have something serious to tell you," Bren imparted. "There was this old cop, Harry Fine, who befriended me when I was a rookie. He told me that for a male cop in New York, the possibilities for wild sex were endless. By age thirty-seven, he had completely lived out his every conceived notion of sexual fantasy. It got to the point that the only thing that could turn him on was watching two women have sex together. That was the only thing he could not participate in and experience personally."

"You think that's what Joey wants, to watch me and Viv make love to each other?" But I don't really care what she thinks or what Harry Fine said because I know something Bren doesn't know. I know something all of them don't know (except maybe Annie) and I'm not telling!

"Not necessarily, this guy said he had tried all kinds of wild sex but he never even hinted that he was coming on to me. Now I don't mind telling you I was hot bootie gorgeous in those days."

"Still are."

She held up her hand to quiet me. "He was always the perfect gentleman."

"Who talked dirty to ya?" *I know about the dungeon, I know about the dungeon, hahahahaha.*

Bren shot me a nasty look. "Listen here, Sophie. Harry told me not to experiment too much too young lest I lose my ability to get aroused like he did. I think that is sage advice from a man who knew what he was talking about. So, if you… " She gently hugged Annie about the shoulders and moved her front and center, "need any advice on kink, you just ask sweet Little Annie here."

"I'll punch you in the nose." She made a fist. "Sophie, pop her one for me, would ya!" But I was running to the bathroom.

They were play wrestling when I returned. Annie had Bren in a mock head lock. "I think that," Annie said as she raised herself up and let go of Bren, "that my advice to you is," she paused to catch her breath, "is that we are old now and cannot *possibly* live out all our fantasies. Go for it, Sophie; may there be many more in your lifetime!"

"There," I turned to Misty, "is a happy and loving thought together in one little package." I went to Annie and hugged her like I meant it because I surely did. "Aren't people from the Midwest supposed to be boring?" I asked.

"Ya, Annie."

Bellamy stood, arched her back and stretched her limbs. "Well, that's enough to fantasize about for one day. I think I'm going home."

"Aw, Bell, stay a while." I finished the last drops in my cup, but she already had her jacket on and was at the door.

"Oh my God! Sophie! Sophie, come here. You're not going to believe this. There is a guy outside dumping trash in your front yard. That's illegal dumping!" She gasped, pointing over the café curtain in the foyer.

"What?" I ran towards the door horrified, wide-eyed and open-mouthed while Bren seized another opportunity to call 911.

Miss Sally ran down the hill with a rake in her hand, yelling something. Joey followed closely behind. Linda and the kids were on their way, and there was, indeed, a dump truck tipping a load of garbage in my front yard.

Stunned, with noses at the storm door, we watched the driver lower the emptied bed, then he climbed down from his seat. He reached back into the cab and pulled out a sign, a hand-painted sign which he planted into the mound. This sign looked like something straight out of *Green Acres*. It was mostly faded blue with big primitive red letters that spelled out the word "PIG". Then he climbed back up into the cab, shifted into first gear and started to pull away. Bren opened the window so we could hear and the smell knocked us back a step.

"Detty Roy, you clean up that pig slough," Sally yelled.

I'd never seen her that angry. He calmly downshifted; and then Sally got directly in front of the truck, put her hands on the hood and yelled, "You gonna run me over, Detty Roy?"

He pulled on his emergency break, got out of the truck and tried to reason with Sally but Sally can be particularly righteous when she's right and she began to lecture him. That was enough time for Kernersville police cruisers to arrive, and they blocked the street just this side of Sally's and Joey's homes. Sally trotted back up the hill to talk to the officers and to see that justice was properly done. I don't think she liked this Detty Roy guy at all.

I snapped out of gape mode, grabbed my jacket and ran out the door and across the front yard with the rest of the gals following. Annie was holding her nose.

"Oh Jaysus, oh, Jaysus." Bren scurried past the heap and up to meet the officers. "I saw the whole thing." I heard her yell. Then she softened and smiled. She walked slower, added a flourish to her gait. Bren-Cop-Flirt strolled up to meet the fit and handsome men in blue with their heads all shaved close and clean.

Joey seemed confused as if he was thinking, *This? Happens? Really?* Miss Sally, a house distance away, was going ape shit yelling at old Detty Roy. His overalls were missing a strap, and too much dingy thermal undershirt was showing. The kids ran around yelling, "Pee yeeew" and making pig sounds while Linda tried to keep them from slinging the foul crap at each other.

I could see Bren's Cop-Flirt smile as she and the officers stood upwind from the stench of this massive puddle-mound of something so disgustingly rotten that a pig would only eat if somebody were holding a gun to its head.

That bitch, I thought. *She got me; she got me good.* I shook my head and bit the inside of my cheek. *That God damned bitch, Letta Steele got me good. She planned and executed one hell of a good practical joke. She punked me, fair and square and she got me good.*

The officers were walking towards us with Detty Roy between them. Miss Sally followed and continued yelling reprimands at this strange little man. The entire company gathered around the rank pile in the front of my home. His hat was in his hand; and about seven long wispy hairs floated up with the breeze from his Gollum-esque balding head. "Ms. Chase, did you see this man, Detty Roy Pocock, dump this pig slough in your yard?"

"Yes, Officer, but this has all been a misunderstanding. You see I paid Detty Roy to deliver this. And I'm so glad you came back because I wanted to give you a tip." I reached into my jeans and pulled out a ten-dollar bill which I handed to him. "Thank you, ah, Detty, for your timely delivery." Who was gaping now?

"Ms. Chase, are you saying you asked for this load of pig slough to be delivered to your yard and dumped in front of your home?"

"Yes sir."

"And this sign? Did you order that also?"

"Oh, that sign ... belongs to me." Bren reached for it.

"And why would you, a retired New York police officer, have a sign that says "pig" on it?"

"I used to keep it on my fire escape back home so all the folks in the back alley knew who lived there. A lot of New York cops have them. It deters crime in the neighborhood. You should get one," she said with a perfectly sober face. "I mean if you had a back alley."

"So let me get this straight. You asked this man to dump pig slough in front of your house and *you*," he pointed at Bren, "stuck your own personal pig sign into it?"

"Yes sir," we both nodded.

"And why would you do that, Ms. Chase?"

"Compost. I was planning to start a garden and the book said I needed compost. Spring is just around the corner, you know."

"You know much about gardening, Ms. Chase?"

"Not much, no."

Officer Roberts conferred privately with Officer Mullens, and then they let Detty Roy Pocock go on his way. The officer then turned to us and said, "You two ladies seem to be in the middle of an awful lot of trouble." He pointed his finger at Bren and then at me. "First there was that incident in the parking lot at El Mejor and I heard firsthand accounts about Ms. Chase, here, beat up some kid in an attempted robbery. You were there too, Bren, and now this? I'm going to have to keep a closer eye on you."

"Oh goody. Can I keep a closer eye on you too?" She checked the handsome officer out from top to bottom and raised her eyebrows in approval.

"Bren," he said as he shook his head, "you're a mess."

After a few minutes more of Bren-Flirting, they went back to doing what small-town cops do between nuisance calls, real life and stupid shit like this.

"Girl, you can't use this slop for compost," Sally said kindly like she was talking to a child, "maybe you could get a load of manure and spread it on top of this... "

"Oh, that will improve it," Annie said with apparent disgust. "You'll have to excuse me, Miss Sally; you know I'm just a dumb city girl."

"Wait-a-minute, something is-rotten here," Joey said.

"And you just figured that out?"

I watched Sally's face morph toward understanding completely. "You didn't order that mess. You covered for Detty Roy," Sally guessed. "You know who he is kin to, don't you? He's that Loretta Steele's Uncle Detty Roy."

"Really?"

"He's her Uncle Detty Roy Pocock on her father's side. She was born a Pocock. But you knew that, didn't you?"

"I had no idea," I said with my stupid face… and then it was my turn to face-morph. "Wait a minute. Are you telling me her name used to be Letta Pocock? I covered an open mouth, my eyes widened as I waited for the gravity, the magnitude of growing up with such a name as Letta Pocock to sink in completely. What kind of teasing did the children in the town of Kernersville give to the little, prickly, birdlike Letta Pocock?

"Oh, my." Annie grasped first.

"Hhhah," Misty inhaled.

"That's horrible!" Bellamy followed.

"That was way, *way* worse than Pap smear," Bren stated with a nod.

"Well, no wonder she's so damned mean!" I said.

"Damn!"

"Poor Letta," Misty said.

"Poor Letta?"

"Bellamy, have you got your phone? I want a video of me in front of this pig slop." Bren placed the sign back in the pile.

"Why would you want a video?" Annie threw her hands up, turned around and walked away from the disgusting heap, shaking her head as if she really did not want to know.

"I want to send a picture of this to Francine DaSilva who is my friend in New York and still on the force. She will think this is the funniest fucking thing in the world."

"This *is* the funniest fucking thing in the world," I affirmed.

"Maybe this is a 'you had to be there' kind of thing," Bellamy said, shaking her head.

"Just start recording, please. Make sure you get the pig sign, and zoom out if you can at the end."

"One second, Bren, okay, rolling… now."

"Francine, am I always telling you how nice it is here? This is a load of pig slop that was just now delivered for free." She changed to a feisty, head-shaking street voice and placed her hand on a hip. "And as God is my witness, Baby, I will never be hungry again." Bellamy backed away as slowly as she could. With the sun setting beyond Bren, Annie, Misty and I picked up our cue and together we sang the Da dum, de dum, of the *Gone with the Wind* background theme music.

This was a day when the North met the South for me, for real, collard greens and chowdah. And this was also a day I gained a measure of respect for a small lonely woman named Loretta Steele. She was a worthy adversary and deserved my regard. It's not like I'm ever going to invite her to coffee klatch or anything but maybe we are more alike than I would like to admit, both struggling spiders traveling across the web we designed.

Joey volunteered to help clean up and transport the mess to the dump if it was all properly bagged and in containers and everything. But it was Sally that helped most. Fortunately, temperatures dropped that night and the garbage was mostly frozen. She and I shoveled the wet heavy mess into bag-lined trash cans. Once we finished the first load, I called Joey to help lift the receptacles into the back of his van and he drove off to the dump.

"You know, Sophie, I got to say something to ya."

"What?" What deep wisdom could I expect? Miss Sally was a well of it.

"When you see a pile of dog doo in the middle of the road, most folks walk around it. Some folks step over it, and some seem to have that special way of dancing around it natural-like. You, Sophie, seem to step right smack into it and track all them dirty footprints cross the whole dang house."

"I can step in some shit," I admitted.

"Why do you think that is?"

"Misty said that I'm perpetuating drama."

"Maybe you like a little drama. There's no shame in that."

"I think you're right. It keeps life interesting."

"Well, at least you know that about yourself. Lots of folks go a whole lifetime not having any idea who or what they're about. And if they do know who they are they usually hide it anyway." She wrapped her scarf around her neck and I wondered if Sally knew about the dungeon. The thought of Sally discovering her inner kink crept into my imagination. I wondered, was that probable... possibly?

"You want to come in?" I offered.

"No, I smell like garbage and I want a hot shower. But I gotta ask you, Sophie, you planning to git her back?"

"You bet I am." Ideas ran wild in my brain.

"You'll be spreading more dog doo."

"Pig shit, Sally. I'll be spreading pig shit."

"You sure that's what you want?"

"Well, I don't see that I have any choice. What would you do?"

"Well, I'm a little like you. I like to see stuff get stirred up now and again, myself, as long as it's interestin' and nobody gets hurt. But to tell you the truth, Darlin', I'd have walked *around* that kind of dog shit a long time ago."

I showered and changed. I was due to meet Misty for fish tacos at Smitty's. I could already hear her saying; *Look what you're creating in your life.*

"Look what you are creating in your life."

"I have created some lovely opportunities that I am particularly looking forward to experiencing. Chuck as a probability, hell, maybe even Joe again. I don't think I am doing too badly here."

"I mean with Letta."

"I know you mean with Letta."

"I'm going to a forgiveness seminar next week. Would you like to go with me?"

"No thanks."

"Think about this. Please, Sophie, think about this, what are you perpetuating?" she grabbed her hair. Then as if she had just had the clearest thought on planet Earth she relaxed her hand. "You know, Sophie? That is exactly the wrong thing to tell you to do."

"What do you mean?"

"I mean, don't think about it. Please, stop feeding the momentum. Just stop thinking about it completely. I am asking you to let it go, and I am asking you to forget about it."

"I have to get back at her, Misty. I've been slimed. I *have* to get her."

"But not today, Sophie, not today."

Saturday morning I walked to the gym. I'd already formed a plan to get even with Letta Steele. So with my boxing gloves over my shoulder I entered the Y like I always do. But I am in the best mood of, let's see, maybe my life because I knew a secret, a really good one.

Rita was between classes and walked toward me. "Hey, Sophie, there was a man asking for you. I just sent him back to the bag room. I think he'd still be there. He might be another reporter. You're big news around here." *Big news for Kernersville,* I thought, *in Miami even the murders don't make it into the newspapers.*

"Thanks, Rita, but not nearly as big as you." Her class was mentioned in the article, and it was filling up fast. *Hmm, it couldn't be Joey,* I thought. *Maybe Chuck has flown in from Florida because he just couldn't bear being parted from me for one moment longer. I love my life. I love my life ...* I turned the corner and I saw *him,* oh... my gosh... It was the man with the sky in his eyes.

"Good morning, Sophie, I'm Kevin, Kevin Lane. Our paths touched briefly in the farmers market last July, I believe."

"I remember."

"The cherries," he said and grinned. There were those slightly crooked teeth I recalled. "I saw your story in the newspapers, and I wanted to meet you. Would you be interested in having dinner with me?"

He seemed a little sure of himself. "Well, you've taken me by surprise, a pleasant surprise." And I'm in my gym clothes, have no make-up on and my hair is a mess. "Can I give it some thought and call you?"

He seemed slightly thrown. Clearly this man expected me to be thrilled with his offer. I was thrilled, but I didn't like that he expected me to be.

"Surely," he said. He reached into his pocket and gave me his card. "Feel free to check my website. I'd like to see you on your own terms." With a hand over his heart, he bowed slightly. "Call me, please. You seem like a very interesting lady."

"Thank you, Kevin." I shook his hand. I could just about feel the sparks of excitement flowing up through my arm and straight down to my...

He walked toward the exit, stopped, turned and considered me for a moment. He nodded his head a little and walked out.

I gotta call Bellamy. I thought. *Oh my God, oh my God!*

I started to stretch, warm up; but I couldn't have been any hotter. I was smoking hot, *smoking hot.* I was jumping and weaving, doing some crazy moves like a cross between fancy footwork and the dance of joy. "Kevin Lane, Kevin Lane, Kevin Lane," I sang it like a cheer.

I threw a few shadow box punches in the mirror, a few combinations. Left, right, left, I'm looking good, feeling great and was headed toward the heavy bag when the door swung open and Kevin Lane walked back in wearing grey shorts and a black muscle shirt. He reached into his gym bag for a pair of Everlast boxing gloves while he stared at me. "Want to go a few rounds, Sophie Chase?"

"Hey, I don't even have a bite guard."

He reached into his bag and tossed me a new one, still in the package. I fumbled to open it with my gloved hands. He took it back, ripped the package open and gingerly lifted it from the plastic and placed it into my mouth.

"Don't worry, luv. I'll go easy on ya." He pulled the second glove over his fist with his teeth.

"Uul go ethsy on me? Baybe ahl go ethsy on uo," I said. I think he understood. So with gloves raised, we began to circle each other.

He was long-limbed, outreached me by half a foot. The only choice I had was to maneuver to the inside where I could work him over. He was also a half a foot taller or more. He was right-handed, leading with his left and he was grinning again… no bite guard and probably trying not to laugh. "C'mon, Sophie," he smiled, "show me what you've got."

You son of a bitch, I thought, *you're laughing at me. You're laughing at me?* He jabbed and I parried. He swung and I ducked, then I came up on his inside and punched him cleanly on the chin with a quick right and a left hook to the jaw.

He jumped back and nodded at me. "Good one."

"Thoo," I corrected.

"Ya, two, but it will be the last two." The element of surprise was gone, and the next shot wouldn't be as easy. I covered. Peering over my gloves I searched for an opening. He threw a left and right combination which I parried and ducked but his right hook grazed my forehead. No worries. His footwork was faster than mine because I was conserving energy. I was in the zone, the zone of awareness where all of his body moves could be observed peripherally and anticipated collectively as I watched his face. I jumped a little, and his eyes moved to my bouncing boobs. That was just enough distraction to know I was in. I parried another right and moved inside. Then his left arm encircled me and I knew immediately that I was going down. But on the way down, I lightly swept his groin and tagged the inside of both knees with my right foot.

I was on the carpet, arms pinned with this heaving hunk of a gorgeous man on top of me and I couldn't have moved even if I'd wanted to.

Half-tongued and half-spit, I blew out the mouthpiece. "Hey, no wrestling, that's cheating!"

"And no kicking, that's dirty fighting. You swept my groin."

"A girl's gotta do what a girl's gotta do."

He helped me up to my feet. I lifted my dukes for another go at him. Then his sky eyes got all soft and... bluer. He pulled off his gloves and charged into me. He had me pinned against the wall with the whole weight of his body pressing on mine. He grabbed the back of my hair, pulled my face up and he kissed me ... hard. His chest against mine, his mouth on mine and deeply... deeply and passionately he kissed me and kissed me and kissed me. It was a rage of a kiss and my knees began to give just a little at first. Limply I began to slide down the wall. He stopped me and he held me in place with my upper arms still pinned.

"Out West Steakhouse, tomorrow night, seven-thirty."

Red-mouthed and gaping I numbly nodded. He released me, picked up his gloves and bag and walked out of the gym.

Chest still heaving, I slid the rest of the way down until I was sitting on the floor with my back still glued to the wall.

"You win," I mumbled, "by a technical knockout."

THE END
maybe

www.ingramcontent.com/pod-product-compliance
Lightning Source LLC
Chambersburg PA
CBHW060424180626
46817CB00007B/2649